Fanged
LOVE

KYLIE GILMORE
MIMI JEAN PAMFILOFF

Cover Design: Earthly Charms
Photography (male model): Wagner LA
Model (male): Juan De La Torre
Developmental Editing: Stephanie Elliot
Copyediting and Proof Reading: Pauline Nolet
Formatting: Paul Salvette

DEDICATION

To men who can wear a cape—or nothing at all,
which is most natural—and own it.

FANGED LOVE

CHAPTER ONE
Boz

Why the devil is there a splinter in my ass? Inside the cozy darkness of my coffin, made from the finest oak an obscenely wealthy Transylvanian prince can buy, I uncross my arms and shift from my back onto my right side.

Ouch! With my eyes closed and still half asleep, I wiggle, feeling nothing but rough hard wood beneath me. *Damn that Cornelia!*

"Neli! Get down here this instant!" Neli is my loyal "human" slave, gifted to me long ago. She is supposed to take care of all the things I do not wish to deal with, which is basically everything. I find her to be lazy and stupid like most humans. For example, I have told her a thousand times not to use the carpenter in our village to refurbish my coffin. He always does such a terrible job reupholstering the cushions, even after I threatened him. And ate two of his three daughters.

It is as if the man has something against me.

I roll onto my bare back once more and sigh. *Well, I suppose I will not be getting my beauty rest.* A shame because I feel especially tired this evening, as if I have not had a wink of sleep today.

I suppose it is the stress of all those pesky peasants demanding I stop drinking their virgins and taxing them for the privilege to farm my land. Land I inherited when my master, the Great Kylgorii Gillmoreanu, perished in a very unfortunate sunshine accident. Yes, yes, I may have been the one to leave the dungeon escape door open, but it was truly an accident when I also forgot to close his coffin.

It is just that his coat was so velvety. As his squire, who wore rags made from potato sacks, I naturally admired the soft, luxurious feel. He was an early-to-bed sort of man—hitting the coffin at four or five each morning—so I often entered the dungeon to admire his fine clothing before I myself slipped into the pig crate I called home during daylight hours. Imagine my shock when I rose on that fateful night to find he was gone and that I had inherited his title, wealth, castle, and problems. That was years ago—far too many to count—and though I had technically been his slave, I still miss him. The way he could suck a neck and drain a flailing woman in three seconds was amazing.

Oh, Kylgorii. Sorry about the coffin, my friend. If he were here now, he would have Neli whipped into shape. Literally. I myself have never been able to whip, tame, or motivate her to do anything she did not wish to do. I would remove her head for her constant insolence, but she has a way with the villagers.

"Neli!" I yell once again and push on the coffin lid. The hinges pop from the wood, and the lid goes flying to the stone floor.

Very poor craftsmanship, indeed. I will have to speak to the carpenter this evening. Kylgorii taught me that to rule is to instill fear. Let up for one moment, and people will begin to think they have power. *Hysterical.*

Naked, I hop from my shabby coffin and grab my black satin cape from the hook on the wall. *Why so dusty?* As I inspect the thing, it disintegrates in my hands and falls to the floor.

What the devil? We must have a moth issue. Very ravenous, from the looks of it. And where is that damned Cornelia? I hadn't really noticed the cobwebs this morning when I went to sleep, but clearly she's been neglecting her cleaning duties. The lack of torches is also unacceptable.

I bet she spent the night with that sheepherder again. That does it.

"Neli!" I march up the stone steps toward the kitchen storeroom, where the entrance to my sleeping chamber is hidden. I am hungry, I feel weak from lack of sleep, and I am in no mood for this bear crap! I push on the concealed door.

Hold the scuppers. What is this? I stand in the middle of my storeroom, smelling flour, sugar, and other familiar ingredients, but nothing looks familiar. I see shiny cylindrical containers with very skillful drawings of vegetables on the outside. There are also boxes of something called "pancake mix," along with many smells I do not recognize.

I crinkle my nose. *What sorts of goods are these?* Have we started trading with those crazy Saxons? I hope not. They are scary. Very savage.

I push on the outer door leading into the kitchen, and I am hit with blinding lights.

Instinctively, I hiss and throw my arms over my face. It takes only a moment to realize that these lights are not from the sun. If they were, I would be charred by now.

Slowly, I lower my arms and take in the strange objects before me. Large shiny metal boxes that hum like a swarm of bees. Lights that give no real heat. Floors made from polished stones I have never seen.

What sorcery is this? "Neli!"

Suddenly, the door from the connecting parlor flies open.

"Boz?" Neli's green eyes are wide with shock. "OMG! You're awake?"

"Yes, girl. Plain to see! Now tell me what the hell is going on. What are these—" I sweep my hand toward the tallest of the shiny metal boxes making all sorts of unnatural noises off in the corner "—objects? And do not tell me you have once again traded my gold for Gypsy trinkets and black magic, or I will skin you alive!"

Neli stands there dumbfounded in her odd-looking clothing—extra-long dark blue breeches and some white shirt that hugs her form, but provides no support. Very indecent. Her long red hair is still the same, however.

"Where is your corset? And, woman, what is on your feet? Put on proper attire this instant!" She appears to be standing on pieces of toasted bread, her toenails painted red and hanging out in the open air. *I never!*

Neli blinks at me and clears her throat, but words do not leave her mouth.

"Well, girl, do not simply stand there like a speechless Carpathian boar. What do you have to say for yourself?" I cross my arms over my chest. That is when I notice something frightful. My arms are thinner than I recall. I glance down at the rest of my body. I resemble a weathered scarecrow.

I whip my gaze to hers, silently demanding an explanation.

"Sir, welcome back."

"Wha-where have I been, Cornelia?"

"Asleep, sir. For five hundred years."

CHAPTER TWO
Boz

Five hundred years? I am in no mood for Cornelia and her silly little games. "Cease with the theatrics, girl, and bring me my supper. I will take it in my quarters." I march from the kitchen, heading for my bedchamber upstairs. While I prefer to slumber somewhere hidden and windowless, I find the luxury of coffins and cellars to be lacking. My chamber is a lavishly appointed suite with two fireplaces, fine tapestries, and oil paintings of my master, his master before him, and some of my own artistic creations. For example, a peach that I am quite proud of. *The fuzz is sublime.* "And tell Bogdana to bring up the water for my bath!" I yell over my shoulder as I enter the parlor and come to a halt.

"What the devil?" I mutter. *Who gave permission to redecorate this room?* My red velvet chairs have been replaced with disgusting beige things with sharp angles and no wood. I poke at one. *Hmm…soft.* I pivot and take in the room, noticing that my fruity artwork has been replaced by enormous paintings of wine bottles. The tall ceiling and fireplace are the only things that remain the same. "Neli!"

"Stop yelling. I'm right behind you."

I startle and jump. "Do not sneak up on me like that. How many times have I told you to…" I notice a flat-looking object behind her on the wall. A man and woman are trapped inside. "What is *that?* How did they get inside?" I point with a shaking finger.

Neli groans and walks over to the thing.

I hold out my hand. "Do not touch it! You do not know what sort of witchcraft those tiny people are capable of."

She ignores me, presses something on the side of the box, and the people disappear.

Where did they go?

"It's not witchcraft." Neli faces me. "It's called a TV, one of many inventions you've missed out on—" she raises her voice and continues "—while you've been *asleep* for five hundred years!"

I stare at her, wondering where my sword is hidden. Clearly, Cornelia has gone mad. I must put her out of her misery and remove her head.

"OMG. What's it going to take for you to believe me?"

"Why do you keep calling me OMG? That is not my title. I am Prince Bozhidar, same as yesterday, girl."

"Ugh. Fine." She marches over to the wall and grabs a beveled mirror that has been placed there for some odd reason. Mirrors belong in the dressing chamber, not in the parlor. She marches back and holds it up in front of me. "Look! Look at your face, Boz."

"But why would I…" I glance at my reflection. *Gods of the night! What has happened to me?* My normally dark eyes are sunken, and the silver flecks have faded to a dull gray. My cheeks resemble animal hides stretched over bone, and my jaw looks like it has a giant woodland critter napping on it. "Get me my razor immediately! The servants cannot see me in such a state. And where the devil is my dinner? Plainly I need nourishment!"

Neli sets down the mirror on a little table next to the chair I was just poking. "Boz, there are no servants—they're all long gone. We have employees now, and they went home for the day. As for your supper, I'm sorry to say that we're fresh out of virgins." She inhales sharply and raises her voice again. "Because you've been asleep for *five centuries*! Hellooo!"

"Hello? But I am right here. Why are you saying hello?"

"Ohmygod. You're impossible." She takes my hand and drags me to the window. "Look outside. You see there? You're not in Kansas anymore, Toto."

"I do not know what a Kansas or Toto is, but—" I gaze at the rolling hills bathed in the golden rays of the late evening sun. Rows of grapevines stretch as far as the eye can see. "Those are mature vines." And mature vines take at least three years to grow. I know this because we have always made wine and grown grapes on my land. We are quite good at it, actually. However, last year a fungus wiped out our entire vineyard, which was why we had to increase the rents. The peasants who farm the rest of my land, growing grains and a variety of vegetables, cannot expect me, their lord, to go without. *And a few of them starved. So what? People die. It is what they do.*

"Now do you see?" Neli asks.

I raise one brow. "Yes. Very clearly. And I have warned you against asking favors of that witch. Now we will have to burn the entire vineyard and start over. I am not about to drink cursed wine from magic vines."

Neli throws her hands in the air. "Fine. You win. Those are magic witchy vines. People are living inside that flat box." She points to that TV thing on the wall. "And you were *not* poisoned by the village witch. You also haven't been asleep for five hundred years while I struggled to keep us safe, put myself through college, and built a multimillion-dollar award-winning winery." She exhales sharply. "Oh, and I didn't have to move you and your stinking castle, brick by brick, to California because your land in Transylvania was seized under eminent domain laws and used to build a huge mall. Nope. None of that happened." She taps her foot.

Neli is a bit of a rascal, but this story goes far beyond her usual tricks. I am beginning to believe her. "So you really have no virgins for my supper? What am I going to eat?"

CHAPTER THREE
Stella

I'm practically a virgin with my current dry spell. It's the only explanation for why I keep having these intense dreams that leave me hot and aching. I lie in bed a moment longer, trying to remember the scraps of dream. A mysterious stranger made me levitate with all the incredibly good orgasmic vibes. I never saw his face, just felt his powerful presence. Sigh. Back to reality. Now that I'm back home from college, I'm not likely to meet a man like that anytime soon.

I get out of bed, opening the bedroom curtains wide to another sunny June day in Napa Valley. I brighten at the view as I keep my gaze focused on the neat lines of well-tended vines. I love neatness and order. Probably the planner in me with my penchant for lists and checking things off them. Most every problem can be solved with the right plan.

Hmm, maybe I should make a plan for meeting a guy. But first I need to focus on my new job here at my family's vineyard.

My gaze is inevitably drawn past the vineyard,

rolling hills, and oak trees to the monstrosity on the other side of the road, a medieval stone castle—complete with towers, turrets, and an actual moat with a drawbridge. Castle Sangria was constructed about five or six years ago and is definitely out of place here. Rumor is an eccentric reclusive billionaire built it as an homage to his ancestral home in Italy. Personally, none of us have ever met the man, but the vineyard manager, Neli, seems friendly enough. And very young—about my age, twenty-two. I have only met her once, about a year ago, when I was home for Christmas break. My mom had me deliver homemade sugar cookies in yet another attempt to make nice with the antisocial neighbors who are rarely seen in public. My parents are the opposite; they've been active members of the community ever since they moved here to start Stellariva Vineyards when I was little (Stella—me; Riva—Italian for creek).

I spend a few moments looking for signs of life across the road like usual. It's really strange that their winery just showed up out of the blue, started growing grapes, making wine, and winning awards left and right, while my family's been at it longer with zero awards. But it's kept our family going for years. I mean, sure, my parents haven't had the money to maintain our old Victorian house, but that's just because they reinvest in the business. Plus, they were paying for my college tuition.

And now I'm back home, after graduating from

UCLA, to work at the family winery as their manager. If Neli can be successful at it, then why can't I? I've been preparing for my role for years. Still, I plan to shadow my father, the master winemaker, to be sure I'm up to date on the production side. Next I'll spend time with my mom, who does the marketing. We're close, and I'm proud to work for the family business.

I turn from the window and shut off my white noise machine that I sleep with every night to ward off ghosts. Ha! Kidding. No such thing as ghosts. I'm much too practical to believe in the otherworldly. It's just that this old Victorian house settles at night, and lately it's been making all kinds of creaks and ghostly moan-like sounds. The white noise machine is to cover those completely explainable noises.

I take a quick shower and then dress in my favorite short-sleeved, pale pink floral maxi dress with black sandals. I love wearing maxi dresses that drape loosely to my ankles. So much more comfortable than jeans or pants. I leave my hair down since I'll be working indoors today. First stop, the kitchen. I'm hoping the twins made something good for breakfast. My seventeen-year-old identical twin sisters—who will be seniors in high school this fall—are culinary geniuses.

In the kitchen, I find my sisters working on their latest recipe. The space is so inviting and cheerful, with honey wood cabinets, a huge center island, and a double-basin farm sink at a window that overlooks the backyard. The scent of warm cinnamon fills the air, and my stomach growls.

My sisters have their long hair up in high pony-tails. We three girls resemble our Italian mother's side with our dark brown hair and eyes, our petite frames, and light olive skin. I'm five feet four, and the twins are an inch shorter. Cute as buttons. Mabel wears an apron with a lemon pattern over her T-shirt and shorts. Eliza sticks with her peppermint-candy-striped apron year-round.

Mabel turns to Eliza. "What do you think about adding—"

"—pureed strawberry," Eliza says.

"Just for the filling," Mabel says.

"Yes!" Eliza exclaims, heading to the refrigera-tor.

"Morning," I say.

"Morning," Mabel says cheerily. "We're work-ing on a dark chocolate cupcake recipe."

Eliza lifts the strawberry container in a little wave. "Less than two weeks until the bake-off."

"I know. It's all I hear about around here." I help myself to a glass of water. "Any chance you made breakfast before the cupcakes?"

Mabel waves toward her twin. "Eliza made cin-namon rolls, but Dad took them out for the staff."

"You snooze, you lose," Eliza says with a grin from the sink, where she's washing the strawberries.

I cross to her. "Guess I'll just steal a few strawberries."

"Back away from the strawberries," Eliza says, lifting the colander and setting it on the counter away from me.

"Just one," I coax.

"Ha! I was kidding before," Eliza says. "I saved a cinnamon roll for you. It's on the dining room table."

I beam. "You're now officially my favorite sister."

Eliza sticks her tongue out at Mabel.

Mabel arches her brows. "Eliza is my favorite sister."

"Oh! Direct hit!" I stagger and pull the pretend knife from my back. Mabel smiles and goes back to measuring ingredients for cupcake batter. The food processor whirs a moment later, and they're back in action.

I take a seat at our glossy cherrywood dining room table and devour the cinnamon roll. Nothing like fresh baked…anything, really. I'm going to have to be careful not to gain a hundred pounds sampling everything they make. My sisters are eager for the state bake-off because the prize is full tuition to culinary school. One of them will use that money to go, while my parents cover the other. Mabel wants to focus on cuisine and Eliza on baking. Their ultimate goal is to open a top-rated restaurant. It would be cool if they did that here at the vineyard, but we'll see where they end up. They're both trying to get into different culinary schools. Mabel in New York and Eliza in France.

My dad appears unexpectedly in the dining room just as I get up from the table. Normally he's tending the vines or in the cellar. His dark brown hair is parted to the side, his round cheeks clean-shaven. He's wearing a faded chambray button-down shirt, khakis, and his beat-up work boots. "Finally, you're up," he says.

"It's not that late," I say. "You're just an early bird."

"Get up with the sun this time of year." He tucks his hands in his pockets. "I thought I'd sit in on your meeting with Mom today."

"Yeah, sure, no problem." I head through the kitchen and outside to Mom's office in the cottage out back as Dad follows. The space was originally an in-law unit, which my parents used to rent out, but then the twins came along, so it became the office.

It's unusual for Dad to want to leave his post overseeing the production of the wine, but hey. It's his vineyard. Mom's too. When they're ready to retire, they'll hand it over to me and my sisters (if they're interested). Until then, Mom and Dad are my bosses. I don't mind working for my parents. I know they value my contribution. They were thrilled that I wanted to work here. Of course I did! The winery means everything to me. It's my namesake, my legacy.

I enter the cottage, and my mom swivels in her

black mesh office chair. "Morning, sweetheart." Her dark brown hair is back in its usual bun, no makeup. She favors T-shirts, jeans, and a beige cardigan that's probably as old as I am.

"Morning." I stop to give our old dog Sadie a scratch behind her big floppy ears. She lifts her soulful bloodhound eyes to me for a moment before resting her head on her drool-covered paws. "No, don't get up," I murmur. She's about ten years old and deaf, but she can still sniff out a rabbit from a mile away.

I straighten to find my dad is already seated in the wooden chair across from the desk. I take the other chair. The cottage is sparsely decorated. Just a long wooden desk with chairs and a few art prints on the white walls. The highlight is a large window with a view of the vineyard.

"So should we start?" Mom asks.

"Oh! I should've brought a notepad and pen." I pull my phone out of the deep pocket in my dress. "I'll jot down anything important in my notes app."

I look up at the silence to find my parents exchanging a look. "What?"

"Let's not write this stuff down," Dad says.

"It's of a delicate nature," Mom says.

"Oh, okay." I look from one to the other, confused. "Is it marketing related? Do you have a new idea for bringing in business?"

"In a way," Mom says. "I'm hoping you can help with that."

"We've done everything we can think of," Dad says with a note of worry that has me sitting up straighter. "Wine club, online sales, the tastings."

Mom shakes her head sadly. "Wine club was a good idea, but only a few people were willing to commit to a monthly membership."

A sense of dread fills me at their tight expressions.

"And tastings are seasonal," Dad adds.

"You said online sales did better than you thought," I say. "Right?"

"At Christmas they were good," Mom says.

"It's just become a very crowded, competitive market," Dad says. "There's so many new wineries coming on the scene, and it's harder to get distribution in stores."

My gut tightens. I remember them talking about how the wineries from Latin America were taking over shelf space in the stores. I didn't realize this was what they meant. "Okay, I'll come up with a plan. Something that shines a new light on Stellariva wines." My mind is already cranking with ideas that won't cost too much, when Mom drops the bombshell.

"Here's the reality, honey," she says. "We're nearly broke. I'm not sure we can keep the winery going much longer."

I suck in air.

"And sending the twins to culinary school next year is looking iffy," Dad says.

My stomach knots into a sickly mess.

My mom opens her laptop. "I'll show you the numbers."

A few moments later, I take the offered laptop and stare cold hard reality in the face. They're not just nearly broke. They're also in debt. I can't believe they kept this from me. They knew I planned on joining them in the family business.

"I don't understand." I swallow hard, looking from one to the other. "You paid for my college."

"We took out a loan against the house," Dad says.

"We didn't want you to leave college in deep debt," Mom says.

My sickly stomach knot turns into a lead weight filled with guilt. I look to the ceiling. Okay, I realize they put themselves in debt just to help me out, but they knew the vineyard was my future, and now it's at risk of falling apart just when I finally come on board. If only they'd been up front with me, I could've told them I'd rather deal with student loans than a business on the brink of collapse. I'm baffled at their logic and angry they kept this from me, but above all, I'm heartbroken. For them. For me. For my sisters. We love this place with all our hearts. It's part of our family.

Wanting to be strong for them, I bury my fear that we could lose Stellariva, and face them again. "How long has this been going on? This decline?"

"Five years," Mom says.

Dad runs a hand through his hair and sighs. "We didn't want you to worry. Now that you're working here, you need to know. We hoped you'd come up with some smart way to save the winery that we hadn't thought of."

Five years? This has been going on for five freaking years? I slowly blink. How could they keep this from me? We've always been so close. They knew I planned on joining the family business, yet they brought me on board a sinking ship. I could've gotten a job elsewhere, started working my way up the corporate ladder. I had an internship at a marketing company last semester that wanted to hire me, but I turned it down in favor of the vineyard. My parents knew that. My nails press into my palms, every muscle in my body tense. I'm pissed, but at the same time, I feel guilty for being so angry, knowing they got me through college debt-free out of love. It was probably an overprotective move on their part to keep me in the dark about their financial problems and let me enjoy college. Still, give me a choice in the matter.

"I can't believe you kept this from me," I say in a low voice, trying to digest this huge blow. I need to be strong and not let my emotions take over, but it feels like a betrayal from the people I love and trust the most. I could've handled the truth and done something about it. Maybe they just don't trust in me as much as I do them.

"I kept hoping it would turn around," Dad says

quietly.

"I didn't want to burden you with our troubles," Mom says.

I lift my palms. "But you knew I planned to come back here. You know how much the vineyard means to me. You named it after me. Of course I want to see it thrive for generations."

"That's what we're counting on," Mom says, glancing at Dad. He nods. Both of them turn to me with hopeful expressions.

I narrow my eyes. "From here on out, no more secrets, no more protecting me from the truth. I'm in this, and I need to know exactly what's going on." Whatever it takes, I *am* going to save this winery.

"Max is retiring at the end of the month," Dad says. That's Dad's assistant manager. The man has been with us from the beginning.

"Anything else?" I ask.

"We need a new hot water heater," Mom says.

"That's it, right?" Dad asks Mom.

Mom knocks on her desk. "Knock wood. That's all I can think of."

Failing winery, deep debt, no culinary school, losing our best employee, and a broken hot water heater. That's plenty!

I stand on shaky legs. "I need some time to think."

The pressure of the survival of the vineyard, my sisters' futures, my legacy, all on my shoulders. It's too much.

"We're happy to talk more when you're ready," Mom says.

I lift a hand in acknowledgment and head back into the main house. Two things are clear—secrets are the worst, and I desperately need a plan.

I spend the better part of the day trying to come up with something, going over the numbers again and again, but the truth stares me straight in the face. Without a miracle, this winery will fold within the year. No, I refuse to allow it. If there's a miracle to be found, I will find it.

I sleep restlessly that night, and I'm up at sunrise, feeling completely out of sorts. I dress quickly in a lavender maxi dress with my taupe ballet flats, deciding a walk will help clear my head. A few minutes later, I head out the front door and down our long driveway. I still can't believe my parents kept something so important from me! The medieval castle across the road looms large as always. I glare at it, a stab of jealousy making my gut tighten. Their winery must be swimming in money. They're constantly featured in all the top wine magazines.

But what makes their wines so special compared to ours? I stop on the road and stare up at the enormous dark castle. A light wind pushes my long hair in front of my face, and I smooth it back. *We practically have the same soil.* The sun and weather are identical. We grow the same varietals, and my dad has a degree in viniculture from Sonoma State.

He even worked at a top-notch winery up in St. Helena before buying our place. He knows what he's doing. The only explanation I can think of is that our neighbor's grapes are simply better. Maybe they brought their plants over from Italy. Lots of wineries do that—pay big bucks to an established vineyard overseas for their vines.

Suddenly, the hairs on the back of my neck rise, and I notice a tall man staring directly at me from a large window on the second floor of the castle. The vineyard manager is Neli, a petite red-haired woman. Is this the reclusive billionaire owner of the vineyard no one's ever seen?

I squint. It kind of looks like he's wearing a top hat. Do people still wear those? *Eccentric all right.* Just the kind of guy who would build a medieval castle in the middle of Napa Valley. It must be him. He may be a little eccentric, but there's no denying he knows how to run a successful winery.

That's it! I'm going over for a neighborly chat. Who knows how long he'll be around before he jets off to whatever other properties he owns?

I blink, and he's gone.

I square my shoulders and head back to my house, a new plan forming. I'll bring some of the twins' cupcakes as a neighborly offering. I need some out-of-the-box thinking to come up with a really good plan, and for that, I need to talk to an experienced successful colleague. So what if he spends all his time in hiding, making unusual wardrobe choices? That's fine by me. It almost guarantees out-of-the-box thinking, right?

A short time later, plastic container of a half dozen dark chocolate cupcakes in hand, I march determinedly down our long driveway in the cool morning air. Just one positive step forward could start the momentum in the right direction for our vineyard. The alternative is too devastating to consider. If the winery fails, where would my parents go? How would they support themselves? And the twins' dream of culinary school? Goodbye. I'm not even sure we could get them loans with my parents' level of debt.

Still deep in thought, I cross the road. Even if the twins did manage to get loans, my parents would probably feel terrible they couldn't do for my sisters what they did for me. Not that I asked them to. What a frigging mess.

Perched up on a sprawling hill, the castle looms in front of me, with its majestic grandeur and old-world-style wealth. This is definitely the place to gain some hint at how to turn things around. It's obviously a successful venture for them.

I ignore the goosebumps rising on my arms as I hike up their cobblestone driveway and approach the drawbridge. I ignore the strange sensation that the air is cooler the closer I get to the castle. I am on a mission. I finally reach the large arched wooden double doors flanked by torches on either side—are those real torches?—and reach for the iron door knocker. I freeze and cautiously look around, ready to duck. I could've sworn I heard flapping wings nearby.

Nothing. Strange.

I turn back and knock twice, eager to meet my neighbor for the very first—and hopefully not last—time. I just know he's got some pearls of wisdom to share. How could he not with such an award-winning successful winery?

CHAPTER FOUR
Boz

After sampling some of our new wines, I slide into my creaky wooden casket, ready to coffin down for the day. I am beat. There is much to learn about this new world that I have woken in. The changes to the winery production alone took me all night to comprehend. Machines now perform the tasks of twenty men, separating fruit from unwanted debris. Enormous steel vats now sit where there were once open wooden mash pits to crush the grapes and initiate fermentation. Neli says humans no longer wish to have "toe jam" with their wine.

Blasphemy! Where do they think the true flavor comes from? Peasants have very flavorful feet.

However, I tasted every batch in production and several barrels in the cellar. I must admit that while our new wines lack notes of blue cheese and earth, they are quite good.

I remove my evening wear. I had been wearing a pair of Neli's black "sweat pants" (that were very tight and hardly reached my calves) and a top hat and black cape Neli scrounged up from a bag of All Hallows' Eve garments from her closet. I am pleased that my favorite religious holiday is still observed in these modern times. In any case, my own clothing has long disintegrated, and Neli has promised to bring me an additional outfit for tonight from something called a "thrift store," as she claims it is the only place to find ruffled shirts and clothing that suits my taste on such short notice. She also mentioned procuring some additional outfits "on line." I believe she means to steal them from a neighbor's clothing line. I wonder what sort of leather pants are washed and dried in such a way.

Now, appropriately naked, I lie down flat on my back, and a splinter pokes me right in my backside. *Ouch!* I must have Neli procure a new coffin immediately. This thing is about to fall apart. Yet, I almost do not care. I am simply that exhausted from my evening of learning. Oh, and hunting.

Neli warned me not to venture out alone—too many things have changed, she said—but I am the Great Prince Bozhidar. I fear nothing and no one. Well, except those automobiles. Dear gods of the night, they travel almost as fast as I do! Almost. Which is why I am still with my head. I had been strolling near town, taking in some of the large, oddly rectangular buildings, when one of these vehicles nearly ran me over. Thank the gods for my fast reflexes.

I then found a tavern where the female patrons dressed in what appeared to be undergarments— trousers with the legs missing and tops that exposed everything but the bosom. *So indecent!* Especially because they claimed not to be whores.

I press my hand to my cheek. That blonde woman hit hard. But how was I to know she was not for sale? She also made fun of my "funky getup"—whatever that means. Hungry and weak, I had no choice but to wait around back and grab the first person who walked by: an older woman with a very bad flavor. I loathe dining on grandmothers. Or any sort of woman who is not a virgin.

I wince and flick my tongue over my upper lip. *So bitter.* If it were not for that, I would have drained her dead. Instead, I used the age-old trick to wipe her mind of any memory of me, and sent her on her way. Tonight, I shall hunt again and find something sweet and tender to fill my belly.

My mind quickly wanders to that woman I spotted walking outside moments ago. Her long brown hair was loose and wild, and her sun-kissed skin was concealed by a long dress meant to tease a gentleman's imagination—*sexy little vixen!*—but even through the glass, with her at a distance, I could smell the virginal blood pulsing beneath her skin. So sweet.

I will ask Neli about her when I wake tonight. To be sure, I have many questions about this new world, including how a vampire conceals himself, or more accurately stated, how he conceals his kills. Neli was very clear that in this day and age, my kind is nothing more than a myth. The villagers do not offer slaves or virgins or any of the perks I once enjoyed. Vampires have receded into the shadows, and nothing feels familiar except the constant ache in my belly. A vampire's hunger is never quelled.

My eyes start to close as the sun rises over the horizon.

Gong! Gong!

My eyes pop open. Someone is at the front door. I am sure Neli will get it. I cross my arms over my chest, which is now back to its gloriously muscular shape along with the rest of me. The silver speckles have returned to my dark eyes too. Even my long black hair has regained its lustrous shine. I am once again the grand stallion of the night, worshipped by every female who lays eyes on—

Gong! Gong!

Dammit. What does a prince of the night have to do around here to get his beauty rest? I push on the lid of my wobbly coffin. "Cornelia!"

Silence answers me. Where is that girl? She has forgotten her place. I am her master, never to be disobeyed or displeased.

The door gongs for a third time. *That does it.* Someone must want to be my bedtime snack.

I hop from my coffin, zip up the stairs, and go to the front door, giving it a hard yank to yell at whatever merchant is peddling their wares at such an ungodly hour. "What the devil do you…" My voice trails off.

Standing before me is the woman I saw through

my window earlier. Her potent, sweet floral scent slams into me like a mallet to the face. It is painfully delicious.

I step back and pinch my nose. Otherwise, I will have to pull her inside and devour her—not the wisest decision when I am now a stranger in a strange land. Killing so close to home in such unfamiliar surroundings may prove problematic, if I am to heed Neli's warnings.

The young beauty with her silky dark hair and wide inquisitive eyes looks up at my face. Her gaze then begins the journey south until she realizes I am in my nightclothes. "Oh! Oh, God! You're naked!"

"Yes. As you can see," I say, still holding my nose, "I am a man, and real men do not wear garments to bed. Now what may I do for you?"

Cheeks red, she closes her eyes and holds out an odd-looking container of pastries. "I, uh…uh…just came by to introduce myself. I'm your neighbor from across the road, Stella Baker. I brought homemade cupcakes."

A baker at a vineyard? "I do not eat sugar, but I thank you all the same." Suddenly, I realize two things. One, pinching my nose is completely useless. Her sweet, virginal scent is still entering my lungs and calling to me. And second, I am nude, which is normally no concern of mine—I am a man and modesty is for women—but for some odd reason my shaft is beginning to thicken.

Must be due to my five-century slumber. I have

not made love to a woman in a very, very long time. Otherwise, I am always in complete control of my body, including my generous manhood.

"Very nice to make your acquaintance, but I am a busy man who needs a nap. Good day." I slam the door in her face and glance down at my firmly standing erection.

"Who was at the door…" Cornelia appears, her eyes glued to my nether region. "Boz! Seriously? Please tell me you did not answer the door naked with a giant boner."

I frown and grumble an ungentlemanly word. "Next time, answer the goddamned door."

There is a knock on the door. "Hello? Are you still there?" That persistent baker woman is still outside.

Neli's big green eyes go wide. "Who's that?" she whispers.

"A neighbor," I reply, "coming to poke her nose around, under the guise of good tidings and offering baked goods she calls *cupcakes*."

"Oh great. And you just had to answer the door naked before slamming it in her face?"

I shrug unapologetically. "It is my castle. I will do as I please."

Neli narrows her eyes at me. "We need to act like normal people running a normal winery. You don't understand how quickly rumors spread these days."

"Hello?" The woman knocks once again.

My, my. She is a persistent little thing. "Answer the door," I whisper to Neli. "Tell her if she wishes to see another sunrise, she must never return." My growling stomach takes no prisoners, and at the moment, it is painfully aware of the delectable treat just on the other side of that door.

Neli gives me a look. "What's that supposed to mean?"

I mouth the word *virgin* and point to the door.

Neli's eyes go wider, and she shakes a pale finger at me. "You keep your fangs off her. I am not picking up this castle and moving again because you can't keep 'em in your mouth!"

"Then make her leave," I say.

"Fine." Neli opens the door, and I hide behind it, carefully twisting my body so my still very frisky manhood is not injured. "Oh, it's you! Great to see you again, Stella."

Stella is a name that rolls off the tongue like my beautiful native language. I like it. *Wait. No, I hate it.* As I hate her.

I glance down at my groin, which calls my bluff.

"Neli, right?" Stella asks.

"Yes. Long time no see, Stella. What can I do for you?"

Stella goes on to explain that she just returned home from her studies and is now working at her family's vineyard across the way. This is not good. Avoiding such a tasty treat so close to home will prove challenging.

"Anyway," Stella continues, "I just stopped by to see if I could chat with the owner—maybe pick his brain a little on some marketing stuff, but I think I caught him at a bad time." She adds with a whisper, "He was naked."

Neli coughs. "Was he? Darn it. Must be sleep-walking again. He works such long hours during the day, and sometimes at night too, dealing with our distributors overseas. It messes with his sleep patterns. I should go check on him, but thanks for coming by."

"These cupcakes are for you guys."

Neli takes them. "Thank you. You shouldn't have."

"It's nothing," Stella says, "but I was still hoping for that chat. Is there a better time for me to come back?"

"Um…maybe around seven tonight? Prince Bozhidar has a late meeting, but I'm sure he'd love to help you in any way he can."

What the devil? I almost reach for Neli's neck and slam the door in Stella's face again. What is Neli up to? As is, I am ready to claw my way through the heavy wooden door just for a nibble of this woman. Why would Neli agree to have me meet with her?

"Prince Bozhidar? The owner is royalty?" Stella asks.

"Oh, uh…no, no. His first name is Prince, like the singer—rest in peace."

What? I am too a prince! Prince Bozhidar Alexandru of Transylvania.

"Interesting. Well, tell Prince I said thank you. And please don't mention the whole naked sleep-walking thing. I don't want him to feel uncomfortable talking business with me, and it's not his fault he has a problem."

"I won't say a word," Neli replies. "And he goes by Mr. Bozhidar. Just letting you know so the meeting goes well. He's old-school when it comes to manners. I mean *really*, really old-school."

Stella laughs. "I'll remember to curtsy, then."

Yes. And you should also offer me your body to feast on. Wait. No, no. I must remember not to eat the neighbors.

"All right, well, see you then, Neli," Stella says.

"Sure. And thanks again for the treats. He'll love them." Neli shuts the door.

I wait for the footsteps outside to fade into the distance before giving Neli a piece of my mind at full volume. "What has gotten into you, girl?"

Neli flips her long red hair over her shoulder and folds her arms over her chest. I hate that she is still wearing men's clothing—snug breeches and a white shirt with buttons down the front. So inappropriate. Women should always wear modest dresses, except when in my bedchamber. Then they should wear nothing.

"She obviously wasn't going to leave until I said yes," Neli explains. "Besides, all you have to do is meet with her for one minute, and she'll see you don't know diddly-squat about marketing and go on her way."

"I know not what a diddly-squat is," I snarl under my breath, "but you mean to make me look a fool, and I will not stand for it. I may be out of my element when it comes to living in this new world, but I know people, I know what entices them, and I know how to make the sort of wine that makes a person's soul weep with joy."

Neli rolls her insolent eyes. "Fine. You're the best, Boz. But we can't afford to have her poking around, so you'll have to get rid of her. Also, you need to keep that thing in your trousers." Neli points to my erection. "I know how much you like virgins and what you do to them."

She is referring to the fact that I can never quite stop myself from drinking them to death. They taste too good.

"First of all, I am not wearing any trousers. Second, you forget who is in charge. It is my castle, and I will do as I please." I march off toward the kitchen. "And order me a new coffin! I want it delivered before I wake."

I return to the cellar and climb into my extremely uncomfortable coffin, forced to lie there for another hour before I can close the damned lid, lest I risk injuring my very stiff, very uncomfortable situation.

I would take care of it myself, but I am a vampire. I can get any woman I want, and it is far more pleasurable to be serviced.

Yes, tonight, I shall find someone to sate a different kind of hunger. And I shall stay far away from that baker woman with the pastries. *Meeting. Hrrmph! Foolish Neli.* It is a ridiculous idea. That human, Stella, has no idea how close she came to dying just now, and the last thing I want is to begin killing the town's peasants. Not yet. Not until I am situated in this new time and place.

Nevertheless, I drift off to sleep, thinking of Stella's long flowing dress and sweet delicious scent.

CHAPTER FIVE
Stella

Naked hot man is *really* hard to get past. He was young too, maybe thirty at the most. No, not going there. I need to keep this professional. Stellariva Vineyards is not shutting down on my watch.

Seeing Prince in all his sexy muscular—stop. He has a *condition*. A sleepwalking, fully erect condition, but that is beside the point. The only reason I'm thinking about him naked so much is because it was a shock. Yes, that's why. Any woman would feel the same, even if they weren't going through a sexual drought. *Ahem.* At our meeting tonight I'll pretend I know nothing about his wide rounded shoulders, muscular chest, and impressive...other things. I flush with heat. He must hit the gym hard to get those six-pack abs and the deep V at the waist leading to—

Business. This is business. I have a plan and a backup plan. I'm determined to get something useful out of this meeting. I can't afford to be distracted. Not by how much younger he is than I thought he'd be, considering his level of success.

Not by that body.

And certainly not by his huge, thick…*that!*

I follow my dad to our wine cellar to pick out two of our best vintage bottles—a pinot noir and a cabernet sauvignon—as a gift for my neighbor Prince. I mean Mr. Bozhidar. Neli says it's important to use formal address because he appreciates old-school manners. No problem. If that's all it takes to get in with him, I'll consider myself lucky.

The cellar is dim and cramped with barrels and wine-making equipment. My parents use the outdoor patio for the wine tastings instead of the cellar. Unfortunately, there's not enough of those tasting visitors to keep us in the black.

My dad takes the bottles out and hands them to me. "Are you sure you don't want me to go to the meeting with you?"

"You and Mom said you're hoping I'll turn things around, so let me do my job." My tone is a little snippy, but I can't help it. I'm still so angry they kept the truth about the financial state of the winery from me, and I'd really appreciate it if they could show some trust. "Please," I add belatedly.

His brow furrows over kindly hazel eyes. "My gut says something's off about this Prince Bozhidar guy. What kind of name is that anyway? I couldn't find anything about him online. And we've been neighbors for years, yet we've never seen him—only Neli."

"You never *visited* him." My parents only sent me the one time to drop off cookies at Christmas.

"Today I stopped by, and he answered the door himself. All it took was a little neighborly friendliness to bridge the gap." *Or cross the moat.* I keep that to myself. Dad doesn't need any more ammunition against the one person who could help save our winery. I don't expect Mr. Bozhidar to spill all his secrets on what makes his wine so good, but I'm hoping to get his opinion on ours and how to improve it. I mean, obviously if his secret is the source of their vines, that's not going to help us. It takes several years to grow new ones that produce fruit. I can only hope he's willing to share a few marketing ideas. We'll talk shop, businessman to businesswoman. Under less dire financial circumstances, this kind of meeting would be fun for me.

Dad continues, his tone still suspicious. "And what kind of person builds a medieval-style castle in the middle of California wine country?"

Guess there's no hiding the moat.

"A very *rich* person. He can build whatever he wants if he's got the funds. And you know what? I think it's great that he does what makes him happy." *Like wear top hats.* I keep that to myself too. Really, our neighbor just walks to the tune of his own bagpipes (seems appropriate for a castle dweller).

I head upstairs, cradling the bottles in one arm. My dad follows behind me. I don't care if our neighbor is a little eccentric. Maybe that's what makes him so good at crafting award-winning wines.

Maybe *not* following the crowd is the key to standing out in the competitive wine business.

"Stella, you don't need to go over there," my dad says once we get upstairs. "I mean, he can't be doing anything that different from us. We're growing grapes in the same soil conditions, the same rainfall. It's probably just his connections that gave him a leg up."

"He's obviously doing something right. I'm going to find out what. As for your concern about me going over there, I'll be fine. I'm a grown woman. I can handle a business meeting."

He lifts a finger. "That's another thing. Why does he want to meet you at night? I don't like it."

"He works late to deal with his overseas distributors. Really, it's *fine*. I have my phone, and the manager, Neli, lives there too. What time is it?"

"You've got ten minutes."

"Okay, I'm heading over there."

"How long will you be?"

I barely hold back on rolling my eyes. I've only been home for a few days, and I'm already starting to feel like I'm back in high school. I know my parents see me as capable, they just need to let up on the overprotective stuff.

"I don't know," I mutter. "I'll text when I'm on my way back. Bye!" I head out the door of the wine annex and take the shortcut through the side yard to the road.

Checking in with my dad feels like overkill, but

the closer I get to the castle, the more my heart pounds to the tune of *naked man, naked man, naked man.* I have to get a hold of myself. So much rides on this meeting, and I can't let anything throw me. I have to let any eccentricity or condition he may have sail right on by. Even if the image of his gorgeous muscular perfection is burned into my brain.

The sun is setting as I cross the drawbridge once more. I think cooling thoughts and lift the heavy metal knocker. A shiver courses through me. Wow, it wasn't just my mind that made me cool off. The air definitely feels colder close to the castle. Probably something to do with the stone construction. I'm also wearing another of my long maxi dresses—plain white—and matching sandals, so the cool air goes right to my skin.

I wait in breathless anticipation, my heart drumming to its new favorite tune with a little fluttery add-on: *naked sexy man, naked sexy man.*

One of the large arched wooden doors slowly creaks open. *Is it him? Is he naked?*

Neli's small frame appears in the doorway. She's wearing a white blouse, jeans, and pink flip-flops. Her red hair is in a high ponytail.

"Hi, Neli." I try not to show my disappointment that her boss didn't open the door. Sans pants.

She smiles. "Hi, Stella, come on in."

I step inside, and the door shuts behind me with an ominous thud, echoing through the large two-story foyer.

She takes a step back. "I'll let him know you're here."

"I have arrived," a deep voice announces, startling me. He must move fast. I didn't even notice him approaching. He's dressed, which is good, of course, but his clothes are rather unusual. Like a goth musician in a black top hat, white frilly shirt, black velvet cape, and snug black pants that outline his powerful, ahem, thighs.

I jerk my gaze up to his eyes. Silver glints sparkle back at me in black eyes. How exotic. I guess I didn't notice them before. Maybe I was too distracted by his defined muscular chest with a smattering of dark chest hair, his washboard abs, and his thick penis with a throbbing vein pointing right at me.

I flush hot and try to focus on something else, like his black hair reaching down to his shoulders and his pale skin. Maybe he's a musician in seclusion from his rabid fan base. It would explain so much.

Neli whirls and whispers something to him in a fierce low tone.

"Leave us," he commands. He doesn't raise his voice, but the soft edge of authority is unmistakable.

"I'm the manager here," she says to him. "It's important I'm in on business meetings."

He doesn't reply. Instead, he merely looks at her as though he expects to be obeyed. She turns back to me and then to him before throwing her hands up.

"I'll be nearby if anyone needs me," she says, looking right at me.

I nod. Strange. It seems like Mr. Bozhidar would be the one who needs her assistance not me. I face the man who's the key to getting Stellariva Vineyards out of the hole we're in and back to the light. Out of the red and into the black. Or something like that. I may be a wee bit nervous now that we're face-to-face. He's just so much man (don't think about it), and he exudes power.

I stare as he removes his top hat with a flourish.

"Good evening," he drawls in a deep silky voice that wraps around me like a dark caress.

I step closer, drawn in, and then remember the old-school manners Neli told me were important to him. I drop into an awkward curtsy as I clutch the wine bottles against my chest, my purse dropping forward off my shoulder and hitting the floor. My planner spills out of it, exposing one of my many lists. "Good evening, Mr. Bozhidar."

I go for my purse and planner, but he's faster, tucking the planner back in and snagging the strap with a single finger.

"Quite a long list," he says.

I straighten, meeting those glittering black eyes that seem to hint at something mysterious. "I'm a planner. Love to make a plan and check stuff off my list. It's kinda my thing."

He sets my purse back on my shoulder, his touch through the thin fabric of my dress sending a spark through me.

I lick my lips. "Thank you so much for taking the time to meet with me. I brought two of our best vintages as a gift." I offer him the wine. "Would you like a tasting?"

He leans close, his black eyes gleaming. "A taste?"

My heart is in my throat, a distant warning of danger sounding in my mind. I take a step back.

Wait. I'm being silly. I'm just feeling intimidated. Who wouldn't be in his presence? Good looking, successful, wealthy.

I gather my nerves and remain focused on the prize. "Yes, I'd love to get your opinion on our wine."

"The wine, yes, of course," he murmurs. "We shall have some."

I offer him the bottles, but he doesn't take them. Instead he snaps his fingers, announcing, "Bring these to the parlor."

I glance around. Does he have a maid or a butler who appears at the snap of his fingers? Neli appears. She must've stayed close like she said. I guess she helps him a lot.

He hands her his top hat and gestures for her to take the wine bottles.

She tucks his hat under one arm and takes the bottles from me. "The great hall would be more comfortable than the parlor. Right this way, Stella."

I follow her, sensing Mr. Bozhidar's looming

presence behind me more than hearing it. He moves quietly for a man of his size.

We step through a large archway into what is truly a great hall with a long wooden table and enough room to accommodate—fifty people, at least. There's a line of wooden chairs with intricate scrollwork carved into the top of each one. An enormous candelabra overhead brings out the gold motif in the post and beam ceiling. A stone hearth dominates the opposite end of the hall. Sconces that resemble torches line the walls between arched mullioned windows.

Wow. No detail was spared to make it feel like an authentic castle.

Mr. Bozhidar pulls out a chair for me adjacent to the head of the table, and I take the offered seat. He really does value manners. *And bathing. Mmm…* I inhale deeply, taking in the clean scent of his fresh woodsy aftershave. Oddly, it's somehow familiar. Maybe my ex used it.

He takes the seat at the head of the table, and I try to focus my attention back on the matter at hand. I'm here for business. Not smelling his smooth clean skin.

"I'll be right back with glasses and a cheese platter," Neli says.

Mr. Bozhidar stares at her. "Cheese platter? Just bring the silver platter with the cheese on top. I do not know how—"

"Boz." Neli smiles tightly. "I'm sure Stella

would like to hear about our latest award-winning vintage." She gives him a significant look. *Some kind of problem with the cheese platter around here?*

"I would," I say enthusiastically. "You must be very proud to take the gold medal at last year's Challenge International du Vin, in France." I did my research on the latest news from their winery earlier today. Our winery could never compete at their level internationally; however, there's a big competition in New York coming up next month for domestic wines. I'm hoping we can scrape up the entry fee and submit our best wine. It's a long shot, but now is not the time to be careful. It'll take big, bold ideas and a miracle to save Stellariva.

Neli quickly walks from the room. I think she doesn't want to miss much of our meeting. Maybe she's afraid he'll share all his wine-making secrets. I can feel his stare as I set my purse over the back of the chair, waiting for him to tell me about his recent win. Those black eyes. For a moment there, he felt dangerous. Maybe there *is* something off about him like my dad said. *No, no. Don't be silly.*

Again, I fight back my nerves. I'm sitting in the room with a wine-industry legend, but he's still just a man who puts his pants on one leg at a time. When he wears pants.

"Your gold medal win?" I prompt.

He steeples his long fingers together on the table. "Ah, yes. Our merlot."

"I'm so impressed. That's a very prestigious

competition."

"Yes, yes, would you like to try our winning wine?"

The jitters return. Why can't I seem to settle down? "Sure. That would be wonderful."

He stands. "Let's take this to the cellar. I will give you a tour."

"Should we wait for Neli?" I ask. "She's bringing us a cheese platter." Or a silver platter with cheese on it or something with cheese. I'm really not sure.

"I have no use for that. Come." He crooks his elbow for me to take, like a gentleman from a more courtly era. It's unusual, but I actually like his old-school ways. It makes me feel like we're in another world—like you see in those movies about knights in armor, sword fights, and lavish feasts. Kind of exciting, really. *Must be the medieval atmosphere.*

I cross to him and rest my hand on his arm, meeting hard muscle. My heart starts its lusty drumbeat once more.

We're barely through the front hall when Neli appears with a platter of cheese, olives, and crackers. She holds two wineglasses by the stems in her other hand. "Where're you going?"

"The cellars," Mr. Bozhidar says. "We will dine later."

"Just a minute," she says. "I'll go with you."

"No need," he says at the same time as I say, "That would be nice."

He stiffens and looks down at me. "You wish for a chaperone?"

Chaperone? Now that's *really* old-school. "Uh, I thought it would be nice for her to join us. Isn't Neli a critical part of the success of your winery?"

"Why, yes, I am," she says, setting the glasses and platter on a hall table before rushing back to us. "Thank you, Stella, for saying so. It seems Mr. Bozhidar is eager to show off our wine."

"As he should be," I say.

A few minutes later, I step into the most spectacular cellar I've ever seen. It's an enormous vaulted space, made entirely of pale stone bricks with multiple archways, and lit with candelabras overhead and sconces along the sides of every archway. "Whoa," I breathe as we walk through the space, my hand still tucked in the crook of Mr. Bozhidar's arm.

He gives me a strange look. "Do you wish for me to slow down?"

"No, I'm fine." I inhale and take in the sweet musty scent of fermenting wine and oak barrels.

Neli snorts.

I look around. "Do you ever hold events down here? It's an amazing space."

"Events?" he asks.

"Yeah, you know, like a fun Halloween masquerade or a New Year's Eve party."

"Never," he says. "Though I am an avid observer of all variations of All Hallows' Eve, especially

Day of the Dead, but a party would invite too much temptation."

I lower my voice, though we're the only three here. "You mean people who would steal from you?"

"I cannot imagine anyone would dare. In my castle, we deal with thieves in the usual way," he says dismissively.

"What's the usual way?" I hope he means they call the police, but I'm sensing he's talking about something very different. Something much worse. *Damn. I really need to stop this.* There is nothing to be afraid of—with him or this place. *The creepy vibe is all in my head. The creepy vibe is all in my—*

"At Castle Sangria, we take a long piece of rope and—"

"Tie them up, of course!" Neli interjects from behind with a nervous tone. "Then we call the authorities. But we rarely hold any events. Our main focus is on production. Let's get on with the tour so we can get to the good part—the tastings for Stella."

He gestures to the sides of the vaulted archway we pass through, where there are various rooms. "Production area, armory, torture chamber, barrel room—"

"Sorry, what?" I interrupt. "Did you say torture chamber?"

"*Tasting* chamber," Neli chirps. "He calls it a chamber because it's such a large area, bigger than a room. It's under renovation now."

I glance to my right at a dimly lit space, where I

can barely make out glints of metal, but she rushes to my side and blocks my view.

I lick my dry lips. "Th-then you must do a lot of tastings here if you have such a large room for it." *Not creepy. Not creepy. Not cree—*

"We did before the renovation," she says.

I'm about to ask what kind of advertising they used for that, but I'm distracted by the quick movement of Mr. Bozhidar. One moment he's by my side, and the next he's pulling a dusty bottle of wine from the large rack in a nearby side chamber. The man is like a goth ninja.

He holds it up from where he stands by the wine rack. "Here it is, the best merlot in the world."

He's very proud, as he should be. We join him. Neli produces a corkscrew from a nearby cabinet along with some glasses and pops open the bottle. She pours us each a small sample. I swirl it around in my glass, smell it, and then sip.

They both wait for my reaction.

"It's wonderful, very smooth with notes of cherries and cocoa." I sip again because it's so good, as is feeling Mr. Bozhidar's intense gaze on me. It simultaneously soothes and excites me. "Some hints of vanilla and cedar from aging in oak barrels."

"Excellent," he says, filling my glass.

"We're glad you like it," Neli adds.

"Finish your wine, Stella," he says. "I have a cabernet sauvignon you must try."

I sip again, and he watches my throat as I swallow. I almost feel like I need to chug to get to the cabernet he's so eager for me to try. "Aren't you going to drink yours?"

He swallows his wine and wipes the red drops from his lips with a linen napkin Neli hands him. He tosses it carelessly to a nearby end table. He certainly acts like he's the king of the castle. Well, if he funded the entire venture, maybe he is.

Neli sighs, stuffs the napkin in her pocket, and sets her glass down on the end table, searching the rack for our next tasting wine.

By the time I've sampled his six reserve wines, I'm feeling tipsy. I practically float upstairs on Mr. Bozhidar's arm. "Now you should try my wine," I tell him. "I'd love your opinion on it. It's important that our wine wins some awards too. It's not looking good for our winery right now. Major financial troubles." *Oops! Did I say that out loud?* Here's my plan and backup plan—first, make the wine as great as it can be for the future of Stellariva. But that takes a while with the fermenting and all that, which is why I have a backup plan to win an award with our current wine. Even a smaller wine competition could help. I found one in the Finger Lakes of New York that looks promising. We already missed the major competitions here in California.

"Of course I will be happy to give you my opinion," he says, gesturing toward the great hall. His cape lifts as he moves, and I breathe in his fresh woodsy scent. "Let's return to the table, dine, and drink your wine."

I smile, feeling happily buzzed, and confide, "You smell wonderful, like your wine, sort of woodsy."

He leans close, his lips curving up, his white teeth gleaming. "Your scent is also intoxicating."

"Must be the wine cellar making us all smell so good," Neli announces as she passes us.

I giggle. I probably should eat something to go with all the wine sloshing around in my belly. I barely picked at my dinner earlier because I was so preoccupied with my meeting tonight. And look how wonderfully it's going so far!

We settle back at the long banquet table in the great hall. This time Neli joins us, pouring the pinot noir I brought, and offering a glass to me.

"Why don't you have mine?" I say to her. "I've had my fill for the night, and I'd like your opinion on the wine too."

"Don't mind if I do." She takes the chair across the table from me. "Cheers," she says, lifting her glass.

"Cheers," I say.

She sniffs, swirls, and sips. "Mmm-hmm."

I wait, hoping for more.

"Full-bodied," she adds, setting her glass down.

"Yes, I thought so," I say. "Do you have any tips for improvement?"

Neli stares at her glass. "Let me think on that."

That sounds promising. It's so good, she's not

sure how to improve it. Maybe we do have a shot at winning an award for our wine.

I turn to Mr. Bozhidar expectantly. He lifts the glass and sniffs, his brows knitting together.

I hold my breath.

He sips and spews the wine back in the glass. "Horse piss!"

I gasp.

He shoves the glass away, grimacing. "Horse piss mixed with putrid fish entrails."

"Boz, that was harsh," Neli says.

"What?" He shrugs casually. "I would not serve that swill to the prisoners in my dungeon. It is an insult to my lips. The Baker family should have stuck to their proper vocation—baking."

"Bakers? We're winemakers," I say with contempt.

"Are you so certain? Because the contents of that bottle say otherwise."

My eyes and cheeks are hot, nausea rising in my throat. I stand, completely mortified, unable to make eye contact.

"Stella, I'm sure he didn't mean that the way it came out," Neli says.

"No, I asked for his opinion." I swallow down bile and walk stiffly to the door. Only pride keeps me from bolting.

All the good feelings that built up around the eccentric Mr. Bozhidar vanish. He doesn't care about helping me, and he insulted our wine. I push the front door open through a blur of tears. Did he have to be so harsh? *Horrible, horrible man.*

The night air is cool as I pass the moat and cross my arms against the chill, hugging myself. *Horse piss? Putrid fish entrails?* Our wine can't be that bad, or my parents would've been out of business years ago. Right? I try to comfort myself with that thought. I like our wine, though I'm no expert.

My limbs are heavy as I trudge toward home. My parents pinned all their hopes on me to save the winery, and I've got nothing. Maybe it's time to face the hard truth. Our wine is good but not good enough. There's no hope to win an award. There's no hope for Stellariva.

CHAPTER SIX
Boz

Stella takes her leave, and I immediately notice a shift in the air, an emptiness in the room that was not there before. The realization triggers a pang in my gut. Or perhaps I am simply peckish. *Stella does smell rather delicious.* And while my body may have returned to its usual masculine perfection, something inside me does not feel quite right. Call it a thirst or hunger, but the sensation goes deeper than that, as if my soul has a boundless craving.

Must be a hangover from this goddamned sleeping curse. Whatever the reason, I now need to hunt, which means a change of clothes is required.

I leave the great hall only to find Neli waiting for me at the base of the staircase.

"Seriously, Boz?" Neli taps her foot with that strange little sandal. "Horse piss?"

I raise a brow. "How else would you describe her wine?" *Rancid ball sweat could work.* "And would you please procure yourself a proper pair of shoes to hide your toes? I am not running a brothel." In my village, only women open to courtship or harlots were allowed to show their toes in public. Neli is a slave and not permitted to marry. On the other hand, I was quite turned on by Stella's pink little feet, nearly naked in her white sandals—a sinful little preview of what lies beneath her virginal white dress. *She must be hinting that she wishes to offer herself to me.*

"Boz," snaps Neli, "you need to get over the whole toe modesty thing. It died along with corsets and hoopskirts, thank God. But you know what didn't change? Good manners. Why in the world would you call her wine 'horse piss'? It's really rude, and you hurt the poor woman's feelings."

"Yes, about that. I think you should invite her back for dinner tomorrow."

"Whyyy?" Neli growls with suspicion.

"I want to apologize." *With my fangs.*

Neli gives me one of her judgmental huffs. "You're thinking about biting her, aren't you?"

"No…" *Yes.*

"Uh-huh. Sure. Well, thankfully, after your insults, she's probably never coming back."

The words "never coming back" reverberate through my chest. Surprisingly, I do not like that idea. Must be the allure of her untouched body and virginal blood.

"Then you must go to her and fix it so she returns. For dinner. Tomorrow." My mouth begins to water at the thought of watching her eat. *Those lips…so full and sensual.* After she dines, I will enjoy her smile as I sip from her delicate neck. I am told

my bite is the best. Quite pleasurable. As long as I
do not kill them. Yes, as shocking as it sounds, some
women protest dying. *Should they not be honored to
perish in the arms of such a virile beast?*

I turn and head up the stone staircase to my
bedchamber. Nothing gets me in a good hunting
mood like a velvet cape and a pair of black leather
trousers, which Neli stole for me today. *I hope the
neighbors do not realize their clothing line has been
plundered by her on line shopping.*

I hear Neli's light footsteps close in as I push
open the heavy wooden door to my chamber. The
room itself is quite grand with a vaulted ceiling and
exquisite stonework throughout, but the real gem is
a large four-poster bed made of hand-carved
mahogany. *Very fine quality that has stood the test of
time.* The blood-red curtains on all four sides of the
bed are new—thank you, Neli, for doing at least one
thing correctly—and are perfect for my evenings of
seduction. (The red comes in handy to hide the
blood.) The other notable features in the room are
the paintings. My favorite is the portrait of my
master, the Great Kylgorii Gillmoreanu. His pale
face, with bony features and dark soulless eyes, gives
me great comfort. Like home. Then there is the
painting of his master, Prince Pamfilovamimivich.
He died after a very large bookshelf fell on top of
him. Apparently, he was knocked unconscious and
did not make it to his coffin before sunrise. *Poor
man.* The other pieces of art are all my own. I

particularly enjoy painting fruit. Round fruit. Bosom-esque fruit.

"Boz! Are you even listening to me?" Neli barks.

"Except for that last part, no." I continue walking toward my dressing chamber, a smaller room just behind one of the fireplaces. There is also a hidden staircase leading out to the garden. One must always have an escape.

"I said, Boz, I am *not* letting you seduce our neighbor. Things aren't like they used to be when you could just snack on anyone you like. Nowadays, they have technologies to catch criminals—satellites in the sky, home security systems, GPS tracking on phones. People notice when other people go missing or end up in a ditch, drained of blood. If you're not careful, you'll leave a footprint that'll lead the police right back here."

I haven't the faintest clue what she is talking about nor who these *technologenies* are. They sound rather annoying. "Silly girl, I do not leave footprints. Not if I do not wish to. I am a vampire." I do not fly, but I am quite skilled at the fine art of levitating. *Take that, technologenie!* "And the last time I checked, you are my slave for all eternity and must obey my every command or face shaming your family name." I start undressing from my formal attire by kicking off my new boots. Neli says the soles are made from a tree called "rubber," an appropriate name because I have blisters on my heels from all of the rubbing. *Nothing beats shoes made by the soft hands of tiny Transylvanian orphans forced to work in exchange for bread crusts.* Their attention to detail is unmatched. Hunger is a wonderful motivator.

"Yeah, about that, Boz. I think it's time to renegotiate."

I lift my brows and get to unbuttoning my fine lacy shirt.

She continues. "Look, times have changed. People just don't go around owning other people."

"I am not a people. Neither are you." Neli's soul is bound to mine—I have had her blood, and she has had mine. As long as she remains loyal to me in mind, body, and heart, she remains alive and, more importantly, ageless. If she were to betray me or walk away, she would suffer immeasurable pain and feel as though she were being burned alive. Another fun fact: Only I, her master, can give her the true death. Death by any other hand, including her own, will turn her into a vampire. Her choice. But until then, if I perish, she perishes. Therefore, my survival is critical to her own well-being, and by that, I mean she can continue to eat human food for sustenance. She can live forever, have children, walk in the sunlight, and do everything a regular human does without having to become a vampire. *Perhaps Cornelia requires a reminder of this.*

I add, "Neli, if you are no longer satisfied with our arrangement, I could offer to release your soul from its tether and send you on your way."

Neli narrows her green eyes. "Of all the vampires my parents had to donate me to, they chose the only one incapable of evolving."

"Do not be so damned dramatic, woman. We both know I was the only dark-prince game in town. I killed all of my rivals in my country." *Good times.*

"Maybe so, but I've come across quite a few vampires while you were snoozing, and trust me, you're an unchanged relic compared to them. I mean, you'd hardly even know they were hundreds of years old. They embrace change, and you've always resisted it. Even before you took your lengthy siesta, you were like an unmovable rock—always blabbing about the good old days and tradition and beheadings. You don't know how to grow as a person, and that, my friend, is a problem."

"Or, perhaps, it makes me a fine wine—better with age." Has she not seen how handsome I look with my long black mane and pale skin? It is very elegant. Then there are my eyes with their silver flecks, like a moonless night twinkling with stars. Finally, there is my physique. A Roman statue but without the baby-sized pecker. I am all man, all stallion. *And all vampire!*

"Boz, you're not listen—"

"Cease your complaining, Cornelia." I flick my wrist. "You have enjoyed centuries of life thanks to me. And might I remind you that when it comes to masters, you could have done worse. I never beat you, did I? I never made you wash my genitals or shave my scrotum during the hot summer months. I never forced you to lie with me when I felt the need to blow off a little steam." I am a gentleman, and a gentleman never forces a woman to his bed. Besides, I never felt an attraction for Cornelia.

"Thank God for small favors," she mutters under her breath.

"I heard that."

"Sorry, Boz. Not that you're unappealing or don't deserve to have a tender touch when it comes to manscaping your undercarriage. And yes, we all know there's a reason your looks are legendary—people once sang campfire songs about your ass in those leather pants—but frankly, I'm attracted to men who don't force me to lure young women to their deaths and then make me hide the bodies." She crinkles her pert nose.

She should be honored to do my evil bidding. It is all part of the fun. "I did not see you complaining when my protection afforded you your pick of cocks in the village." Neli had quite the sexual appetite. She slept with at least three different men over two hundred years—very provocative for a woman in the 1400s. Yet, did I call her a whore? No. I did not. *Not until she started flaunting her toes all over the goddamned place.*

"Has it ever occurred to you that men like sleeping with me because"—she holds up a finger—"they're men, and men are horny. And B"—she holds up a second finger—"I'm hot. But that's not the point of this conversation. I have more than served my time, Boz. I saved your castle, I built a small empire, and I kept you safe. For five centuries! Not including all the years before you pissed off that witch."

"So?" This is Neli's job. Do you see me seeking a pat on the back for culling the weak from the human population? No. I serve. I kill. I move on.

I kick off my cloth trousers and slide on my leather ones. The leather is easier to clean after I hunt. *And they emphasize my manly endowment. This is something that never goes out of style with women. You're welcome, ladies.*

"*So,*" she says, "I want more freedom. I want to be treated like an equal partner."

I stare at her oval face and then explode with laughter. "Very amusing."

"But, Boz—"

"But nothing!" I bark, my patience snapping like a twig. "I am your master. I will always be your master. And you will obey me, or I will find another—"

"Person who's the key to accessing all your money? Will you find another business-savvy human who puts up with your bullcrap too? How about a manager for your award-winning winery that pulls in millions of dollars each year?"

"What is a dollar?"

She rolls her eyes. "Help me, Jesus."

"You keep him out of this!" I look over my shoulder and then the other. She knows I fear anything that rises from the dead. Besides other vampires. It is very unnatural. Why does she think vampires fear the cross? We do not wish to summon *him.*

"Sorry." She holds up her hands in the surrender position. "All I'm saying is that if you want to appear as a normal man in this day and age, then you have to treat women as equals, starting with me. Otherwise"—she shrugs—"I'm afraid Stella won't be the last woman to run out of here, hating you with a fiery passion for your rude, antiquated, caveman-like ways."

Hmmm… She does make a valid point. Blending in will be critical to my survival. Neli has already explained that our kind now lives in the shadows.

I raise my strong, manly chin to let her know who's boss. "I will consider *pretending* you are my equal, but for appearances only."

She sighs. "I guess it's a start."

Wrong. It is an end. To Neli's irrational notions of vampire-human equality. Laughable. *I'd sooner become a fruit bat.* The faster she realizes that I am and always will be superior, the better. "And now, you must go to see that Stella woman and convince her I am a wise, trustworthy man of honor who most definitely does not want to suck her virginal blood."

"But—"

"Do it or I will send you to the dungeon without any supper."

"We don't have a dungeon," she throws back.

"What! No dungeon?" What sort of castle has no dungeon? "Where will I imprison my enemies?"

"We needed the space to store more wine. I figured with the extra revenue, you could rent a place—a mine shaft or empty warehouse—to vanquish your foe."

I bob my head. "You are very efficient, Neli."

She looks away, her posture rigid. I cannot deny that it makes me unhappy to see her feeling wounded, but if I do not assert myself as master, all hell will break loose. *The natural order must be obeyed.*

"Jeez. Thanks."

"Neli," I soften my tone, "I am a man. A very strong, handsome, and powerful man with a tempting sexual aura. Nevertheless, I do have compassion for the predicament you face in having such a small inferior female brain. Living in the shadow of such greatness is never easy, but I have faith. You will overcome."

She silently snarls up at me.

I bow my head and reach for my cape hanging on a hook. "I am glad to see we are in agreement. Now, you must excuse me. I need to finish dressing and prepare to hunt a snack in town." I am in the mood for a chardonnay. And by that, I mean a human whose bloodstream is saturated with it. "You will apologize to the virgin and have her back here tomorrow night at seven sharp." I know I said that I should resist drinking my neighbors, but that was before I realized that Stella might just be the most delicious woman on the planet.

CHAPTER SEVEN
Stella

"There you are!" Mom exclaims the moment I step inside the house after my humiliating meeting across the street.

My dad hovers behind her, looking anxious from the archway of the living room. "You didn't text, and we were getting worried."

I let out a breath of exasperation. "I forgot. I had some of their award-winning wine and got a little tipsy."

"You want something to eat?" Mom points over her shoulder toward the kitchen. "There's cherry pie."

My stomach feels sour. "No, thanks."

"Well? How did it go with our neighbor?" Dad asks.

They both look at me expectantly. I can't tell them the truth. That he spit out our wine and insulted it.

I rub the back of my neck. "It wasn't as helpful as I hoped. He didn't share any wine-making secrets, and their marketing seems to exclusively rest on their reputation from all their awards," I lie.

Honestly, we never got that far in the conversation.

"We tried to win something in a few local competitions last year," Dad says.

"Nothing," Mom says. "I think the judges are biased toward previous years' winners."

"Ah." What else can I say? That maybe our wine isn't so good? "I'll come up with something. Maybe a newly designed label to make the vineyard look like an old European estate. Sometimes perception makes all the difference."

"I like our label," Mom says.

My shoulders slump. I just feel so defeated by tonight, so damn tired. "I'll think on it more. Good night."

"You're going to bed already? It's not even nine." My mom glances at the grandfather clock in the corner of the living room. It's an old family heirloom and oddly reminds me of the stuffy, pompous jerk across the road.

"Just need to relax and unwind," I say and head upstairs. My only other idea is hard-core grassroots marketing. Showing up at every shop in the area to try to place our wine, calling every distributor and offering them a deal. We may lose some profit, but it could give us a foothold. Tomorrow. I'll get started tomorrow.

The next morning I drive off in a van full of our

wine for my in-person selling campaign. I'm wearing a flowing maxi dress in a light red and white block pattern that I hope says sophisticated and professional. I've got my list of potential customers that I'm eager to put check marks next to with each successful sale. Just because our wine hasn't won any awards doesn't mean it's horse piss. Jeez.

Yet, time after depressing time, it's a no. No one will even *try* the wine. They tell me there's no shelf space, or they want me to pay for a display. I'm tempted to slip a few bottles onto the shelf when they're not looking, but it's not like we'd profit from it. The heavy pit in my stomach is growing bigger by the second, and I'm starting to feel a little desperate.

I drive home in the late afternoon, trying to psych myself up for pitching the wine to distributors in a long cold-calling session. My parents already tried the main distributors. I'll hit up the little guys. Any niche I can get us into is a step in the right direction.

When I let myself into the house, the welcome scent of the twins' famous oatmeal chocolate chunk cookies hits me. *Yes, please.* Exactly the sugar-filled comfort food I need before my long slog on the phone.

I head to the kitchen, eager to dive in. "Just what I needed…" I trail off at the shock of seeing Neli sitting on a stool at the island counter next to my mom. Neli looks relaxed and refreshed—the exact opposite of me at the moment—in a white peasant blouse and white capris. Mom's in her usual T-shirt and jeans. They're having tea. *What the hell?*

"Hi, honey," Mom says. "Neli stopped by to see you, so I invited her to stay for tea. Your sisters made your favorite cookies."

Mabel turns from the sink, where she's washing dishes. "Mom said you needed a pick-me-up."

Eliza nods, looking worried.

"I'm fine," I say firmly, mostly for Neli's benefit. I don't want her to know how much last night rattled me. "But thank you for the cookies." I take one from the large cooling rack and bite into warm gooey perfection. I close my eyes, giving myself this moment of pleasure before having to deal with Neli. I'm sure she hated our wine as much as Goth Man, but was too polite to say so. Maybe she came over to apologize for him, but I don't want to hear it. Just thinking about his insulting manner makes me angry all over again. He's already sucked all the positive energy out of me, and I won't allow him to drain me dry.

I finish my cookie and take a seat at the island counter next to my mom.

"Neli was just saying how much she enjoyed our pinot noir," Mom says.

I stare at Neli, disbelieving. *What game is she playing?* "Oh, yeah?"

"Yes, I hoped we might collaborate on a project," Neli says cheerfully.

I stiffen. "Collaborate?" There's no way I'm working on anything that involves the horrible man next door. I don't know how Neli puts up with him. He's insufferable, insulting, indecent! So many "in" words fit that *inhumane* man.

Metal cupcake pans hit the floor with a clatter. "Sorry!" Eliza chirps. "Just getting things ready for our new cinnamon bun cupcake recipe."

"Maybe we should take this to the patio," Mom suggests.

I shake my head. "Actually, that won't be necessary. I'm not interested in collaborating. We're going in another direction." I stand. "Excuse me, I have some calls to make." I walk out.

"Stella, what's wrong?" my mom calls after me. "Don't you even want to hear her idea for collaborating? She waited all this time to tell you."

I keep walking, heading toward the stairs. "No, thank you."

"Stella!"

"I've got work to do," I say.

I'm halfway up the stairs when Neli appears in the front hall below. "Stella, wait. Can we take a walk?"

I grip the handrail tightly, trying to rein in my temper. I don't want to lash out at Neli when I'm mad at *him*. "I'm really very busy."

"Five minutes, okay? I think you'll find it worth your while."

I clench my teeth, pride and curiosity battling it out within my mind. "Okay, five minutes."

I go downstairs and lead her through the front door. We take the brick path toward our flagstone patio, where we host tastings. It's set back a ways from the vineyard. My sisters and I used to play in the grassy yard next to the patio, on a swing set that's long gone.

I gesture for Neli to take one of the cushioned swivel chairs under a large patio umbrella. I deliberately choose the chair that will keep my back to the castle across the street. I know the reminder will just piss me off.

"First, let me just say your wine is not horse piss," she says.

"Gee, thanks."

"Boz shouldn't have said that. He's going through something right now. Some massive, uh, life changes, and it's made him a little loopy. We're both very sorry about the way things ended last night. He asked me to come over today and make it right."

"You did nothing wrong, Neli. There's nothing to forgive. As for him, he can apologize for himself if he really means it."

"He's sun sensitive because of some…medication, but maybe he can stop by one night to do just that."

I instantly feel bad for despising the man. He has a sleepwalking condition *and* he takes heavy-duty medication. My brows draw together, thinking a little more about his eccentricities. Neli also said he works a lot at night too. So many things that don't quite fit—avoids sunlight, works nights, sleepwalks in the early morning, on heavy medication. He sounds like an oddball nocturnal animal. "What's wrong with him?"

"What's *not* wrong with him is a better question," she replies.

"Sorry to hear it." I lean forward. "I appreciate you coming over to follow up, but I don't feel comfortable collaborating on anything. I don't think it's in my best interest to spend any more time with Mr. Bozhidar."

"I see." She shrugs one shoulder. "Okay, well, I tried. So, uh, nice chatting with you. Sorry it won't work out. Bye." She stands abruptly and heads back the way we came.

I stare at her rapidly retreating back. Funny. She didn't sound sorry. She sounded kind of cheerful when she left. I shake my head. What an odd pair those two are.

Guess we didn't miss anything never spending time with our neighbors.

Boz

"What do you mean she's not interested in spending the evening with me?" I roar. This is the gravest insult. And I put on my new velvety cape for this? After a wonderful slumber and an arduous time selecting the perfect outfit for Stella's visit this evening, Neli has brought nothing but disappointment. "Did you tell her the pinot noir doesn't taste like horse piss?" I gave Neli strict instructions to say just that.

"Yes, Boz, I did exactly as you asked. And I said we were sorry about the way things ended last night."

"Did she forgive you?" A vampire never apologizes, so Stella had better appreciate the gesture.

Neli looks to the floor, finally submissive, as my servant should be. "I think so."

"Then what is the problem? I demand you bring the virgin here tonight."

Her head jerks up. "Boz, it's different now. You can't just summon a virgin. And how do you even know she *is* a virgin? A modern woman in her twenties probably isn't."

My nostrils flare. "It's in her scent. Roses."

"Roses," she mumbles.

Does she not recall the distinct odor of purity? Perhaps she's forgotten after sleeping with so many men over the centuries. I politely decline from mentioning her open-toed shoes and whoring ways with those three men. *Three!* Quite scandalous. The important thing is that Stella shows up as I've planned.

"Did you tell her I summoned her here this evening, yes or no?" I demand.

She holds up a palm. "In so many words."

"How many words does it take? It is a simple phrase. My master summons you."

She grimaces, most likely at the reminder of her incompetence. "People don't say summons nowadays. I mentioned collaborating."

"Collaborating." I try the word out on my tongue, not liking the feel of it. "What does this mean?"

"Never mind." She takes a deep breath. "Bottom line—she says it's not in her best interest to spend time with you, and I have to say she's not wrong."

"You speak in riddles, woman! I am never at the bottom. I am on top. I am the Great Prince Bozhidar Alexandru and must be obeyed." I flash my fangs in displeasure.

She backs away, cringing at my display of power. This doesn't make me feel as good as I hoped. The Stella problem harps on me. For some reason, her abrupt departure last night made a hollow ache in my chest area. I thought her virgin blood would help the ache, but perhaps it is her presence I crave too. Why else would I feel like howling at the moon like a lowly werewolf? They don't know their head from their ass the way they chase their tails.

"Neli, you must solve the Stella problem."

She lets out a long breath that I assume is necessary for her to summon the strength to face me again after I intimidated her so with my fangs. "Why her, Boz? She's got enough troubles without adding a hungry vampire to the mix. Her mom says their winery isn't doing well, and they're hoping Stella's marketing know-how is going to bring them back from the dead, so to speak." *Zombies?* At my horrified expression, she adds, "Not literally." Most unnatural the way decaying corpses walk the earth.

Neli blows out another harsh breath.

I am beginning to wonder if Neli has contracted consumption. It would explain her unusually insolent behavior lately. *That would be most inconvenient.* Not that she would die, since she is practically immortal, but that does not mean she can fall ill. Who would brush my hair before bed?

She adds, "I feel like you need to catch up with modern speech. Maybe I'll have you watch all ten seasons of *Friends*. That's where I learned the most about current dating customs."

I cock my head. "Dating customs? Is there some sort of exchange of fruit? I don't believe we grow dates anymore."

She laughs and promptly quiets at my glare. "I'm talking about how modern men and women spend time together."

Finally. She is fixing the problem. "That is what I need. Bring me these friends of yours, and then tomorrow I will be prepared for Stella."

"To do what?"

"For the dating."

She blows out another breath. *Definitely consumption.* I'd better have her call for the leecher.

"The only way I'm going to arrange for you to spend time with Stella is if you help her with her family's winery. Not bite her, not mate with her. *Help her.*"

"You must assist me with the dating. I command it."

"What if we work on a wine blend from our varietal and hers? Maybe then she'd have a chance at actually making a decent wine."

I arch a brow. I have my doubts. Mixing a fine wine with horse piss will taste like fruity horse piss, but my need to see Stella again trumps any argument against it. "And then Stella will spend time with me once more?"

She hesitates.

If I had a beating heart, it would be pounding in anticipation. As it is, every muscle in my spectacular body tenses.

Finally, she says, "If you let me help you adapt to modern times—"

I gesture impatiently, waving her on. "Yes, yes, watching your friends, but not for ten seasons, just the one night. I cannot wait ten long seasons to see Stella again."

She makes a strange face, almost like she wants to smile except her lips are smashed tightly together. "Then yes. I think she'll agree to spend time with you."

Fire shoots through me, the fire of victory. I will have what is mine. Stella.

CHAPTER EIGHT
Boz

I spend the entire evening watching the tiny friends perform several stage plays through the magical window on this "TV" Neli has installed in my bedchamber near my reading chair. I do not know when they sleep or where they hide the audience, who seems to laugh every few seconds, but I find no humor in any of it. To the contrary, this group of very old adults—in their late twenties—are very peculiar. They are unwed, own no land, have no servants, and the females are well past their childbearing years. Also, apparently no one works despite claiming to have jobs.

The most shocking thing, however, is the state of these very castrated, docile men. *The horror!* They do not speak directly to a woman when they desire her, and instead try to woo her with polite conversation while drinking coffee. Weak coffee. With milk. What sort of man puts the juice from the teat of a lactating cow in their coffee? And, pray tell, what is the matter with simply telling a woman what you desire? *Come here to my chamber, wench, I wish to plow you.* Why not offer her father something of value in exchange for her? A goat. Or a pig, perhaps. I simply see no point in being a man of means if one does not wish to barter for goods and the sexual companionship of a woman. *Or for handing over their tasty virgin daughters to the local vampire.*

"I bid you good evening, friends," I say with a malcontented sigh to the actors, though they stay in character even when I press the little red button on the handheld box that controls the TV's stage curtain.

I sit quietly in my chair next to the dwindling fire and contemplate the uneasiness in my chest. *What is the matter with me?* It is almost sunrise, and I have not fed, yet I have no appetite. Not for the local fare I have been sipping outside the pubs. The startling truth is I only wish to sink my fangs, and perhaps another part of my anatomy, into a certain female across the road.

Hmmm… I rub my rough chin, mulling over the idea of paying her a visit. I have about one hour before sunrise. *Yes. I will go in through her window and take a whiff. That should sate me for today.* But what about tomorrow? Or the day after?

Another idea hits. If Stella will not agree to engage in this collaboration, then I will use my powers of suggestion. By tomorrow, she will be begging to see me.

Knowing I must be discreet if I am to sneak into her bedchamber unnoticed, I undo the buttons of my white shirt and enter my dressing room in search of something darker to go with my black leather trousers. On the shelf are soft stretchy woven things Neli calls *sweaters*. I hold up the dark blue one with long sleeves. *Ick.* It has no ruffles or fine buttons made of those iridescent seashells I favor, but it will have to do. I have not gone to the tailor just yet.

I slide on the garment—*oh, very soft*—and glide my hands over my torso while I gaze into the large beveled mirror mounted to the wall. The clothing nicely displays my strong muscles and broad chest.

I turn and look at my firm backside, now also on display since my long shirt no longer conceals it. *Could split firewood with that ass.* I still prefer formal attire, but I do believe this sort of outfit will assist me in enticing a certain human to my bed—something I would want her to do willingly. It is one thing to use my abilities of persuasion to make a human want to spend time with me, but it is very unsportsmanlike to hypnotize a female into sex. *Where's the fun in that?*

"Eh-hem! And just where do you think you're going?" Neli snaps, appearing in the doorway of my dressing room, wearing a very unusual fuzzy robe with animal print. *Women's fashion is very strange in these times.*

"Out for a little stroll."

She raises one red brow. "So close to dawn?"

I pull back my long hair and grab a piece of leather from my grooming drawer to tether it. I do not want it in my way when I scale Stella's home.

Wait. "Is Stella's bedchamber on the first or second floor?"

"Boz, no!" Fire shoots from Neli's green eyes. "Don't you dare go over there."

"Calm your feathers, little hen. I am merely going to treat myself to a whiff of her delicious scent before I go to coffin." I finish tying off my locks and glance once more in the mirror at my pale face. The high cheekbones are nice, as is my strong jaw and brow line; however, I have been told by many women that my full lips are very sexually enticing. *Perhaps I should use this to my advantage and draw more attention to them.*

"Do you think I should cut my hair and go for a more modern look?" I ask Neli. "Like those Joey and Ross men?" I also cannot help noticing the lack of chalkiness of their skin. In my time, being supremely pasty was a sign of grandeur and influence. *Or the bubonic plague?* In any case, people of stature did not spend their days outside, working the fields or tending to cattle. The paler the better. Now, after seeing these friends perform their daily peasant duties, I am beginning to understand that the common man of this era spends his days inside very large buildings, slaving away on their electronic devices. The outdoors is reserved for those with free time, wishing to relax. "I also understand there is a product to give a man's skin the darkened appearance of one who enjoys leisurely afternoons by the ocean or on a yacht. Do I have a yacht? If not, please procure five before I wake, and ensure they are very glamorous."

Neli's eyes flicker with agitation, and her face turns an angry shade of red. I am now wondering if I have misdiagnosed her consumption. *Perhaps she is in need of a long walk outside to feel more fashionable.*

"Boz," she growls.

Ah! I suddenly realize why she is upset. "You may borrow my boat on your annual day off, if this concerns you."

"No! For fuck's sake, you do not have a yacht, and if you did, I wouldn't want to borrow it."

"Then what vexes you, girl? Out with it." I flick my wrist in her general direction.

She crosses the room and shakes a finger in my face. "If you go over to Stella's, we both know you'll be tempted to take more than a whiff and—"

"And what?" I sneer, growing impatient with her lectures.

"Your score with virgins is: Boz, eight hundred plus. Virgins, zero."

Of course it is. I am the master and always get my way. "I want you to make an appointment with the barber and a good tailor today while I sleep. I wish to look like gentlemen of this era. Perhaps a nice suit made of leather, but with more modern lines. I would also like to know the location of one of these sorceresses who can give my skin a golden luster." I shall spare no expense to impress Stella so she will submit fully to me.

Neli rolls her eyes. "You're totally going over there and ignoring everything I said, aren't you?"

"Yes." I am going to use my gifts to ensure Stella wants to spend time with me, but that is all. I will have to depend on good old-fashioned seduction for the rest. "And if you had done your job to convince her to come to the castle this evening, I would not be forced to take matters into my own hands, now would I?" I open the door that leads to a concealed staircase behind my mirror and head for the stone steps leading downstairs to the garden.

"Fine! Guess I'll start packing, then, since we'll be on the run after you kill her! Thanks, master!" Neli yells from inside the castle.

I do not understand why she believes I lack control. Have I killed a single human since I rose from my lengthy slumber? No. Not even when I felt ravenous.

Of course, this Stella is a temptation like no other. But how is this my fault? If Stella does not wish to be seduced by a vampire, she should try being less desirable. Maybe cover herself in cow dung or stop bathing altogether to mask that intoxicating scent.

Mmmm…roses mixed with notes of wine and sunshine. My entire body quakes with anticipation.

I zip through the hedges that border the castle's property line, and cross the dark road. The moment I step foot on Stella's property, a bloodhound howls from upstairs. I move swiftly to find the old hound in Stella's parents' room and stop the alarm.

Using my beastly hypnotizing spell, I command it. "Rabbit."

The dog settles to slumber, happily dreaming of chasing a rabbit. Such a simple joy.

I move swiftly to Stella's room, so close I am already salivating. My pulse will not slow. The ache in my veins turns to an excruciating fire burning out of control.

I must have her. I must have a bite.

Yes, just one. One nibble and then I will be satisfied until I can have her in my bed and drink all of her.

꙳ ꙳

Stella

I seriously shouldn't have taken that ZzzQuil. Because I just had this insane dream of a shadow walking around the room. *Next time, I'll drink warm milk instead.*

It's just that with so much pressure to save Stellariva, I can't seem to relax. Everything's riding on me.

Eyes closed and half-dozing, I roll onto my back, willing my mind to find a happier place to dream. Beach. Sunshine. Coconut trees growing giant bags of money so I can save Stellariva.

"You are so lovely," says a low, deep voice, causing me to jackknife upright.

Shit. "Who's there?" I listen carefully over the quiet whirr of my white noise machine and open my eyes as wide as possible, but I don't see anything in my room aside from the pale moonlight bathing the foot of the bed. "I'm losing my mind."

"No, my sweet Stella, I am the one who's losing his mind."

I blink, wanting to run or scream or do something even though I'm aware it's a dream. *Yet, that voice...* The way it fills my mind is hypnotic.

"Who are you? Who's there?" I ask, but deep down inside, I know the answer. My brain just won't let the name come out. It's like there's a wall inside my head.

A cool hand presses my chest, pushing me back down. "Rest now, my lovely Stella. You will forget I was here and fall into a deep sleep until the sun rises. Then you shall wake with an insatiable desire to spend every waking moment with your stunningly handsome and *irresistible* neighbor, Mr. Bozhidar. Also, you will *not* notice the small hickey on your neck and will tell everyone who asks that you were attacked by a very aggressive mosquito."

What? I chuckle. *What a freakin' hilarious dream.*

"What do you find amusing, woman?" the deep voice snaps.

"My neighbor? Irresistible? I'd sooner have sex with a toad or marry an old shoe." Not that my neighbor is an ugly man. In fact, at first glance, he's actually pretty beautiful. But then he opens his mouth, and it's like a train wreck of rudeness. *Thank God I never have to see him again and this is a dream.* I sigh with relief. I know it's not real, but maybe I needed this. Laughter is the best cure for stress.

"I am no toad or shoe." The voice grows louder. "I am the night. The darkness. The sin you have desired your entire life."

The raised volume in his voice jars me from my twilight state. *Or am I still dreaming?* Unsure, I sit upright again and see the shadow standing at the foot of my bed. It has a distinctive male form— broad shoulders, thick arms, and a narrow waist. *Wait.* "Mr. Bozhidar?"

He grumbles something in a language I do not understand, and then I hear, "Sleep, Stella. Sleep, I command."

I lie back down, my body growing heavy and melting into another dream. I fall into the deepest, most relaxing slumber ever.

When I wake, I feel like a new me, only re-membering tiny pieces of my bizarre night and all the images my mind dreamed up. *Hilarious. Talking shadows that looked like my neighbor...*

I hop from bed and go to the bathroom to get started for the day, but as I pass the mirror, I spot something on my neck.

What the hell? I lean forward over the pedestal sink, inspecting the two bumps and small red marks surrounding them. I must've had a very aggressive mosquito in my room last night.

Suddenly, a vision of Mr. Bozhidar pops in my head, and my stomach does a flip. Lower still, there's an ache of desire.

WTF? I'm just being silly. I don't want that man, and I never will. I'm simply excited about collaborating with him now that I've had time to cool off. It's the perfect solution to Stellariva's problems.

I'll invite him over tonight. He can meet my family, and we can start working together.

CHAPTER NINE
Boz

Challenge accepted! After listening to Stella's ludicrous nocturnal mumbles, comparing me to a wart-covered amphibian, I am now more determined than ever to seduce the virgin across the road. It will require every weapon at my disposal, but when I am done with her, she will be eating out of my cold hand, begging me to bed her.

The battle begins tonight! Neli has arranged for our collaboration, and we will meet Stella at her home this evening.

I have spent the early evening hours preparing, not wasting a moment. When I rose at sunset, a man with short dark brown hair with an unfortunate streak of yellow through the top (perhaps a sorcerer's curse?) was waiting to give me a haircut. It is now cropped short in what Anton calls a "crew cut," though I argued it should be called a "master cut," a term he was forced to agree with in the end, because, as Anton rightly pointed out, the shorter cut draws attention to my supremely handsome features. Neli paid him richly for his time, and I used my power of suggestion to make him forget.

Next, a strange brassy woman with orange hair and a gold hoop through her nostrils invited me to her "mobile tanning station," a large white box on wheels. She sprayed me with a liquid that instantly gave me the look of a man who has the means to spend leisure time outdoors. Joey and Ross have nothing on me. I am now every bit the virile modern man of means. *Well, almost.*

At present, I am preparing for the final step in my transformation. Neli is driving me to see the tailor whose shop is inside the marketplace. Very odd.

"I am enjoying the speed of this horseless wagon," I say, exploring the levers on the door that lower and raise the window. There is also a device that plays any sort of music one wishes to hear. *The marvels of the modern world.*

"The horseless wagon is called a Beemer," Neli replies, her eyes keenly focused on the well-groomed road.

"It is a definite improvement over traveling by carriage."

"I'm glad you're enjoying some of the perks modern life has to offer. Maybe keep that in mind when we're shopping for your clothes."

"Why? What is it that I will find?"

"I don't know how to break it to you, but…"

"Well? Out with it, girl." I snap my fingers.

"Leather pants are no longer in fashion for men."

"What? This is criminal! How are men supposed to protect their cocks while pillaging or plundering?" That used to be my favorite pastime when I was a young vampire. Obviously, we did not have TVs back then, so one had to have a hobby. Later, as I grew into a more sophisticated and kinder vampire warlord, I enjoyed reading and painting.

"Pillaging is illegal now. You can't just burn down people's homes and take things because you feel like it. Plundering is still in, though, but they call it *income taxes*, and it's done by the government."

"This era is no fun." Perhaps I can improve things by bringing back leather trousers. I have been known to start a fashion trend or two in my day. For example, capes. That was all me. Those other vampires were copycats.

"I'm sure you'll find other things to entertain you, Boz."

Yes. Her name is Stella. "And what else may I expect to find at this marketplace?" Perhaps I will buy my sweet little human a trinket. Or a monkey. Or a monkey wearing a trinket.

"The marketplace is called *a mall*. They have a little of everything, but mostly people go to buy clothes—they have about twenty or thirty shops to choose from."

"So many tailors in one location?" How extravagant.

"The clothes are already made. You just buy

them and take them home to enjoy."

"Well," I grumble, "I will insist on trying them on before I make my purchases, as I doubt the tailors of this time are accustomed to dressing a man of my spectacular physique."

Neli mumbles something about a bloated ego-maniac—one of the other drivers must have offended her in some way.

The Beemer comes to a halt next to several other Beemers in a large open stable of sorts. I look around, searching for the stalls and tents of the merchants displaying their wares, but all I see is a large beige structure that reminds me of a box.

"Where is the marketplace?" I ask impatiently. She knows time is of the essence. Tonight I shall see my Stella and take one final sip of her delicious virgin blood before her deflowering. Ah, the delights of seducing a maiden.

"Everything is indoors, inside that building." She points to the structure. "Are you sure you don't want me to pick an outfit for you? It's a little bright in there with all the lights."

"Nonsense. I am even more attractive by candle-light."

"It's not candlelight, Boz. It's artificial light, like we have inside the house, but brighter, like a thousand mini suns."

I stare at her in horror. "Do you have a death wish?" She knows my well-being is tied to hers, and artificial or not, so much light cannot be healthy.

"It won't kill you. I've seen other vampires here before, but they protect themselves."

"If I had known, I would have worn my hooded cape. You have been remiss in your duties."

"I couldn't let you wear a cape. Those aren't in style any longer either."

Sacrilege! What is wrong with these modern humans?

Neli reaches into her large leather bag and hands me an odd-looking black hat with a long brim only in front.

I study it from different angles and stare at a strange orange symbol. An incantation of sorts? I toss it back to her. "Is this witchcraft?"

She puts it on her head. "It's an S and an F together for the San Francisco Giants."

I take it from her and put it on since she was not instantly burned by its magic. "I thought giants were a myth. Do the people wear their symbol to ward them off? Are the giants fond of the mall?"

"It's a baseball team. A game of sport the locals enjoy." She hands me a pair of black glasses. "Put these on too. It'll help with the light."

"And do they fight to the death in this baseball?" *Perhaps I will join in this game. Nothing better than a fresh kill.*

"No. Can you please put on the shades?"

How clever. Shade for the eyes. I slide them on. "But how will the shopkeepers admire my striking black eyes? How am I to hypnotize them into giving me the best price?"

She blows out a breath, muttering, "Patience."

Another overly long breath from Neli. I simply cannot have a sick servant waiting on me hand and foot. She will be much too slow. "If you insist on not calling the leecher—"

"I'm not sick!"

"Then you must need more fresh air. I insist you take a long walk outdoors on your annual day off." When I was first gifted Neli, I was not the generous master you see today. There was no such thing as a day off. If a slave wished to eat, they worked. If they wished to live, they obeyed. Of course, Neli was an obstinate, disrespectful, wild beast of a girl when her family gave her to me. They were tenants on my land, farming various grains and squashes. One year, there was a drought and they could not pay their rent, so they offered Cornelia.

"Do you mean to tell me," I said to her mother, "that is not a large rat?" She was covered from head to toe in mud. I could not even tell she had red hair underneath it all.

"Her name is Cornelia." Her mother pushed her through the back door of my castle. "She is a good girl. Hard worker."

Who were we kidding? The locals knew what I was. This child could not have been more than ten summers, and she was *not* being offered up as a servant.

"I am sorry," I had told her mother. I pushed

the dirty runt back outside, using the tip of my finger to avoid getting grime on myself. "I do not require additional labor." I dropped my voice. "She is too young." In other words, I did not drink children. Even evil vampires must have limits.

"Well," her mother pushed her back inside and said, "I have nothing else to pay you with—no other children, no cattle, no money—so take it or leave it."

My patience grew thin. I was in the middle of my painting lesson. "The answer is no. I will not accept her as payment. You have one day to return with gold, or you must vacate your land."

I reached for the runt, but this time she ducked, stepped to the side, and kicked me in the shin. "Ugly bastard!"

I looked down at her and raised my hand, intent on giving her a smack on top of her mud-caked head as a warning, but then our eyes met. She did not shrink away from me. She did not show fear. Just...defiance and fire. *With a delicious evil streak. Mmm...*

"Well, I suppose I could let her work in the kitchen." She would not be a child forever and could make for a nice snack in a decade or so. "Off you go, now. Find Alina in the kitchen. Tell her she is to bathe you, feed you, and find you a clean dress."

Cornelia stuck out her tongue and ran off.

When I turned to her mother to bid farewell, I

will never forget the joyous gleam in her eyes.

Oh, I see. Offer the unruly child to the local vampire. In that moment, I realized why I, too, had been offered to my master as a boy. I was the runt. I was the wild, disobedient, unwanted child.

They sent me to my death. At the time I received Neli, I had been a vampire for centuries, yet I had never realized this. I believed I'd been offered as a servant, and never considered I was intended to be a meal. My master, the Great Kylgorii Gillmoreanu, took pity on me. He did not believe in eating children, a rule I learned from him. Later, once I reached my early twenties, he would find me invaluable and turn me.

In any case, the rage I felt in that moment, while staring at Cornelia's cruel mother, would lead me to a dark place that night. I never did tell Neli how her parents perished, or that they sent her to her death, but from that day forward, I felt protective of her. Perhaps because I saw her as a version of myself. *Left behind by those who were supposed to care for her.* When she came of age, I never even considered eating her as a snack. She was smart, feisty, and as close to family as a vampire like myself would ever get.

Then, on her twenty-third birthday, she asked me to change her, but I did not wish to curse her to a life in the darkness. There was, however, something appealing about the notion of never having to be alone again. A platonic forever companion. So I told Neli that I would give her my blood, and I would take hers. If she wanted to turn, she would have to do it herself by taking her own life. Until then, she would remain human, bound to me, ageless.

Looking back, I am pleased that I did not change her. I think once she saw all the benefits to being my immortal human slave, what was the point? She is afforded many luxuries, including one slice of bread and cheese each day. Her annual day off is also another lavish perk.

Neli smiles sweetly, grateful for my generous suggestion. "Yes, I'll look forward to fresh air on my day off next year. Can we get this over with?"

"Yes, I am ready for the final step in my transformation into a modern man. Stella will not know what hit her."

Neli rolls her eyes and mumbles, "It'll take a hell of a lot more than a suit and a spray tan to make you into a modern man."

"I am a fierce, deadly vampire. And last time I checked, being an alpha male never goes out of style." This battle is as good as won. "And now for my victory suit!"

CHAPTER TEN
Boz

The moment I step inside the mall, my senses are assaulted by the tiny suns and a cacophony of sound. I stay close to the edges of the space, passing by a variety of food stands with scents of meat, bread, and something spicy.

"Fortunately, it's a Thursday, so it's not too crowded," Neli says. "We should be in and out in no time. I'll point out the men's clothing stores, and if you like the outfits in the display window, we'll go in."

I follow her, uncertain of the right direction. How confusing this place is with the many paths and multiple floors. I stare at a moving staircase. There is definitely some witchcraft at play here. I will not be fooled so easily.

A few shops later, I find a store that is dim inside with pulsing music that reminds me of the delicious rhythm of a fresh vein.

"This is the place, Neli." I step inside a shop that is split down the middle—men's outfits on one side and women's on the other. What a talented tailor to attempt both.

"This store is for teens," Neli says under her breath.

I do not know who these teens are, and I do not care. This place is for me. I find it relaxing. A young man with blond hair that sticks up like a field of spikes approaches.

He stops in front of us, slouches, and shoves his hands in the pockets of worn light blue trousers with holes in several places. They must not pay the staff adequately here. "'Sup, can I help you?"

"I am Mr. Bozhidar, not a 'sup.' Please tell your tailor I will need an outfit in my size for this evening."

He gives me a lopsided smile and slowly nods his head. Perhaps the village idiot has been employed for the distributing of outfits already made in the proper sizes. It seems a simple job. "Sure, man. You look like a large. What's the occasion?"

I smile, pleased that I know all the modern lingo. "A date with a virgin."

"Big man! High five!" He holds his hand in the air.

High what? I flick my finger at Neli. I cannot deal with the idiot any longer.

Neli steps forward. "He means a first date. So how about you get us some jeans for a six-foot guy, bring a measuring tape if you've got it for his waist, and I'll help him with the shirts."

He nods, smiling for no reason. "I got you." He turns to me, still smiling widely. "There's a sale on our button-downs and some polo shirts up front that could be good for a virgin date." He chuckles and walks in a slow stroll toward the shelves in the back of the shop. His trousers are so ill-fitting I can see his underclothes with bright yellow faces sporting idiot smiles. Is this intentional to match his expression? His tailor boss has made a fool of him.

No matter. I turn and stride over to the shirts he indicated at the front of the shop. The buttons are only on top, and there is a formal collar. The sleeves are cut short. *Perhaps these shirts are meant exclusively for strong men, like myself, to display our arms in a show of muscular prowess.*

"I will take one of these in every color." I turn to Neli standing nearby. "Did you bring sufficient gold coins to cover it?"

She leans close. "They don't use gold coins anymore. It's more convenient to use this." She reaches into her bag and pulls out a small leather holder. From this she removes a slim black rectangle that shimmers in the dim space. I do not know what it is made of, but it is unlike anything I have ever seen before. "Here. I got one in your name. It's called a credit card. Basically, it's like an electronic banknote. You give it to the merchant and they use it to draft a note to the bank, who pays them on your behalf. You settle your account with the credit card company later."

I take the item and notice that my name is imprinted on it along with the words American

Express. "Very ingenious." Sounds like something I would have invented. "Please bring my items to the money man," I tell her. "Perhaps I will look for more of these shirts with short sleeves." I peruse the wares of "Must Have Tees" and take a white tee in large. Just to be sure, I remove my SF hat and sweater to try it on.

The store idiot approaches with a stack of blue trousers. "These jeans are super popular right now. They keep selling out, but we got a new shipment in this morning."

These "jeans" have holes in them, indicating that it is perhaps in fashion to not display one's wealth. A silly idea, but fine. I am here because I wish to blend in. I remove my shoes and leather trousers.

"Dear God!" An older woman covers the eyes of a younger woman. She must be protecting her virgin eyes. Ah, see, this is why men and women usually go to different tailors—the tender eyes of young maidens. When you are as well-endowed as I am, underclothes cannot be worn with leather trousers.

"Whoa, dude," says the idiot.

"Boz, no!" Neli exclaims, rushing toward me. "Put your trousers back on, please. There are dressing rooms for that."

"A whole room to dress? Why didn't you say so?" In my day, one simply stood in the middle of the tailor's shop while he fitted you.

The young man holding the light blue trousers

gestures toward the back, and I follow him. I can hear giggling from the women's side of the store, and that only makes me stand taller. Maidenly virtue is one of the highest delights.

"What is taking you so long?" I demand irritably as we walk through the mall toward the doors leading outside. "We must get to Stella's home within the hour." Yes, I finally figured out how to tell time using their clocks. It makes sense that they abandoned the sundial since the peasants spend so little time outdoors.

"Some help would be nice," Neli says from under a pile of bags hanging from her shoulders, wrists, and gathered against her chest.

"Yes, well, help cannot be found at the moment. I have not had time to procure another servant since I have just woken from a five-hundred-year nap." Could I *be* more sarcastic? I chuckle to myself. Chandler has taught me well.

Neli does not laugh. I could order her to, but I am suddenly halted by the most wondrous sight. There, across the indoor courtyard, a shop with a large portrait of a man and woman embracing. They are about to kiss.

A moment later, I peer into the shop and find jewels displayed on black velvet. It is perfect. A gift for Stella.

I stride forward confidently with my American card and stop in front of an elderly crone wearing a gray dress. "Hello, I am Mr. Bozhidar. I would like your finest jewelry as a gift for my virgin date."

"First date," Neli chimes in from behind me.

The crone indicates a chair in the corner. "Miss, why don't you have a seat and set your bags down?"

"Thank you," Neli says and shuffles to the corner.

"Perhaps you would like a simple silver bracelet?" the crone asks.

I suppress a shudder. Silver and I do not get along. "I prefer gold."

She points to a gold chain with a heart fastened on one end. "A sweetheart necklace could be good for a first date. Would you like to see it?"

I incline my head, and she pulls a key out from a drawer, unlocking the jewelry case. She removes the heart and opens it. "You can put a picture in there."

It is very nice, but I do not have time to sit for a portrait. "Perhaps another piece with jewels might be better."

"Wait, hold up," Neli says, rising from her chair. "Can you give us a moment?" she says to the crone.

"Of course," the crone says, stepping to the far side of the counter.

"What is it now?" I demand. "First you insist I wear these trousers that look worn by many others, and then you insist on underclothes, which confine my very large—"

"Boz, please! We need to get going. You're eager to see Stella, right?"

"Of course. But I must bring her a gift."

"Okay, but you can't bring her jewels on a first, uh, meeting."

"Date," I correct.

"Collaborative time together."

I suppress a sinister smile. *Soon, Stella, soon.*

"Just go with something simple," Neli says. "You know what modern girls like? These charm bracelets." She indicates a display case. "You can go with the gold, and later she'll enjoy adding charms to it."

I can hypnotize Stella, so I do not see the need for charms, but I will defer to Neli's knowledge of modern women. "Yes, I will go with this charmed bracelet."

I snap my fingers at the crone. "A gold bracelet and all your best charms."

Our time at the mall ends soon after that, and I am pleased with my purchases. After we are both seated in the Beemer, I begin to wonder if the bracelet will truly be enough. "Are you certain Stella would not want a pygmy finger monkey? Or a stable of albino horses?" I want her to know how beautiful she is, and what better way to show it than buying her exotic animals from faraway lands? Something to show off to her friends and make them envious.

Neli stifles a smile. "Yes, I'm sure. The gift you got her will definitely be enough."

I relax, removing my odd hat and black glasses. And now to seduce—no, I need to use modern lingo—to *collaborate* with my date for eternity.

CHAPTER ELEVEN
Stella

I've been weirdly anxious today, watching the clock in anticipation of Neli and Mr. Bozhidar's arrival tonight. Despite him being rude before, the thought of seeing him now sets off butterflies in my stomach.

What's up with that? Must be because I'm so excited about their willingness to collaborate with us. *A jointly produced wine! With the Castle Sangria Winery! How exciting! And doesn't Castle Sangria sound like a party place already?* Neli called to float the idea of a wine blend this morning, and I jumped on it, inviting them over to discuss the details. Nights work better for Mr. Bozhidar with his schedule and sensitivity to sunlight from his medication. (I wonder if he has Lyme disease. I've heard the antibiotics can make you sensitive to the sun. He otherwise seems to be the picture of health.) Anyway, I can be as flexible as they need if it means a solution to Stellariva's problems.

The twins made fresh-baked bruschetta with tomatoes and mozzarella. Mr. Bozhidar doesn't care for sweets.

My parents are settled on the sofa in the living room, but I'm too anxious to sit, so I pace the first floor, stopping to peek out the front window every ten seconds. Mabel and Eliza are hanging out in the kitchen, waiting to meet Boz for the first time. They'll make themselves scarce for the business part of the evening. I smooth nonexistent wrinkles out of my white maxi dress with light blue floral toile print. I love this dress with its cascading capelet short sleeves. I paired it with white open-toed heels. My long dark brown hair is down to cover the red mosquito bites that appeared on my neck this morning. I hope I look okay. *Oh, I can't wait to see him.*

Wait. I mean...I can't wait to discuss this new wine! Yes, that's what I meant. Because it would be silly to *want* to spend time with Mr. Bozhidar. He's rudeness personified. A barbarian in the body of an ancient warlord.

That doesn't make any sense either. But for some strange reason, every time I think of Bozhidar, I have a vision of him riding a dark stallion on a moonlit night, his black cape flapping in the wind. His eyes are intense, filled with fury and despair.

"Stella, you're going to wear a hole in the hardwood," my dad calls in a teasing voice, snapping me out of my weird thoughts.

I stop in the archway of the living room. "I'm too wound up."

"Clearly," says Mom, who is holding hands with

my dad on the couch. I hope one day I can find the kind of love they have, but for the moment, I'll take not seeing my family having to live in a cardboard box.

The doorbell rings, and I dart from the room, yelling over my shoulder, "I got it."

I open the door and my breath hitches. My gaze locks on the glowing black eyes smoldering down at me. He looks different somehow. More unbearably handsome and sexier. How's it possible? He's the same contemptible man I met earlier this week.

But everything about him feels different now. Maybe it's because I'm a huge sucker for unpretentious men with big hearts, and despite his impolite words about our wine, the fact he's willing to help strangers—my family—in a time of crisis speaks volumes about who Mr. Bozhidar really is. He has nothing to gain from helping us. *Nothing.* If anything, he's a very busy man, and we're pulling him away from his important business. Bottom line: Actions speak louder than words. Actions and honesty. In fact, now that I'm thinking about it; how can I be upset over that whole horse-piss incident? It was his *honest* opinion. I should respect him for his candor. Especially since he offered to help us instead of walking away like most people would. There are no words for how grateful I'm feeling right now!

Sadie shuffles forward, her bloodhound nose sniffing madly. As soon as she reaches Mr. Bozhidar, she goes crazy sniffing him from crotch to toes. Her head jerks up, and she bares her teeth in a low growl.

My mom gets a hold of Sadie's collar. "Sorry. I don't know what's come over her. She's usually so docile. She's getting old and senile." She pulls Sadie away to the far side of the living room and makes her sit.

Mr. Bozhidar looks down at me and flashes a smile that makes my knees weak. *Have his lips always been this sensual and full?* Maybe he got stung by a bee.

"Oh! You got a haircut," I say, though that's not quite it. My pulse is racing, and all of my nerve endings are tingling. "It looks good on you."

"You also look lovely, sweet Stella."

"Invite them in," Dad says from behind me.

"Sorry. Yes, come in. Hi, Neli, good to see you too." I was so taken with Mr. Bozhidar that I didn't notice her standing there. My parents introduce themselves and my sisters to Mr. Bozhidar with no help from me. I can't take my eyes off him. He's wearing a black polo shirt with faded jeans that cling to his muscular thighs. He doesn't look goth anymore. Maybe that's what has me so enthralled. Before he covered himself in a strange costume, and the full beauty of his face was hidden by his long raven hair. But now he's showing off every breathtaking, virile, manly inch. It reminds me exactly what lies beneath those formfitting clothes. I can barely think straight with the lust coursing through my veins.

And then Sadie stands up and howls. Mr. Bozhidar grimaces. *So strange.*

"Must be a full moon tonight," Dad says jovially. "I'll put her in our room." He guides Sadie up the stairs to their bedroom, where she normally sleeps.

"Stella," my mom snaps, drawing my attention, "everyone's going to the living room for drinks. Could you help me bring the bruschetta in?"

"Yes, of course," I mumble. The twins must've left.

I follow her, the hairs on the back of my neck rising. I stop and slowly turn my head to find Mr. Bozhidar standing in the archway of the living room, his legs shoulder width apart. He looks powerful, confident, and his gaze is eating me up. I flush hot and quickly turn away, heading into the kitchen.

I wonder what it would be like to feel those powerful-looking shoulders and chest—*ow!* I knocked into a kitchen stool.

"Are you okay?" Mom asks. "Did you have enough to eat today? You seem really out of it."

I stare at the counter, not really seeing it. Everything's a blur, like I'm swimming in a fog. "I'm fine. Maybe I'll have some coffee. I'm a little unfocused."

"You're working too hard." She gives my arm a squeeze. "I think things are going to start turning around for us now that we have a working relation-ship with Castle Sangria Vineyards. Knock wood." She knocks on her head.

I smile. "Okay, let's do this."

A short while later, we're all settled in the living room with sparkling water and a platter of bruschet-ta. The twins too, who apparently didn't leave, instead settling in the living room to not so casually check out Mr. Bozhidar. Our living room is a cozy space with a fireplace, built-in bookcases behind glass doors, and ornate crown molding typical of old Victorian homes. I'm on the plush blue sofa with my parents, the twins are perched on the arms of the sofa, and Neli and Mr. Bozhidar are on the adjacent light blue upholstered armchairs. Neli has been explaining about the process of mixing different varietals, but I can barely focus. My gaze is drawn again and again to Mr. Bozhidar sitting in his chair like he's the king. This is not a man who slouches. He owns the space. He hasn't taken a single sip of sparkling water or eaten a bite of bruschetta. For some reason it bothers me. Like maybe he thinks our food and drink are substandard just like he said about our wine.

Horse piss mixed with putrid fish entrails.

Such a rude person. *Wait. No.* He's an *honest* man. Which explains why I'm suddenly finding him so attractive. I despise lying men. *Learned that the hard way.* And I haven't met any guys who appealed in a long while, and here's this gorgeous muscled manly perfection right here in my living room, who lives across the street.

His eye catches mine, his lips twitching, and I turn away, blushing. That's the second time he caught me ogling him. I need to get a hold of myself. It's just that his new haircut really brings out his unusual eyes and the strong lines of his jaw and sensual mouth. And his formfitting clothes—

"Stella, honey."

I blink, glancing up in surprise at my mom, who's standing next to me. "Huh?"

"We're going outside to the storeroom now. Do you want to lie down? You don't look so good." She puts the back of her hand on my forehead. "And you feel a little warm."

I hear the faintest growl, and my head whips toward Mr. Bozhidar instinctively. His eyes gleam, the silver in them seeming to glow. I can barely breathe as I rise from the sofa, lost in those eyes. *What is happening?*

"I-I'm fine. Let's do the tour," I say, trying to shake it off.

My sisters stay behind, whispering to each other, uninterested in the business part of the evening.

Neli hooks her arm through mine and ushers me quickly from the room. "Can't wait to see how you're set up over here. Your mom had this great idea about you guys hosting private tasting parties on your patio using our wine. We never host. Way too busy. You can take a percent of the profits for the hassle, and we'll probably sell more wine. Already I feel good about this collaboration."

I snap out of it and focus fully on Neli. Somehow I missed the entire conversation. "I love that idea. You saw our patio the last time you were here. It's a nice covered space with a view of the vineyards and your castle too. If you're happy with the arrangement down the line, I could host special events in your barrel room, as well. I think a masquerade would be perfect for the ancient-looking space."

"You're full of great ideas," she says, pulling me along even faster.

The front door opens ahead of us. Mr. Bozhidar moved so quickly I didn't even hear him approach from behind.

I smile up at him as I pass, and he leans toward me, breathing deep.

Did he just smell me? I shiver as I step out into the warm night air. Neli appears by my side, chattering away, but this time I'm fully conscious of Mr. Bozhidar's powerful presence behind me. Where are my parents?

I glance over my shoulder. They're trailing behind, talking quietly to each other. Guess I'll have to be the one to show off Stellariva.

After a brief tour of our manufacturing facility on the east side of the property, which thankfully my dad took the time to explain, my mom offers our guests tastes of different wines to help narrow down the best option for mixing with theirs.

I watch Mr. Bozhidar closely for telltale signs of disgust, but there aren't any. I'm not sure he's even sipping the wine. He draws it to his mouth, tips the glass, and then licks his lips, his glowing black eyes smoldering into mine. I want to know what he thinks of it, if he's even tasting it, but at the same time all I want is to feel those lips tasting me.

This is crazy. I lift my hair off the back of my neck, suddenly fever hot. I can only pray I'm coming down with something. I can't even consider getting involved with the man who's the key to keeping our business afloat. What if things went bad between us? That would really be the end of Stellariva.

The rest of the evening passes by in a strange fog until *he* says his goodbye to my parents and then takes my hand, murmuring in a deep hypnotic voice, "Until we meet again." He brings my hand to his lips and kisses it, and then he turns my hand, palm up, and places something cool and heavy there, gently closing my fingers around it. "A gift for you."

My breath comes faster, my cheeks flushing. I open my palm to find a darling gold charm bracelet with several tiny charms. I'm floored by the sweet gesture. "Thank you, Mr. Bozhidar," I whisper.

His voice is silky. "Please, call me Boz."

He leaves, and I'm suddenly deflated, as if he took all the energy out of the room with him. Still, there's a lingering tingle in my stomach, like some strange afterglow. Whatever happened tonight, I can honestly say that I've never experienced anything like it. *Don't be silly,* I tell myself. *You can't risk getting involved with this guy.*

A moment later, my parents and I are standing in the foyer alone. I slip the bracelet on, admiring it.

"What's that?" Mom asks.

I return to myself with a start. "It's from Mr. Bozhidar. A gift."

"He must really want to work with us," she chirps. "A promising beginning."

"I didn't like the way he was looking at Stella with a hungry look in his eyes," Dad says, scowling. "And he gave her jewelry!"

"Oh, you," Mom says. "It's not like it's a ring. Overprotective dad, step down. So maybe he admired Stella. Any man would. Our daughter is beautiful." She strokes my hair back over my shoulder, smiling.

"Something is off with that guy," Dad grumbles. "Sadie went crazy. I haven't heard her howl like that in a long time."

I stiffen, suddenly feeling defensive. "He might be a little eccentric, but that's only worked in his favor. We can't turn our backs on this opportunity. This could be the answer to all of our problems. We might even win an award with a mixed varietal under our label. That could open doors everywhere."

"She's right," Mom says.

My dad crosses his arms and glares at the door our guests just exited. "I still don't like it. I think we need to be sure Stella's not alone with him."

"Dad! I'm not a kid anymore."

He shakes his head. "I'm telling you, Stella, something's not right with that man."

"Well, too bad," I say, "because he's our way out of this financial situation, and I'm not going to mess it up by insulting him."

My dad gives me a stern look. "I'm going to bring Sadie downstairs. Let's see if she's still acting strange about our eccentric visitor."

The moment Sadie returns, she follows her nose, sniffing everywhere Boz has been, all the way up to my charm bracelet. She growls low in her throat.

"See?" Dad says.

"She's just confused. Mom says she's getting senile in her old age."

My mom tilts her head, watching Sadie return to where Boz was sitting, sniffing again.

Maybe something about Boz *is* off, but the strange thing is, it doesn't scare me. To the contrary, I'm excited by him. Maybe more than I should be. I need to remember my priorities, and nothing is more important than saving my family's winery.

CHAPTER TWELVE
Boz

"Well, I'd say that went rather well other than that lowly bloodhound sniffing around." I remove my black polo shirt—so soft, it's annoying, or maybe it's the golden dye coating my skin?—and toss it on the couch in the parlor. Now gloriously shirtless, I pour myself a glass of red wine. I rarely drink it, blood is my thing, but after inhaling horse piss and pretending to drink it, I need something to cleanse my palate so I can mentally savor my victory.

"Oh no. Don't you dare, Boz." Neli marches into the parlor behind me. "You do not get to toast yourself after that—that—"

"What?" I say, inhaling the fragrant glass of our vineyard's finest in my hand.

"You gave her the whammy." Neli glares with her green eyes.

"Whatever do you mean, girl?"

"I saw the way she was looking at you."

"So?" I shrug.

"So…that wasn't just a reaction to your haircut and clothes."

"Ah." I point my index finger toward the ceiling. "But the tan."

Neli marches over, steals my glass, throws it back, and then stares up at me. "Cut the crap. You went to her room, hypnotized her, and now she's all into you."

I ignore my wench, because she has no understanding of what it is like to live hundreds of years, life growing stale and redundant with every passing day. I have seen the glimmer of a fading sunset and the spark of a new day, but the sunlight itself has eluded me for eight hundred years. "When you've lived as long as I, give me a call on your tiny phell cone."

"Cell phone. And I *have* lived as long as you, Boz. Longer, actually, because you were asleep for the last five hundred years, which means I've technically lived about two centuries more."

I pivot and hiss. "How dare you? Everyone knows that vampire years are like dog years. My one year equals your seven."

"Uh, where the hell did you hear that?"

"On the internet. I hear she is quite reliable."

Neli rolls her eyes.

"Do that again, and I shall pluck one of your eyeballs from your skull and wear it as my codpiece." I grab my discarded shirt and march upstairs to my dressing chamber to change.

"About the right size too," she mumbles at my back.

"I heard that! And we both know I am hung like

an elephant. Many o' woman has run screaming from my bedchamber for fear of being impaled."

Neli follows me. "That was because you showed them your fangs."

"Perhaps, but do not discount the intimidating nature of my large phallus." I chuck my dirty shirt in a large white plastic bin that Neli calls a "hamper." You simply put the soiled clothes inside, and they magically reappear a few days later neatly folded and stored in their proper place. *Modern marvels truly are impressive.*

"That's not the point!" Neli stomps her foot.

"Then what is?" I turn and snarl down at her. "That I cannot pursue the girl across the road because you, a lowly servant who is bound to me, do not approve?"

Neli groans in frustration and presses the heels of her palms to her face. "I'm sick of this, Boz. I'm sick of you not listening to what I have to say. I'm sick of you treating me like a second-class citizen—"

"Third class. Second class would be my valet, whom you allowed to die of old age, apparently." Pure laziness.

"Fine!" Neli throws her fists to her sides. "Third! But that doesn't change the facts."

"Which are?" I cock a brow.

"That you and I are all we have. I can't survive without you, and you can't survive without me."

"Have you been licking toads again, girl? I've warned you to stay away from those."

Neli stares at me, and then, like a candle that's been snuffed out, the fight leaves her. She leaves my chamber and goes over to the long padded armchair called a couch, where she plops down. Her lackluster aura sends a wave of dark chills through me.

I follow, feeling genuinely concerned. She lives to fight with me. "Neli? What is the matter, girl?" I take the place next to her on the couch. A stream of tears runs down her pale cheeks. I won't ever admit it, but I cannot stand to see a woman cry. It feels like nature herself is weeping, and who doesn't care about nature? "Why are you upset? Is it your moon cycle? Have I not given you enough bread and cheese in your daily ration?"

She covers her face and sobs with even more gusto. I want to cringe, but I hold it in.

"I can't do this anymore, Boz. I can't."

"What?"

"I can't babysit a grown man, who also happens to be a powerful vampire that refuses to change."

"What are you saying? I am the prime example of adaptation. Have you not witnessed my very impressive transformation these last few days?" I watched the friends, I used a credit card, and I cut my hair. I even stopped demanding that Neli launder my clothes. *The hamper does it for me now.*

Neli pushes back a lock of red hair behind her ear, her teary green eyes meeting mine. "Release me."

"What?" I jerk my head back.

"You heard me."

"But if I did that, you would turn into a pile of ash and dishonor your name, your family."

"I don't care! I want out."

I lean back into the couch, feeling this odd sensation in my chest. Pain. "I-I do not understand, Cornelia. Why would you choose death over being my major-peon?" I refer to her official title as the head of the servants, a proud moniker from our time long ago. She came up with the idea herself after tiring of being called my slave.

"It's majordomo! Not major-peon!" She inhales sharply and whooshes out a breath. "For the last five centuries, I've been free. Okay, with the exception of having to keep you alive. And figuring out how to move a dormant vampire halfway across the world. And move his castle brick by brick, then have the entire thing put back together because I knew he would never accept anything but the exact castle he inherited from his maker, and I would never hear the end of it if I let it be destroyed. But despite all those challenges, I built a life, Boz. I went to school, I learned about the world and different cultures. I worked hard to give us what you see, and even if I still suck at dating because the world keeps moving faster and faster and I can't keep up, I've learned one thing." She holds up a pale finger. "I don't want to be your slave anymore."

I thought she loved being my slave. This news is shocking. "Then what do you want?"

"I want to find love and live a normal human life." She bows her head and shakes it with a sigh. "But it's just not in the cards for me, so I'll take freedom."

She wants freedom. I allow that to sink in. "But you know there's only one way to make that happen."

She nods. "Yes."

"Become a vampire."

"God no!" Her eyes go wide. "I said I want you to *release* me. I want a swift and painless death."

Death? "No. I will not allow it!" The ache in my chest grows stronger.

"Why?"

"Because…because…you are like family and…" I look away. I might be a vampire, but I am a man first, and it is a well-known fact that men do not discuss their feelings. It is a sign of great weakness. Also, the other men tease you, and nobody likes that.

"What, Boz?" Neli pushes. "Tell me, dammit! I'm like family and *what?*"

"Fine." I meet her teary gaze. "If you wish to hear that I would miss you, then I will say it, but only if you promise to never leave. And bring me virgins when I ask."

She shakes her head again, this time with disgust.

I sense that she's back to wishing for that swift death. "Very well. If it is what you truly desire, Neli,

I will release you, but I ask that you find me a replacement companion first. Stella."

I see the wheels churning in her weak female mouse brain. "If I do that," she says, "do I have your word that you will release me?"

Ha. Hahaha… Never. "Of course."

Her eyes twitch. "I don't believe you."

"Too bad. It is either that or you can take your own life."

"You know I'll just become a vampire if I do that."

Yes. Only one's master can deliver the true death. It is a safety catch. Otherwise, a vampire's human slave could leave at any moment. Death is a gift only I can bring her. Otherwise, she can become like me, though I'm fairly certain that the glamour of becoming a vampire died long ago. She knows this life isn't for everyone. Being the fastest, smartest, deadliest, and above all, best looking is no simple task.

Neli takes my hand and squeezes. "Boz, I need you to promise that if I do this for you, you'll let me die."

I stare into Neli's eyes. I hate to lie to her, but telling the truth is far too demeaning: I would be lost without my Neli. She is like a sister. Who waits on me. And helps me kill people.

"I promise." I hold up my hand. "Now, let us get on with the business at hand."

"You have to remove the whammy."

"Why?" I clear my throat. "Not that there is one." Because it's unsportsmanlike to hypnotize a woman whom you desire in your bed, though, I must give myself credit; I merely hypnotized Stella so that she would want to spend time with me. All right, and I may have told her to think me handsome. So what? It's just that I saw her lying there and couldn't help myself. "Fine. I gave her the whammy, but in my own defense, I never intended to bed her while she remained under my spell. I merely wanted a taste of her attention." It was sweeter than I imagined.

"Good. Because you and I both know you won't be satisfied with winning her if it isn't real."

"Agreed. So what do you suggest is the next step?" I ask.

"First off, remove the whammy. Then get to know her. Spend time together. Show her who you really are. If she still wants you, then maybe she's the one you've been searching for all these years. Your forever companion."

My bride? My forever love? Could Stella truly be the one I've been searching for all these centuries? (At least I was before my forced nap.) I had given up all hope of finding my mate. It's why I decided I wasn't meant to be a one-neck vampire. Lack of hope will do that to your tender immortal soul.

Who wouldn't give up hope after the years dragged on and on with no signs such a woman existed? I was forced to give up any ridiculous notions of finding my bride and embrace my bachelorhood. I accepted that Neli would be my companion and that my manly sexual needs would be met in other ways.

But now, this notion of Stella perhaps being *the one* excites me. *Could she be my soul mate?*

I heard rumors that a vampire knows his forever mate by the intoxicating scent and the taste of their mate's blood. The flavor is said to drive a vampire mad with lust. Stella is the first woman who meets both requirements. "You are right. I must spend time with her to see if she could be the one. And I will go to her room tonight to remove the whammy." I need to be sure her affections are genuine.

"Okay, but no more hanky-panky, Boz. I saw the *huge* hickey on her neck."

"It was a tiny scratch," I argue. "Only about the size of a chicken egg. With holes in it." I shrug. "And a tad purple. All right, fine. It was a massive hickey, but can you blame me? She is very desirable."

"Boz, she's a good girl. And I believe, in my heart, that you are a good man, capable of extreme kindness—when you want. So please don't ruin her life. Find some salty old crow to mess with if Stella isn't the one."

"I am not into birds, but I do not judge."

"I—never mind. Just promise, okay?"

I groan. "Very well. If it will make you happy, I promise I will not ruin her life." *Ah...but a nibble, that is fair game.*

❧ ❦

Later that night, dressed in black, I go to Stella's house. I stop briefly to "rabbit" her bloodhound into slumber before entering Stella's room. Her sweet scent fills my lungs, and my body tenses instantly. I'm beginning to notice that my reactions to her are uncommonly strong. Tonight was no exception. Every time our gazes clashed, it felt like my heart might start beating again, almost like a strange tickle.

I gaze down and admire Stella's ethereal beauty while she sleeps—the way her dark hair fans over the pillow, the way her full lips rest in a sensual pout, and the manner in which her hips curve like a seductive song that speaks to the male in me. *So beautiful. My Stella…*

Enjoying the gentle purr of her soft, rhythmic breaths, I lie down next to her, knowing that if she is roused, I can use my gifts to lull her back to sleep. For the moment, however, I want to feel her warm body close to mine. I want to infuse my mind with the sensations only she has managed to provoke over the course of a very long existence. *But what if she does not have true feelings for me?*

I do not like that idea one little bit.

I roll onto my back, stare at the ceiling, and rest my hands over my stomach. There is a soft whirr from a small machine in the corner that reminds me of a gentle breeze. It is most soothing. I will have

Neli purchase one for my coffin. Perhaps it will make me feel closer to Stella while we are parted during the day.

I sigh. "Stella, Stella, Stella. What are you doing to me?" I should be out there in the new world, exploring all the riches it has to offer, and conquering its terrain. I should be seeking out the company of other vampires and learning their new tricks. Concealment is infinitely more difficult in this day and age, and we must adapt or perish. I am certain not much has changed in the way of vampire hunters, either. They were a pain in the ass when I was three hundred years old, and they are probably a pain in the ass now. But instead of worrying about that, or about acclimating to this new time, I am cutting my hair and going on shopping expeditions. All for a woman.

The most disturbing part is that Neli is right; Stella is a good girl. I can see how deeply she cares for her family—it is in her eyes when she talks about making Stellariva into something grand. She wants to honor her family name.

I sigh and turn my head toward my sleeping goddess. *You are truly a remarkable woman.* And this being my opinion after only a handful of interactions, I can only imagine how much more impressed I might become if we truly spent time together.

Suddenly, there's a niggling stab of guilt in my gut. Despite my desire to drink her virgin blood again tonight and feel her warm, soft body beneath me, I fear my presence will only taint such loveliness.

It pains me to say it, but I do not want her if it means destroying her—such a sweet, perfect flower meant only to be admired. If she were mine, I would want to make her into a vampire, which would destroy her very nature. So beautiful, so kind, so human.

"I am sorry, Stella, but I must not see you again." The realization shocks me. I have never walked away from anything I desired. Not once.

"Boz…" Still deep in slumber, Stella rolls to her side and flings an arm over my torso. "I like you…" she mumbles.

I smile and pat her soft hand. "And I you, Stella. And I you." I let out a long sigh. "You are released from my powers henceforth. Your mind is your own. Your will is your own, now and forever."

I will never again be able to use my powers on her. And she will forever be free of me.

CHAPTER THIRTEEN
Stella

I took some time on my appearance today, carefully applying makeup and styling my dark brown hair to have some body with a nice wave to it. I'm wearing my blue and white maxi dress with spaghetti straps and a scoop neck that shows off my cleavage. *I know, I know, my meeting with Boz and Neli is not a date.* I just want to look my best so I feel more confident. Sure, that's why.

The doorbell rings and my heart races. I stride to the front door, already smiling in anticipation of my visitors. "Hi!" My smile drops as I realize Neli is here alone for our meeting. Her red hair is down, contrasting with her light blue V-neck blouse. "Where's Boz?"

Her brows shoot up over wide green eyes.

My cheeks heat. "He told me to call him that last night." I run my finger along the gold bracelet he gave me, delighting in its darling charms. I peer behind her, hoping he's just running late. "Is he coming?"

"No."

My shoulders droop, and I turn, gesturing her

in. I try to hide my disappointment. I've been looking forward to seeing him all day. He was kind enough to agree to help our winery, he gave me a gift, he was so attentive last night, and, let's face it, he's drop-dead gorgeous. From his dark hair to his unusual silvery eyes to his exquisitely muscular build. The total package.

Oh, man, I'm so easy. Give me a charm bracelet, and I'm charmed.

I refocus on Neli and put some enthusiasm into my voice. "Would you like a drink, or should we go straight to the storeroom?" I invited them over to taste our different vintages in an effort to narrow down the best choice to blend with one of their wines.

"Storeroom is fine by me," she says.

I lead her through the house, heading for the back door, and say a quick hello to my twin sisters in the kitchen, where they're baking red velvet cupcakes. Their futures are never far from my mind. Winning that baking competition would be a blessing, but not something we can count on. My family is counting on me to get this winery back on its feet.

After a short walk to the storeroom in an adjacent building, I remind Neli of our current inventory. She had the tour last night, but I don't expect her to remember every detail.

In no time at all, Neli settles on a cabernet sauvignon she says has potential. "It's bold."

I study her expression, looking for signs of disgust like Boz showed the first time I offered him our wine. Though last night he seemed fine with it. *You know, I hadn't tasted that particular bottle the night we met, already being tipsy from tasting their wine.* Maybe it was just a bad bottle. I relax, feeling so much better about the whole thing.

I smile. "I'm glad you think so. We could blend it with your award-winning merlot."

She rocks her head side to side, and I can tell she's not on board.

"I was being presumptuous. Tell me which wine you think it would blend well with."

She lifts her glass. "How about I take a bottle of this with me, think it over, and try a few?"

"Absolutely." I retrieve a bottle for her, and we head outside.

She tells me about the right flavors for a blend for immediate consumption versus long-term aging potential, but I'm finding it hard to focus. All I can think about is visiting Castle Sangria and seeing *him* again.

I walk her to the well-worn dirt path that leads to the main road. It's a perfect summer day, and the view of Castle Sangria as we walk buoys my spirits even more. "Thanks for your help, Neli. I'd love to try some blends with you." I smooth my hair back, trying not to look too eager. "We could make a night of it, invite Boz to join us too."

She looks off to the castle, back to me, and

cocks her head. "I'm the head of operations, not him."

"Oh, of course, I understand." I play with the wineglass charm on my bracelet, a smile tugging at my lips. "I was also thinking I could take another look at your barrel room to plan an event there." I meet her eyes. "I want to contribute as soon as possible to your winery. This isn't just a one-sided arrangement. We could do a joint harvest celebration outdoors in September, and a spooky ball on Halloween at Castle Sangria would be amazing. Such great atmosphere there. Of course, we'd have to add the spooky touches. Right now Castle Sangria is grand elegance with the great room, the barrel room, not to mention the dining room. I'm sure there's even more that would be wonderful for guests." I'm gushing. I can't help it. I'm excited about our project.

"You sound really enthusiastic about Castle Sangria," she says flatly.

"It's magnificent," I say in a breathy voice. But I mean *he's* magnificent.

"I'll let you know," she says, backing away. "I've got your number."

My gaze trails to the castle again, hoping to glimpse the mysterious man himself. I don't even have his number to thank him for everything.

"Bye, Stella."

I snap to attention. "Bye, thanks again for stopping by. I appreciate you taking the time. I know how busy you must be."

"No rest for the wicked," she says ominously.

My breath catches at her sinister tone.

She flashes a smile, turns, and walks away.

Strange. I rub the goosebumps on my arms and head back inside.

೭ ೩

Boz

"You said you would remove the whammy!" Neli shouts, pacing my bedchamber.

It is much too early to be dealing with my insolent major-doody. I have barely had time to dress and seek out a spicy morsel wandering out of the local pub. The evil ones taste the spiciest.

I summon patience. "What's got your panties in a bunch, wench?"

Her mouth forms a perfect O. I stifle a laugh. I have just proven I am up on the modern lingo. Now the one who said I could not change with the modern era has just been schooled.

She recovers herself. "Boz, you said you would remove the whammy, yet I saw Stella this afternoon, and she was clearly still smitten."

Hmm…this is not good. I already decided not to pursue her for her own protection. "Are you certain?"

She shoves a hand in her hair. "Yes! You were all she could talk about. And she kept hinting about visiting the castle." She shakes her head. "I trusted you. Ugh, why did I trust you to play fair?"

"Cease your complaining. I removed the spell last night."

"Then why is she so eager to see you?"

I spread my arms wide, indicating my masculine perfection displayed in a modern black button-down shirt and black leather trousers. I will bring them back in fashion by example. "If she's smitten with me, I assure you it is by her own choice. It is a curse I must live with, women throwing themselves at my feet—"

"You lure them in."

"Begging me to take them to bed."

"Boz!"

I flash my fangs in displeasure. "I tire of your harsh tone."

She paces the bedchamber again, muttering to herself about playing fair and trust and all kinds of nonsense vampires have no use for. We feed, we kill, we rule. And we protect women in danger, even from ourselves.

I watch Neli wearing a hole in my Persian rug with her pacing. It pains me to say the truth out loud because I do not like to share. Still, it is the only way to silence her incessant complaints and irritating pacing. "I will not be pursuing Stella."

Neli halts, staring in shock for a long moment.

I wait for her mind to assimilate the news. I have never once given up a woman I desired.

"Why?" she finally asks.

I walk to my window and look across the road to Stella's home bathed in moonlight. She and her beloved family all work together for their livelihood. One that I will only destroy by taking her from them. "My presence will only corrupt." I turn at her silence. "She is an innocent. A rare untouched beauty I must admire from afar."

Neli sinks heavily to my reading chair and stares up at one of my finest paintings—two ripe melons. "You really did remove the whammy." Her brows knit together as she lowers her gaze to the floor.

Her belief in the truth of my words brings only a moment's pleasure before the eternity without Stella looms in front of me. She will marry another, bear children, grow old, and die. And still I will go on, never having the woman I have waited centuries to discover.

"Wait a minute," Neli says.

I sigh heavily. Does she not sense my need to gaze longingly at Stella's home without her constant chatter?

"You said you'd release me if I brought you Stella as a companion. How is that supposed to happen if you avoid her?"

I do not reply. Now is not the time to discuss the truth—I could never kill Neli. She is like family. Yes, yes, bound to me against her will, but no one gets to choose their families, now do they? I hope Neli will understand this when the time comes. As for Stella, resisting her will take strength and untested levels of willpower.

Neli appears at my side. "Boz, I think what's really going on is that you're letting insecurity get in the way of making a real connection with the woman who could be your forever mate. I know it's scary—"

"I fear nothing," I growl.

She gives me a patient smile. "What I'm trying to say is that if you really did remove the whammy, and she's still into you, I think there could be something between you two. The best thing to do is spend time helping her with the wine blends, maybe have dinner together, get to know each other." She blows out a breath and relaxes. "This is good. You'll have your bride, and I'll have my freedom just like we talked about."

I cross my arms. "I am sorry, but Stella is out."

She stomps her foot. "We had a deal! You get a replacement for me."

"Perhaps a more suitable candidate will come along in the next century." *Or never. No one can compare to Stella.*

"Fine." She purses her lips, appearing deep in thought.

I can tell by the defiant gleam in her eye, this is not over. Neli is a stubborn one, a trait I happen to admire, except on occasions such as these. She intends to nag me to death until I change my mind, but it is not going to happen. I am determined not to pursue Stella, and Neli will simply have to accept it. "The master has spoken. Now, if you do not mind, I need time to myself to wallow." As any gloomy vampire knows, there is an art to a proper wallow.

I stare out the window, noting that Neli is still standing behind me, stewing, so I give her the orders that will send her away and keep her occupied for a long while: "I will need my new must-have tees pressed by sundown tomorrow." I wonder if this is enough busywork, so I add, "Also, I would like you to establish a falconry. Make that happen immediately. I do enjoy watching a bird of prey at work. It reminds me of my youth." *There. That should keep her busy.* And once she is done with that, I will come up with more frivolous tasks. *Perhaps have her buy some llamas and learn the fine art of weaving wool.* Anything to prevent her from scheming or meddling in my romantic affairs.

"I know what you're doing," Neli says, "so if you truly don't want Stella, I'm willing to accept it. No need to make me start an aviary or menagerie. But in all my years of knowing you, Boz, I've never seen you abandon a friend or ally in distress."

I turn and narrow my eyes. "Stella is neither."

"She is a neighbor, which technically makes her an ally. Even more importantly, you know her family's vineyard is on the verge of going out of business, and you gave Stella your word to help them."

My conscience makes a rare appearance, stabbing me with guilt. I did say I would help Stella, and Neli knows I cannot so easily turn my back on a vow. *Damn my chivalrous nature.* I want to do the impossible—rescue a woman and resist her at the same time.

Neli continues. "Her winery will go under in less than a year. Her family, whom she loves, will be destitute. Her younger sisters will have to give up their dream. Unless you're a man of honor."

Damn that Neli. She knows that maintaining my honor is my Achilles' heel, but this is one of those rare occasions when I am damned if I do, damned if I do not. "I am a vampire of great power. I will get over the tarnish to my stellar reputation."

She smiles. "I'm sure you will, but deep down, I know you'll do the right thing and keep your word to Stella and to me. You help her, get to know her, make her your bride, and let me go. Everlasting love is your reward."

Only my honor prevents me from destroying the delicate perfection of Stella. It is a painful irony.

"Please, Boz, do this for me."

I feel the tugging on my cold, unbeating heart. Neli does not understand what she's truly asking of me, of the risks to Stella. On the other hand, I am Prince Bozhidar. I have never walked away from something simply because it is difficult. For example, during a time of great famine and war in my lands, the humans fled and left me with very little food. Of course, I refused to abandon my castle, so I struck a deal with some unsavory merchant types, who often purchased wine from my vineyard to sell in faraway lands. In exchange for wine, they would bring me women. Food. From where? They did not say, but it seemed like an excellent idea at the time—I *was* pretty hungry. When my shipment finally showed up, I took in the women's dirty, pale, bruised bodies all lashed together with rope. Clearly they had been mistreated. I ate the merchants instead—they tasted horrible. Then I freed the women. Of course, they had no way of getting home—they were many, all from lands I had never heard of, so I had to take them in. I had a very clean castle for many years.

"Very well," I grumble. "I will help Stella in any way she requires." *And then turn away forever.* I am strong. I will endure the temptation.

Neli throws her arms around me. "Thank you!"

I pat her back two times. The display of affection is entirely inappropriate. Still, an unusual glow of warmth spreads through my body. It almost feels like life has returned. *Impossible. But nice.*

CHAPTER FOURTEEN
Stella

I'm still not quite sure why I'm experiencing a sudden fascination with my neighbor, but it's so intense that when I woke the other morning, I could smell him on my pillow—a woodsy aroma that reminds me of the night.

Such a weird thing to think, right? I mean, what does the night smell like? Maybe campfires and hot chocolate? Or...toasted marshmallows? I'm not sure, but his cologne is sweet and delicious. I just don't understand how it got all over my room.

Hmmm... I feel like the answer is right on the top of my head, but I can't quite get at it. There's been a lot of that happening lately. Must be all the stress.

I toss the gray queen-size comforter off and swing my legs over the side of the mattress. The early rays of the sun peek around the curtains on the double window adjacent to my bed. Just behind those curtains is my fabulous view of Castle Sangria. I smile to myself and stand. I feel rested and energetic, like I could take on the world.

Maybe it's because I'm finally seeing a light at

the end of the tunnel. Neli texted last evening and asked me to come over to their winery around seven tonight so we could work on the wine profiles.

Boz will be there, I remind myself. My heart flutters. I think of how incredibly generous he is, considering how he's giving us his time on a Saturday. He has a small wine empire to run, and I know he probably values his downtime. Then I start thinking about how he looked the other night, with his new haircut and clothes. It was almost too painful to look at him—every curve of his ripped chest and biceps on display through his snug polo shirt. And that hard ass in those jeans? *So gorgeous.* My neck tingles. I give it a rub and go into my small bathroom done simply in white tile with blue accent tiles, noting that those weird mosquito bites have already healed. *Strange. Why does the spot still itch?*

Anyway, I have a lot of work to do today—helping my parents pull together promotional materials. Once the new wine blend is finished, there will be an announcement to do and tasting events to host. The key will be creating lots of buzz with the wine influencers. If they get on board, then the wine magazines will follow and start talking about us.

I shower and put on a pink floral maxi dress with black flats, but then change my mind and go for matching pink sandals. It's kind of silly, but I think I caught Boz staring at my toes a few times. Maybe he's a toe man. Either way, I like the idea of him admiring parts of my body, which is why I tie my hair up in a sloppy bun. I noticed he stares at my neck a lot too, and it'll be warm out today.

I spritz a little of my favorite rose perfume behind my ears for the finishing touch and head downstairs to the kitchen with a bounce in my step. Mabel pulls a quiche from the oven.

"Oh no. Is that your bacon gruyere recipe?" I ask, my stomach grumbling.

"Yep!" She sets it on top of the stove.

"You know that's my favorite. I'm going to gain twenty pounds if you guys don't stop cooking all this delicious food."

"Well, the state bake-off is next week."

"I thought Eliza was entering that with one of her cakes," I say.

"They have a savory competition this year. It has a prize of ten thousand dollars, and I know we could really use the money right now."

It breaks my heart that she's even thinking about money. "Shouldn't you put that money aside for school if you win?"

Her mouth pulls to the side. "I overheard Mom and Dad fighting. Is it true we're going to lose the house?"

Ugh. I know I should be honest, but she's still a kid. I don't want her to worry. "No. You must've misheard them. Everything's fine," I lie. "We've got a solid plan in place to grow the business and turn things around quickly." I tap the end of her nose.

"Soon we'll be making enough to send you to the Culinary Institute of America in New York." I know going there is her dream. Eliza wants to go to Le Cordon Bleu in Paris.

"I'm not holding my breath. The tuition alone costs over a hundred grand."

Yikes. That is a lot.

"But the institute here has a summer program— one month, ten thousand dollars," she adds. "Maybe I can go to that? I mean, at least I'll have it on my résumé—that is if you really think things are going to turn around?"

I smile with encouragement. "I think that's a great idea, but let's not give up on getting you into your dream school, okay?" I know we can at least get her into the state university here. They have loans and whatnot. It's not her dream though. "Oh, and hey, I'm looking at what it would take to enter our new wine in the big tasting championship in New York. If we get in, maybe you can come along, and we could tour the school while we're there."

"Seriously?" Her big brown eyes light up. "New York?"

Maybe I spoke too soon. "Well, a lot has to happen first." Having a great wine would be a nice start. Then we need to submit it for consideration. Plus there's travel expenses and a hotel. I'm hoping that Castle Sangria might be willing to front the costs. We could pay them back out of our future profits. "But let's keep that between us for now. I'd hate to get everyone's hopes up." They only take the best of the best wines from around the country. The initial qualifying samples are due next month. They have to be sent in blind with a number, no winery label, and you have to pay a courier to hand carry the entry on a private plane. Shipping wines by car or truck agitates the sediments and changes the flavor. It's even a risk to fly with it, but that's your best bet to deliver the bottle with the flavor fully intact. Flying commercial won't work because they limit the amount of liquids you can carry, and I'm not about to put our wine in the belly of a plane, where the temperature might not be controlled.

"Your secret is safe with me," Mabel says.

"What are we talking about?" Mom enters the kitchen. She looks tired—dark circles under her eyes and a somber vibe.

"Oh, uh…" I think fast. "I'm going over to Castle Sangria later to work on the new wine. I didn't want Dad to get upset. I know he's not a fan of Mr. Bozhidar."

My mom swipes her hand through the air. "Your father just worries, that's all."

Mabel raises a brow. "I dunno, Mom. I'm going to side with Dad on this one. Something about that man feels off."

"Like what?" I laugh. Everyone's so paranoid. I don't get it.

"Like…the way he looks at you," Mabel says, widening her eyes comically. "Reminds me of a wolf sizing up a juicy lamb."

I roll my eyes. "He's just intense. Okay, and he's a little eccentric." But those eyes…they scream bedroom.

"Oh, and let's not forget handsome," Mom chimes in with a swooning effect to her voice.

"Whatever, I have to get ready for work," Mabel says.

Mabel has a summer job at the small French bistro down the road, working in the kitchen.

"Have fun," Mom says to Mabel. She turns to me. "And you don't have too much fun."

I shake my head.

My mom waits until Mabel's out of the kitchen. "Honey, I didn't want to bring this up, because I know how smart you are and how dedicated you are to helping Stellariva, but maybe I should say something. I noticed how Mr. Bozhidar was looking at you too. And you gave him your share of looks back, but is it really wise to get involved with a man when you're planning on doing business together?"

That joyous flutter in my heart, the one that was there when I woke up this morning, dies with a sputter. She's right. It's a terrible idea. Things could go sideways and the deal could blow up. "Don't worry, Mom. I'll keep it professional. I promise." But as soon as those words leave my mouth, I already feel like I've gone back on my word, like it's a forgone conclusion I'm going to be with that man. And yes, I know I hardly know Boz, but these glimpses into his honest, generous heart have me wanting to spend more time with him.

No. You can't blow this, Stella. You can't. I'll do whatever it takes to keep my knees locked together. *No entry, handsome.*

"Thank you, honey. And good luck tonight. Tell Mr. Bozhidar we're very excited to see what he comes up with."

Suddenly, I'm wondering if my mom should go instead. She's the one with the nose. My heart instantly protests. I have to see him. I'm drawn to that place and to that man.

Maybe tonight I'll figure out how to break his hold, because it can only lead to a bad situation. A man like that—rich, smart, generous, and hot—is single for a reason: Because he wants to be. And I'm not going to risk this important venture for a fling, especially when I have zero interest in those. Pursuing anything with Boz will only lead to heartbreak.

That evening, just before seven, I head across the road to the castle. It's a bit of a climb up the driveway to the front door, but it's a warm evening, and I need to work off some of the anxiety that's been building all day in my stomach. I know what I have to do. I know what's right. This partnership is the difference between my family's survival or losing everything.

I walk up the long, cobblestone driveway at a brisk pace. My gaze flashes to the window on the top floor. Part of me hopes to find the silhouette of a tall, strong man watching me, but it's empty.

I sigh, but tell myself it's good. Very good. There can't be any more of those longing glances from across the room and little flirtations.

"Excuse me, ma'am. Hello!" a man's voice calls out from behind me just as I pass the moat.

I stop and turn, thinking it's probably some tourist who's lost. We have tons of people who come from all around the world to visit the valley and the wineries. People get turned around all the time. And, oddly enough, the GPS doesn't always work in this area. It's like a chunk of road is simply missing from all the electronic maps. It's no big deal since both wineries have big signs out, and it's not like anyone's going to miss the huge castle at the top of the hill, but it is strange.

"Hi," I say. "Can I help you?" The man is wearing thick glasses and a very unusual outfit—a long brown trench coat and a wide-brimmed hat made from straw. First of all, it's pretty warm out this evening. Second, why wear a summer hat with a winter coat? *Oh well.*

"Yes, yes. Thank you. I'm from the local water conservation agency. I'm doing surveys about the various wineries and was wondering if you could answer a few questions about your neighbors."

Huh. That's odd. How does he know I live across the road? And all of the wineries are strictly regulated in the valley in terms of water usage. The county monitors compliance to usage limits and conservation law; for example, we're only allowed to water our plants at certain times of the day. Once a year, an inspector comes out to make sure all our sprinklers and irrigation systems are functioning properly. But that's usually in the early spring. "I'm sorry, but who did you say you work for again?"

He pushes his thick glasses up his nose. "The water conservation agency. We're a private group. We monitor the wetlands. You know, for bird and animal migration. I'm in charge of tracking nocturnal species. Have you noticed any unusual wildlife activity at night? Animals being eaten? How about bats? Have you seen bats on your neighbor's property?"

Okay. This dude is cuckoo. We have no wetland in this area, and I don't like his beady eyes. "I'm sorry. I really couldn't say. You'll have to ask them." I turn and continue on my way, walking even faster toward the front door.

"How about bloodsucking bats?" he calls out.

Ohmygod. I shake my head and keep walking.

The front door of the castle jerks open. Neli's about to greet me but notices the man. Her eyes go wide, like she's surprised, and then they narrow into tight little slits.

Does she know this creep? I look over my shoulder, and the guy turns and walks quickly to his black truck, where one man is waiting behind the wheel and another is seated on the passenger side.

"What did they want?" Neli asks when I get to the door.

"That man was asking about your vineyard. They're some looney bat activists or something. I don't know."

She nods slowly, looking irritated.

"Everything okay?" I say.

"Oh. Yeah. Great. Come on in. Boz is waiting for you down in the cellar. You know the way."

"Aren't you joining us?" The last thing I need is to be left alone with him.

She reaches out, fixes a stray lock from my hair, and then pinches my cheeks.

"Ow. Hey!" I push her hands away.

"Sorry. You had a bug on your face."

On both cheeks? And why's she fixing my hair?

"I'll be along shortly. Now run along." She practically pushes me toward the staircase that leads down into the cellar.

What the hell is with people tonight? I shrug and take a big breath, knowing what awaits me down in the dark, intimate space. *Be strong, Stella. Be strong...*

CHAPTER FIFTEEN
Boz

I have Neli answer the door so I can limit the time I spend alone with Stella. I hear them approaching the cellar now, where I wait. Perhaps I will let Neli take charge and merely watch the proceedings so that I may keep Stella at a safe distance. It is the only way to resist her.

I lean against a nearby column, arms crossed. A single look will convey to Neli what I need from her—she has to be the one to offer the blends for Stella to enjoy. I don't want Stella to take offense at my subtle request not to be too near her.

"Hello?" a soft feminine voice calls. Stella. Has Neli left her alone?

I stay where I am, considering if I should step farther into the room or wait. Maybe Stella will think no one is here and go back upstairs for Neli. But then she steps close enough for me to catch her intoxicating rose scent, the scent of purity.

Mmmm…delicious. Her virgin blood tempts me fiercely.

She steps farther into the space, peering into the dark shadows at our various rooms and rubbing her arms as though she's chilled. With the movement, light reflects off the gold bracelet I gave her, and a deep sense of satisfaction fills me. I like seeing her wear my gift. It means she likes it, and pleasing her pleases me. Then my gaze catches on the long line of her neck exposed with her hair up, and hunger takes over, clawing at me. I must remember how special she is, a rare gem that is going to require all of my willpower to resist tonight. My honor demands it.

I straighten away from the column and remove my black blazer. "You seem chilled."

She yelps and slaps a hand over her mouth, her brown eyes wide. "Oh God. It's you." She drops her hand and sighs with relief.

"Forgive me for scaring you. I merely wanted to offer my jacket." I approach her slowly and offer my blazer, not trusting myself to wrap it around her.

She beams up at me. "I'm okay, thanks. I was just a little spooked by the shadows. Silly imagination."

"Nothing to fear here. You are as safe as a lamb in a lion-less meadow." *Welcome to the lion's den. I promise to keep my fangs to myself.* I set my blazer over the back of a chair. "Please, take a seat. We have arranged three blends for you to try." I gesture toward the long table that Neli has prepared in the center of the barrel room.

Speaking of Neli, where is she? I should text her to join us with my new communication device she calls an eye-phone. I prefer to call it "the Summoner," as that is its purpose for me.

Stella takes a seat and looks all around. The cellar is a large vaulted space with multiple archways lit by candelabras overhead and sconces along every wall. It is one of the more comfortable spots in the castle with its dim lighting and privacy. Alarm shoots through me. That nearly sounds as intimate as my bedchamber. I send an urgent message to Neli.

> **Prince Bozhidar:** *Your presence is required for the tastings.*

I wait for the Summoner to serve its purpose, and then I wait some more, but there is no response from Neli. *Is this thing broken?* I give the device a shake and stare at the small screen. *How can this be?* Neli always responds to every chiming notification. She is a slave to her eye-phone.

I want to track her down, but don't want to be rude to our guest. Surely, Neli will be along shortly. *If she knows what's good for her.*

I turn my attention back to Stella, who is rubbing the side of her neck in the spot where I took a sip. The memory sends more sharp need rushing through me, but I resist my urge and make a note to always feed before I see her in the future, to prevent temptation.

"Will Neli be joining us?" she asks hesitantly.

"She'll be down shortly."

Her head lifts, and she looks up at me under her lashes, seeming almost shy. The delight I always feel in the presence of maidenly virtue is nearly eclipsed by primal lust, but I cannot allow the beast in me to emerge.

"Would you like to sit with me while we wait?" she asks.

"I-I…" I am about to tell her that I prefer to stand, but what can I say? I am a complicated male who, on top of wanting to protect her, also believes in being a gentleman. And what is the number one rule of a gentleman? *Always be a gracious host.* Of course, the vampire version of that rule includes the added phrase: *before you eat your guest.*

No, no, I tell myself. *I am better than that. I am an ancient powerful vampire with unmatched self-control.* I can handle anything Stella throws my way, even a little naked toe action.

"It would be my pleasure." I take the seat across from her so that Neli can sit at the head of the table and provide a buffer between us.

"I'm so glad we're working together," she says.

"I am happy to help a neighbor." The air between us fills with an awkward energy, which is unknown territory for me. I am a creature of the night. We don't do awkward. My little friend Chandler does awkward all day long. That is no help. I must consider how Joey or Ross would handle this. *Ah, my friends, I fear you have never faced such temptation.*

I know. I look away and pretend to study the wall.

Stella does the same, looking around.

Yep. Just two regular people, sitting together in a dark, private wine cellar. One of them absolutely does not wish to drink the other's blood.

"So," Stella finally says, breaking the long silence, "I would love to plan some future events here. Your barrel room is just spectacular. I really appreciate your help and would like to give something in return. Plus it would bring publicity to both our wineries. What do you think of a harvest celebration in September?"

I cannot have too many visitors here now that I am awakened from my five-hundred-year slumber because there would be questions about where I have been all these years, and questions lead to lies. Lies lead to a risk of exposure given how easy it is in this day and age for anyone to check the facts. "How many people would attend an event like that?"

"Tons! It could be a real moneymaker." She smiles. "I'm sure you'd sell a lot of wine, and some of our blends would be good to sell too."

"That is an idea," I say diplomatically, not wanting to squash her good spirits. Also, she smiled her sweet smile for me, and now my unbeating heart is all tingles and manly flutter. Quite unusual. The flutters, I mean. Being manly comes naturally.

She gestures overhead to the nearest candelabra,

continuing with her creative ideas. "And with all these cool candles around, it's a great vibe for a Halloween masquerade ball, which I think I mentioned before. Add some cobwebs in the corners, maybe some spooky ghost sounds." She shivers and then chuckles. "Look at me, creeping myself out with ghosts. I know they're not real, but sometimes my imagination runs away with me. Like the other night I could swear I heard strange noises in the house. I ended up sleeping with my head under the covers. Ridiculous, right? Honestly, I'm much too practical to believe in the otherworldly. My sisters like to watch all those paranormal shows—anything with ghosts, witches, vampires, werewolves—but I can never suspend disbelief long enough to enjoy them."

I find her comments most intriguing, considering she's sitting next to a vampire and seems to be exceptionally responsive to me. At least, on a subconscious level.

"Which creature is your favorite?" I ask, more than a little curious if she will say vampire.

Stella's cheeks flush. "This is a little embarrassing, but the real reason I keep away from all things supernatural related is because when I was nine, my cousin Kevin snuck up on me the day before Halloween wearing fake vampire teeth and a cape, of course—his dark hair slicked back for the full effect—and popped out at me from the corner of the living room. I was legit terrified. I didn't know he was visiting, and I'd just seen *Dracula* the night before. I had nightmares for *years* about a vampire coming out of nowhere to suck my blood. Strange how deep a memory can get into your psyche and really mess with you. Anyway, I stay away from any books, movies, or TV shows that might remind me of the otherworldly. The real world is scary enough." She laughs a little, but I cannot join her mirth.

If she knew I was a vampire, I strongly sense she would run screaming from the room. Childhood fears are very powerful things in humans, and she just told me that vampires are essentially her equivalent of Muma Pădurii—basically an old heinous forest hag I feared as a child. My mother used to tell stories in order to prevent me from wandering off alone in the nearby forest: *"Do not go beyond our farm, Bozhidar, or Muma Pădurii will nibble off your toes and make soup out of your knee-caps."* It took several centuries to overcome my fear of pine trees, and do not get me started on the smell of kneecap soup. I still cannot go near it. In any case, if Stella fears vampires even one tenth of how much I feared Muma, then it is safe to assume that Stella will never accept me. *Perhaps this is a blessing in disguise—for Stella's sake.*

I decide a bit of small talk and sharing can do no harm. "I am also 'creeped out' by certain creatures—forest hags especially. Also, ghosts." I suppress a shudder. It is unnatural to move about without a body. Then I wonder if the strange noise she heard at night was me during one of my nocturnal visits. Perhaps I was distracted by her beauty and did not cast an effective memory erasure on her. "By the way, that noise you mentioned; what did it sound like?"

She waves that away. "Oh, it's just the creaking of the floorboards in our old house as it settles."

I move with great stealth, so I know for a fact that was not me. Not a creak to be heard. *Perhaps it is simply the old house settling, as she said.*

"So, what do you think?" she asks. "Would it be okay for me to start planning some events here for the fall? I really want to do my part in repaying you for all the kindness."

I absolutely cannot allow random people to roam the castle. Vampires must remain in the shadows of modern society. "You give back simply by being you."

She blushes prettily, her lashes fluttering down. "Thank you, Boz. That's so nice of you to say."

I cannot tear my gaze from her, at a complete loss for words in the face of her sweetness. It is as if *she* has cast a whammy on *me*.

"I brought a snack," Neli announces from behind me.

My head whips toward her. I was so distracted by Stella, I did not hear Neli approach. I must be more careful. Distraction is the quickest way for your enemies to take advantage. Not that Neli is an enemy. She is family, whom I currently wish to strangle for leaving me alone this long with Stella.

"Neli, so good to have you here," I say with the sharp edge of authority to my voice. "Have a seat. Now we can finally begin the tastings."

She sets down a platter with a bowl of glossy dark red cherries, small plates, and napkins. "Stella, I think you'll find the cherries are a nice complement to the red blends I've made."

"They look delicious," Stella says.

Damn that Neli. Yes, they do look juicy, which means blood-red cherry juice on Stella's sensual lips.

I tear my gaze away and turn to Neli. "Join us," I command. I'm tempted to put her under my trance, but I don't dare do anything suspicious in front of Stella. Now that I know about her fear of the supernatural world, she must remain unknowing of my powers. Not that I ever intended to tell her what I am.

Neli ignores me, instead smiling at Stella. "Boz and I have already tried these blends, but I think it's best if it's a blind taste test for you. Would you mind?" She takes a purple ball of cloth from the platter and shakes it out, holding it up to Stella.

Seriously, Neli? A scarf? Neli is diabolical.

Neli continues. "All right now. Just turn your head a little, Stella, so I can put this on you for a true blind taste test. I just want to be sure you're happy with the perfect blend—no influence from us."

"Oh. Sounds fun," Stella says.

Fun? I think being staked in the gonads would be more enjoyable. I snarl silently at Neli as she goes behind Stella to tie it on and completely ignores my warning.

Once Stella's eyes are covered, I start making a slicing motion with my finger across my throat. *You are a dead dorko, Neli.*

Neli smirks like the evil female she is and finishes tying the scarf securely, placing her finger over her lips in a shushing gesture to me.

Did she just shush me? A vampire? I never! But Neli is smart. She knows I cannot do a thing. *Not now anyway.* There is always later. Perhaps I will revoke her yacht privileges.

"Okay." Neli leans down to Stella's ear. "How's that?"

Stella holds her fingers up in front of her eyes. "I can't see a thing."

"Great. Try this one first." Neli puts a glass in her hand.

I whip my finger through the air and point angrily to the empty chair at the head of the table, ordering Neli to take a seat.

Like she did when we first met, Neli sticks her tongue out and runs away, racing up the stairs. *Damn her speedy and crafty insolent ways!* I should have made a meal of her when she was eighteen. But nooo…I had to make her my major-dingo.

"Mmm," Stella says after sipping. "That was

very good. Just a splash of merlot, right?"

"Correct," I say.

She beams a smile that stuns me. No woman has ever smiled at me like that. Like she is thrilled just to be with me. She looks like an innocent captive virgin awaiting my command in her blindfold and pink dress. Soft, feminine—

Clumsy. I shoot a hand out with my lightning-fast reflexes to catch the bowl of cherries she nearly knocked over as she reached for one.

She holds up the cherry, unaware she nearly tossed the lot of them. "Palate cleanser." She pops it in her mouth and chews. "These are amazing. Where did you get them, Neli?"

I pause, enthralled as Stella licks a drop of cherry juice from her full lower lip.

"Neli?" Stella asks.

My voice is hoarse. "Neli had to see to some business upstairs." *Sharpening her horns or something.* "She will be back shortly." I pull out the Summoner under the table and discreetly pound out another message to the impudent major-dodo. This time she responds: *Spend some time with her. I promise I'll return soon.*

Stella pats around the table. "Where's the napkin?"

"Here." I place it in her hand, and her fingers close partially around my hand, the touch firing through my senses.

"Thank you." She wipes her mouth and discards

the pit, discreetly wrapping the napkin closed. "Did you like this blend too?"

"I have my opinion, but Neli and I would like to hear yours first."

I have already decided that decanter three is the superior blend. Neli agrees, but she wants Stella to come to the conclusion on her own. Of course, none of that matters right now, since all I can think of is adding a fourth blend to our tasting fun this evening: Stella.

Number four—I mean, *Stella* holds out her palm blindly, smiling sweetly. I find myself leaning forward—to kiss or breathe her in or taste? *Yes. I want it all.* "I'm ready for the second glass."

I pour it for her and place the glass in her hand, taking the opportunity to let my fingertips brush against hers again. I know I shouldn't. I know I am only torturing myself with the morsels of intimacy, but I cannot seem to help myself.

Her cheeks and neck flush pink. My touch affects her as much as it affects me, and I do not know what to make of it fully. I have never experienced anything like this with a woman, where her every move, her every breath leaves me hypnotized.

I watch as Stella sips the next blend, my gaze fixated on her sensual lips. "It's a little too fruity," she says.

Most likely from the cherry she just ate. "Yes." I refrain from correcting her. She is perfect just as she is.

"Please tell me it's not just me sipping delicious wine and scarfing down cherries." She picks up a cherry, her lips closing around it as she sucks it off the stem.

"Sweet Stella, enjoy." I am losing my damn mind, torn between wanting her and protecting her innocence. Also, my leather trousers are suddenly unbearably tight. I am so tempted to storm up the stairs, grab Neli by the scruff of the neck, and bring her down here to sit with Stella and make her watch Stella's sensual lips dripping with blood-red juice. But that would mean leaving Stella blindfolded and alone. She might take it as an insult.

She fingers her charm bracelet, looking so content. I wonder if this is how she looks when she first awakens from slumber. The words are out of my mouth before I can stop myself. "Do you enjoy sunsets?" It is when darkness descends, my favorite time.

She takes off the blindfold, her brown eyes meeting mine, sending a jolt through me that makes me feel alive. "I love sunsets! Especially over the vineyard when the last rays of sun paint everything in a soft glow."

"I paint." I never share so much about myself. It is just that there is such a strong connection, and I keep finding things we both like. She likes the sun's rays painting a glow, and I enjoy painting. We both love sunsets and beauty. Other than the fact that she is human, we match. Of course, that could be changed. *No. You are stronger than that.*

She props her chin on her hand, smiling at me. "Aren't you multitalented? An expert winemaker and an artist." A drop of red cherry juice rests on the corner of her mouth. My mind flashes to her as my vampire bride, a drop of blood lingering from her feeding on me. I would make her stronger, sharing my incredible powers as a vampire of eight hundred years.

"He sure is," Neli says cheerfully, surprising me once again by her sudden appearance. Stella has me enthralled. "Boz, you should show her some of your paintings."

My paintings are in my bedchamber, which Neli knows. She also knows I cannot allow Stella anywhere near my chamber of pleasure and seduction. That would be "game over," to use a more modern term.

"I'd love that," Stella says. "Maybe you could design the label for our new blend. Ooh, a sunset would be cool."

"You must try the last blend." I need to remove myself from her presence before I do something that cannot be undone.

"Close your eyes, Stella!" Neli says, taking a seat at the head of the table.

Stella complies.

I pour Stella the wine and hand it to her. Neli gestures for me to pour some for her. I ignore her, just as she has ignored my every command.

Stella's eyes pop open. "This is it!"

Neli squeezes her arm. "We think so too."

Stella lets out a happy laugh. "I'm getting better at this wine stuff if I'm in agreement with you two. We've got to enter this in the wine competition in New York." She holds up a palm. "Sorry, I'm getting ahead of myself. I'm just so excited about what this could mean for Stellariva. It's really, really good."

The best competition is in France, but I keep that to myself. Neli tells me she has sent someone in our stead these past few years since we began entering, due to the fact she is bound to me and must remain by my side, which made travel quite difficult. Now that I am awake from my curse, we shall most definitely attend in person.

Neli smiles her especially evil smile. "Actually, I think a wine competition is a great way to build buzz and really put Stellariva on the map. Don't you agree, Boz?"

Stella turns to me, hope shining in her big brown eyes.

"Of course, recognition can always help," I say, careful not to commit to a competition.

Neli raises her hands over her head in a grand gesture. "We should think big!" She leans toward Stella. "How do you feel about France? We compete every year. You could join us."

Join us?

Stella gasps and slaps a hand over her mouth,

her eyes wide. She drops her hand. "Seriously?"

I freeze, unable to steal Stella's obvious joy but also unable to agree to the competition.

"Seriously!" Neli exclaims, jumping from her seat and opening her arms to Stella.

Stella jumps up, and they hug and laugh together. I cannot be part of this. I will not allow myself to be so close to temptation for so long. The pull to her is too strong. Also, the risk of her discovering what I really am would be too great, considering how keenly aware she is of me. It's as though our sensations are heightened in each other's presence.

I stand, prepared to take my leave.

They break apart and turn to me. Neli shoots me an urgent look. Stella's smile falls at my serious demeanor. "Are you not on board?"

"Of course he is," Neli says. "He wants to help you out because he's an *honorable* man. It's a calling for him. Truly."

Stella's expression turns hopeful once more.

I am torn. What is more honorable—agreeing to France, which could help Stella immensely, or walking away for Stella's own good? Both could help her in very different ways.

Likely noting my lack of enthusiasm, Stella looks down, her shoulders slumping. "It's okay."

An empty ache deep inside tells me what I must do. I cannot steal her joy or ruin her chance to save her vineyard.

"We will go, and we will win," I pronounce.

"And I will cover all expenses. Of course, I will ask your parents for permission, as is proper."

Stella puts her hand over her heart, smiling at me. I will do anything for that smile. "Thank you. I owe you big time."

That is a debt I can never collect, because surely I'd ask for the one thing I cannot have: Her.

CHAPTER SIXTEEN
Boz

After Neli shows Stella out, I quickly realize from the sweat gathering in my nether region that I have backed myself into a very precarious corner. A trip to France? With Stella? What in the name of the dark gods was I thinking?

This connection between us is growing stronger by the minute, like a force I cannot control. And, as anyone who knows vampires will tell you, an out-of-control vampire is a very bad vampire. *Prince Bozhidar might be dangerous and handsome, but he is no rogue.* I do not kill haphazardly. I weigh the risks and adhere to my rules. I am not a savage.

Yet, every moment that passes in Stella's presence leaves me feeling increasingly vulnerable to temptation. *I want to be bad. I want to be a bad, dirty vampire with Stella.*

"Neli! Come here, you insolent major-dorko!"

It takes several moments until I hear her footsteps approaching the kitchen, where I am currently collecting ice from that rectangular food-cooling box and depositing it into a cloth.

The kitchen door swings open. "It's majordomo. And what do you want?"

"Yes. Major-dodo. Is this not what I said?" I grunt. "And do not distract me from the subject at hand; I cannot accompany Stella to France." I place the ice in a cloth and shove it down the front of my trousers. *Christ almighty, that's cold!*

"Ummm…what the hell are you doing, Boz?"

"What does it look like? I am cooling my loins." I yelp as one cube works its way free and slides down the interior of my trouser leg.

"Strange way to deal with your horniness, but oddly, I'm not shocked by anything you do these days." She exhales and folds her arms over her chest. "Now, what's this about not going to France?"

I wince, feeling my gonads shrink into tight stones. "It is too risky. My desire for her blood is overwhelmingly powerful, and I fear I will kill her."

Neli lifts one red brow. "You're an eight-hundred-year-old vampire, and you're telling me you can't control yourself around a girl?"

"Yes. Exactly." I yank the icy cloth from my breeches and toss the bundle into the sink. "It is no use! The fire in my loins will not extinguish."

Neli chuckles. "Told you so."

"Told me what?" I snarl.

"She's your mate."

"Sorry to disappoint you, but she is not. I was perfectly able to resist her this evening, as you saw with your very own eyes."

"Says the man shoving ice down his pants."

"I admit that my attraction to Stella is extremely strong, but that does not make her my mate."

Neli shakes her head and whooshes out a frustrated breath. If I agree with Neli, then I will have to accept making Stella mine, and I cannot have that. Stella is meant to be human—beautiful, kind, delicate. "No. Impossible."

"Ohmygod. Why are you always so stubborn, Boz?"

"It is in my nature. Just as asking ridiculous questions is in yours."

Neli rolls her eyes. "I'm telling you, she's the one. Think about it. You get all flustered when she's around. You think she smells and tastes like a virgin, but I've yet to meet a twenty-two-year-old woman who's that hot and hasn't managed to get laid."

The thought of her with another man makes my blood boil.

"See!" Neli points a finger in my face. "You're getting jealous right now, aren't you? I said she's not a virgin, and you jumped to thinking about some other guy boning her."

"No. No. I thought of another man having sex with her." Why would Stella require additional bones? She was born perfect. "And this is not proof of her being my mate."

Neli grips my forearm. "Boz," she says sternly, "you woke up almost immediately after I spotted Stella arriving home from college with all those boxes piled up in her parents' car. It's a sign."

"And?" I push.

"I'm not stupid."

"Yes, I am aware you have your moments of male-like intelligence, but I fail to see your point."

Neli's face turns a bitter shade of red. "I know about the witch. I know about her curse."

Oh. That. I vowed never to think of Olga or the curse again. Reliving unpleasant memories are of no use to me. "Then, if you are aware of her curse, you know that it was a farce—a ruse."

"She cursed you to sleep until 'a woman came into your life, capable of breaking your heart.'"

"That is not exactly what she said. And, trust me, I was there when the curse was exacted." Many years had passed since I overcame my forest-hag phobia, but I still felt a lingering unease around witches. And what better way to overcome a fear than to immerse one's self in it. So I decided to pursue Olga, and we became lovers. Very briefly. Until she began asking me to kill her enemies and I realized her interest in me was a self-serving power grab. Yes, she claimed to love me too, but I believe she was simply enthralled by my massive cock. I could not fault her for that, but I could for her attempts to manipulate me. When I informed her it was over and that I would never do her bidding, she told the town that I had taken all of the virgins, of every age, and eaten them. In truth, *she* kidnapped them, ate their toes, and boiled their kneecaps into a broth, which she served that very evening to the town's poor while she spun her lies.

I should have listened to Mother about hags.

The next evening, the village's peasants came looking to burn my castle—all right, looking to burn everything in it. Stone is very difficult to ignite. I explained the situation to them, holding nothing back. Yes, I did enjoy my virgins, but I would never take the children. The peasants took me at my word, as I had never lied to them in the past, and they turned on the witch. When Olga saw that her plan to ruin me had failed, she stormed my castle and laid a curse:

"Prince Bozhidar, I curse you to sleep until a woman is born who will teach you humility and kindness, whose beauty is so majestic, it will bring you to your knees. She will break your heart, and you will feel the misery, same as I."

"That is a bit harsh, do you not think?" I said. "We only fucked a few times, and it was quite underwhelming."

I believe that was the part that pissed her off the most. Apparently, she enjoyed the sex. The underwhelming perception came from me and me alone. Oops. The point to all this is that Olga knocked me out, and I awoke five hundred years later to the day.

"So what does any of that mean?" Neli asks after I relay the exact wording of the curse. "Why do you think I'm wrong about Stella?"

I lift my chin with confidence. "It is far more likely that Olga's magic simply expired rather than

Stella being the woman who was born to wreck me."

"Go on." Neli swirls her index finger through the air. "I'm listening."

"Stella grew up in that house right across the road from us. Why did I only just wake a few days ago?" I realize through conversations with Neli that Stella had been away studying for several years, but I am certain there were many occasions where she was here with her family and I was slumbering in my basement.

"Easy. Because she wasn't a woman then. And clearly she hadn't yet become *the* gal meant to break you. Now she is. Have you forgotten all about how witches and curses work? They're very cryptic, yet incredibly precise in their meanings." Neli shrugs.

Could Neli be right? Could Stella be the woman who was born to best me, subdue me, break me? "Then…if she is the one who lifted the curse, what should I do? She means to destroy me."

"No, Boz. She doesn't. The witch just said the woman would break your heart. She would teach you humility and kindness."

"Exactly. Are those not the ingredients to an epic vampire destruction?"

"Look. All I know is that since you've met her, you've embraced change, albeit in baby steps, and not nearly enough to change my mind about wanting death, but you have attempted to adapt. Overnight, you've decided to put the well-being of another person—Stella—above your own. All of this means you are learning humility and kindness, just as the curse prescribed. Change is upon you."

"It is true, I do enjoy my new tan as well as the new cologne in a big blue spray can in the bathroom."

Neli gives me a look. "You've been wearing Glade?"

I nod.

"I thought it smelled familiar."

"The scent is very woodsy and fresh." I wave my hand through the air to disperse more of the scent clinging to my skin.

She nods. "Yes. Yes it is."

"But my acceptance of a few minor gadgets, such as the Summoner and a new cologne, does not signify I should take Stella to France. I do not trust myself not to lose control and kill her."

"Then…" Neli groans, "you should turn her."

I blink rapidly. "Why would I do that?"

"If she is who I think, then you're right. You won't be able to resist her. And, eventually, you'll make her a vampire anyway. You'll have to if you want to spend eternity with her."

I groan with dread. Turning Stella is not as simple as shoving ice down one's trousers. There is a dance to be had. There is a process of introduction to our world. *Well, unless your parents gift you to a vampire, in which case, it is pretty much a go-with-the-flow sort of thing.* Nevertheless, I cannot wrap my ancient mind around one simple fact: I do not wish to harm my beautiful human. I wish to protect her. Even if that means shielding her from myself.

"No. I will not do it," I say firmly. "You will need to tell her that France cannot happen and—"

A blaring noise sounds, and I cup my hands over my ears.

"Fuck." Neli's green eyes go wide. "I think they're here."

"They? They who?"

"Those pesky asshole vampire hunters," she replies.

"What do you speak of, girl?" I say loudly over the noise.

"Remember that lame cult of vampire hunters? They're still around."

"The Van Helsings? But how did they find me so soon?" I frown.

Neli rolls her eyes. "Luck. They've been lurking around for a few months. They set up an observation post across the road."

"Where across the road?"

"In the attic over at Stella's house."

Jesus. Stella mentioned hearing strange noises in her house, but it is not due to a ghost. It is due to a very large cockroach infestation. And her old dog is too deaf to have noticed. Some watchdog. Stella needs a team of young hellhounds. In the meantime, I will draw first blood.

"Neli," I growl through my teeth, "why did you not mention this before?"

"You forget, I've been on my own for five centuries. They're not the first hunters to come sniffing around, and in my experience, the best defense is to just carry on like regular humans."

This is no excuse. "Neli!"

"I'm sorry I didn't say anything. Okay? But they usually get bored and leave on their own. I've only had to kill, like—" she holds out her hands and counts on her fingers "—eighty."

Oh gods.

The alarm continues blaring through the house. "Shut that thing off," I command. "I will deal with the intruders."

"Are you sure?"

I give her a look that indicates I am about to kill her too along with the hunters.

"Okeydokey. Shutting it off." She disappears into the parlor, and I go out the back door so I can sneak up on them from the outside. But after ten minutes of levitating from window to window, there is no sign of these Van Bastard vampire hunters. I go back inside and do a sweep of the rooms just to be sure. No one.

Standing in the foyer, I exhale slowly. Who knows what these hunters have seen? If they have proof that I have risen, they will never leave us alone. Not until they've put a stake through my heart.

"Anything?" Neli comes up behind me, panting.

"No. They have fled." I would chase after them,

but it may be a trap. "I will have to survey the situation tomorrow—find out how many there are."

"No need." Neli waves her hand through the air as if dispelling a foul smell. "I have a private security company on retainer."

I cock a brow.

"What? We're rich. And, honestly, I got super tired of killing all those hunters."

"So a company does it for you?"

"Pretty much." Neli taps the side of her head. "The modern supernatural world has its perks."

"I am not so sure I want to pay others to do my dirty work. Also, I rather enjoy capturing vampire hunters and torturing them. It is especially fun when you pluck out an eyeball and make them eat it." *Or send them to the hags for pedicures.*

"Sorry, Boz, but we are running a very legiti-mate, very successful business. The last thing we need is to play torture with our enemies. Better to let the pros deal with them. I hired otherworldly mercenaries. They'll make sure none of it traces back to us. Especially since there are eyes and ears everywhere."

Ah yes. The technologenie. "How long will it take these mercenaries to catch the intruders?"

"Not sure. But I suggest we vacate the castle until they do."

Oh hell. It dawns on me that the infestation ac-tually lies across the road. Of course, the hunters are of no threat to Stella and her family, but we must get them out of the house if we wish to clean up the menace.

"It looks as though you and I are heading to France a bit early, Neli. We will send word to Stella and her family to join us there. Make up some excuse for our hasty departure." I pause, thinking it over. Yes, this is an excellent plan. Castle Sangria is the defending champion and has already paid for several entries. Our daytime staff is perfectly capable of managing the winery in our absence. Stellariva has no business, so no one will notice if they shut down for a few days. And having Stella's family around will help keep her safe from me. "Arrange to have them stay at a villa near us, and then send a private plane to get them. Say...in a week. Tell them they need to hand carry our new wines for the competition." Neli had explained the process to me earlier when I questioned her on why she had not already sent our wine by ship, as I knew it would take months to arrive.

Neli flashes a devious smile, and I know it is because fate is playing into her hands. She wants to be free of me. She wants me to mate with Stella. As for me, I no longer know what I want. I cannot kill Neli. I cannot harm Stella. And, unfortunately, I'm beginning to believe I will do both.

CHAPTER SEVENTEEN
Stella

I can hardly believe I'm on a private jet with my family on our way to Bordeaux, France. It's dark now as we fly over the Atlantic Ocean. I know I should sleep, but I'm too excited. The furthest I've traveled is Phoenix, Arizona, to visit a friend. (Seems they still have some diehard hippies living there. I saw a sign for the Society of Sunshine Love.) Unfortunately, my excitement over attending the best wine competition in the world, in one of the best wine-growing regions, is tempered by the fact that yesterday's bake-off didn't go as we hoped for the twins. No full-tuition scholarship to culinary school or big prize money. I'm proud of my sisters' efforts, though, and they did win something—Eliza took second place in the sweet category ($500 prize), and Mabel earned an honorable mention in the savory category (a ribbon). Now it's even more important for Stellariva to gain recognition at this wine competition. It's a ticking clock before my family's winery goes under, taking everyone's hopes, dreams, and livelihood down with it. No pressure.

I blink gritty eyes in the dimly lit cabin and

check on my family. Everyone's sleeping. I sigh. If this wine competition doesn't yield any good results, it's over. Bankruptcy. We'll probably have to sell everything just to keep food on the table. The twins will have to take some low-level job at a restaurant after graduation and just hope to have a chance to work their way up. A process that could take years if it happens at all. I want better for them.

I close my eyes. My father left our winery in the care of our assistant manager, Max, who'll be taking retirement when we return. I'll miss him; he's been with us since the beginning. At least we won't have to worry about keeping him on payroll. *Enough.* I need to focus on the awesomeness of this moment. There's plenty of time for worrying later.

Right now I'm living a dream. Neli arranged everything for our family at no cost to us, from the limo ride to the private airport to the jet and hotel. We'll be arriving in Bordeaux at seven a.m. local time tomorrow, which is Thursday. The competition is Friday, there's an auction and a formal ball on Saturday, and we return home on Sunday. My sisters say Bordeaux is known for incredible food too. They want to try a few restaurants with the money Eliza won. By the time of the auction, the prizes will already be announced. The auction is open to the public, which gives Stellariva another chance to shine. We brought several cases of wine for it. You never know who'll show up. Maybe a sommelier from a famous Parisian restaurant, or a huge international wine distributor.

My mind drifts to Boz in formal wear at the ball. Gorgeous perfection in black. He defines tall, dark, and mysterious. Since he left for France ahead of us, there's been a strange hollowness in my chest. I've missed him, which says a lot. In the past, it's taken months for me to get to know a guy before I felt even a hint of attachment. With Boz, it's like our connection was already there. All I needed to do was to open my eyes and let it in.

I drift to sleep, finally, the thought of his powerfully confident take on the world making me relax. I'm so glad he's in my life. He's brought hope to a dark situation. His generosity and strong character have inspired me. Simply put, I've never met a man who's more honest, genuine, and giving. His physical attributes aren't so bad either.

I wake to a fresh woodsy scent that smells just like Boz's cologne. My pulse races until I realize I'm still on the jet. I glance around. My dad waves to me as he exits the jet's bathroom.

"Morning," he whispers as he takes his seat across from me. Mom and the twins are still sleeping.

"Morning. Are you excited about the competition? It's amazing what Boz did for us."

He leans across the aisle. "I am. I have to admit I had my doubts about Boz, but his generosity and Neli's competent manner, well, it really puts my mind at ease. What do they have to gain from helping us, after all? This is what good neighbors and community are all about." He gestures, raising his palms. "Lifting each other up."

I smile. "I'm glad you came around. I told you they were good people."

"Still, I don't want you dating him. He's a little off. Fine to be friendly, but, err, not someone I'd like as part of the family. Understand?"

I scrunch my nose. "You make it sound like I'm about to marry the guy." A flutter of excitement in my stomach surprises me. Me and Boz—being married, intimate. I flush at the thought.

My dad shakes his head. "Better not to head down that road. Maybe you'll meet someone cool at this wine competition. Hopefully, a local from California wine country so you can stick close to home."

Someone "cool" by Dad's standards is my high school boyfriend, Tyler, a chaste relationship since he used me to cover up that he was gay. Dad hoped we'd marry. Unfortunately, so did I. Secrets are the worst, though I understand now the pressure Tyler was under at the time. Tyler promised me we'd be engaged the year after we graduated high school, and I believed him. He broke it off on graduation night, finally admitting the truth. My heart was shattered. When I finally got the courage to try dating again in college, I fell for a medical student at a nearby university. Turned out he was an unemployed, married con man. Another devastating breakup. Secrets and lies. I learned a hard lesson, and I learned it well. Now I have zero tolerance for liars. I don't need anyone in my life like that ever again. Boz is the exact opposite, honest even when the truth is sometimes hard to hear. I appreciate that.

"Thanks for the advice, Dr. Love Genius," I tease Dad.

"That's what dads are for." He crosses his eyes, making me laugh. "I can't help looking out for you. I just want you to be happy." He jabs a finger at me. "So no dating guys that set off my Danger, Will Robinson alert."

I roll my eyes and settle back in my seat.

"Psst, you think we'll win something?"

I shift to meet his eyes, and he looks so hopeful I know there's only one right answer. "Absolutely."

I walk with my family to the restaurant where we're meeting Neli and Boz for dinner. We're really here! Bordeaux is beautiful with so many well-preserved majestic buildings. I've already seen a cathedral, a palace, and an opera house in the neoclassical style with impressive Greek columns. The wine competition takes place at a modern-looking conference center and exhibit hall with lots of glass to let the light shine in.

My pulse thrums through my veins in my eagerness to see Boz again. I spent extra time getting ready tonight. I'm wearing my long hair down, and I applied just enough makeup for a subtle glow. My dress is new—a steal from Target—but I think it says elegant sophistication. It's a pale pink floral dress with cap sleeves and a shallow V neck in the formfitting bodice. The hem ends at my knees, falling in a diagonal to my ankles in back. Light beige open-toed high-heeled sandals complete the look. *Will he notice?*

My dad stops at an elegant-looking restaurant, ornate carved pillars flanking the door. He holds the door for us and ushers us in. "Ladies."

I step in first, noticing the crisp white tablecloths and expensive-looking art on the walls—all colorful abstract splashes or clumpy portraits of people holding black umbrellas. But none of that holds my attention as my body starts to tingle, sensing Boz is near. How or why I react physically to him in such a strange way, I don't know.

My eyes search the dimly lit space for the man I can't seem to stop thinking about. And Neli, of course. I spot them at a long banquette table in the back. Neli's glaring at a man sitting alone at a nearby table.

I wave to her. She immediately smiles and stands. "*Bonsoir!* Glad you found the place."

Boz stands and inclines his head in greeting. My breath catches. He's stunning in an expensive-looking navy suit tailored to his exquisite muscular perfection. Every nerve ending sparks to life.

My mom rushes forward, thanking them both profusely for everything.

"It is nothing," Boz says modestly.

"It's *everything*," I say.

His silvery eyes lock on mine for an intense moment. I fight the urge to draw closer. His pull is magnetic.

Eliza and Mabel bound forward, hugging Neli and thanking her for everything. Then they gush over Boz.

"You're so generous," Eliza says, looking up at him under her lashes.

Oh my God, is my baby sister flirting with him? She's seventeen!

"We can't thank you enough," Mabel says in a high reedy voice.

Boz holds up a hand. "Consider me thanked, girls. We are happy to have you as our guests."

"Killer suit," Eliza says, looking up and down Boz's body.

Boz shoots Neli a questioning look. She does a quick head shake.

"You look…" Mabel starts.

"So hot," my sisters say in appreciative unison and then giggle madly. *So embarrassing.*

Boz studies the ceiling, refraining from comment.

"Girls, take a seat," Mom says, shooing them over to sit by Neli. "You're embarrassing yourselves." She follows closely behind, whispering in a low fierce tone to them. *Mom lecture on manners coming right up!*

Boz holds out the chair next to him and catches my eye, gesturing toward it. I take the seat, smiling at his old-fashioned manners. My dad takes the chair on my other side.

After we're all seated and the waiter takes our drink order, Mom fills Neli and Boz in on the safe delivery of the wine to the judging area. My parents took care of that while I took a much-needed nap. I definitely shouldn't have slept because now I feel wide awake and wired. Like I could stay up all night.

Neli's gaze lands again on the man sitting alone. I glance over, and he quickly brings a newspaper up in front of his face. I only caught a glimpse of thick glasses, but something about him seems familiar.

I lean across the table to whisper to Neli, "Is that someone from home? He looks familiar, but I can't place him."

"Who?" Neli asks, shooting a glance at Boz.

I point toward my own palm to indicate the guy without directly pointing. "The guy you keep looking at sitting alone with the thick glasses."

She shakes her head. "Never seen him before. I caught him checking me out and was letting him know I'm *not* interested." She sounds tense.

"Oh."

Boz slowly turns, his steely gaze settling on the

man. The guy peeks around his newspaper and startles, dropping it. He quickly leaves.

Wow. Boz is better than my dad at getting guys to leave. He sure looks out for Neli. Wait, is Boz involved with Neli? She is beautiful with her red hair and sparkling green eyes. Smart too. I rub the wine charm on my bracelet, as I often do when I think of Boz. He gave me jewelry. Did he also give Neli the pearl necklace she's wearing? Have I been pining for a man whose heart is already taken?

For the rest of dinner, in between my father's and Boz's entertaining debates about the best grapes from Europe, I find myself studying Boz and Neli. First thing I notice is that Boz barely touches his food, and when he does, I'm pretty sure he tucks it into his napkin. Maybe he's one of those health nuts, who only eats a few select items to keep up their spectacular physique. *Really working for him.* The second thing that hits me is how close Boz and Neli seem, often following the same line of thinking. Sometimes it sounds like playful banter, though the playfulness is on Neli's side. Boz seems to take everything seriously. Maybe he secretly enjoys it, but he's one of those manly men who don't show much emotion.

After the meal concludes, we thank Boz for the fantastic food, which he paid for before my parents even got the chance to contribute. I linger behind on our way out, hoping to talk to Boz alone. I need to thank him personally for his incredible generosity—it's a lot, and my family needs to find a way to repay him someday—but also, I want to know what the story is with him and Neli.

Luckily, my mom is talking Neli's ear off. My dad and the twins are already on the sidewalk, waiting outside, probably coming up with ideas about pastry recipes to name after Boz. I love that they adore him as much as I do, given where things started, but now I worry about how attached I've become so quickly. Is it a mistake? Did I jump before I looked?

Before I can come up with a subtle way to ask about the situation, Boz says, "You were very quiet at dinner. Is something not to your liking?"

"Oh, no. I loved everything. Not one single word of complaint about anything. This restaurant has such a romantic ambiance with the dark wood paneling and soft lighting." I suddenly realize how much I wish it were just the two of us for a romantic night. I fear my secret longing for him is too obvious, so I quickly add, "This whole trip is like a dream come true for my family."

A smile tugs at his lips. "A happy dream, I hope."

"Yes," I breathe, taken in once again by his rare smile. Then I remember myself. "You and Neli seem close."

"We have a bond that cannot be broken," he says matter-of-factly.

"Ah. Are you two more than just coworkers?" I

ask.

I hold my breath, praying he says no.

He lifts a shoulder in a casual shrug.

And it seems he's done talking about that. I don't press. But she must mean a lot to him. I mean, what guy talks about a bond that can't be broken if they're not serious about a woman? Plus they live together. I don't know why I hadn't considered it before. I was so caught up in his magnetism, his sexy good looks, his incredible kindness toward me and my family, I was blind to the truth. Now I feel like an idiot. And I'm crushed.

He holds the door open for me. I brush past him, ignoring the spike of raw lust that goes through me. I would never be the reason a couple breaks up, but I can't shut off my feelings. I can only try to hide them.

My mom turns to us the moment Boz and I step outside to join everyone. "Neli just told us the hotel we're staying at is supposed to be haunted. They have a tour of the suite where they say you can feel the chill of the old widow pass through you."

I cross my arms, rubbing the goosebumps. "No, thank you. Bad enough I hear creaks in our old house at night. I might not believe in ghosts, but I could still have nightmares."

My dad wags his finger at me. "Remember when Stella used to have that recurring vampire nightmare after Kevin snuck up on her the day before Halloween—"

"Wearing his fake vampire teeth!" Mom finishes. "Oh, Lord, it took forever to convince her it was just Kevin. And even longer for the nightmares to stop."

I sigh. "I'm fine as long as I stay away from creepy stuff."

My parents shake their head over the memory. The twins are busy whispering to each other, shooting glances over at Boz, their new crush. Boz gazes into my eyes somberly. He already knew about my childish nightmares, but clearly he feels bad that I'm being reminded of it now.

"We'll skip the ghost tour," Neli says. "Let's head back for a nightcap at the hotel lounge. It's a beautiful space." We're all staying at the same historic hotel.

"I'll take the twins on the tour and back to bed," Mom says as we head toward the hotel.

"I'm beat," Dad says. "Jet lag's catching up to me."

"I could go for a drink," I say. "I napped this afternoon, and I'm wide awake."

"Perfect!" Neli says.

Boz gives me a sideways look that almost seems sad. "I too have the jet lag. You and Neli should go discuss whatever women discuss."

"Mostly we talk about men," I say casually before catching up to Neli. I don't miss his dropped jaw.

That's right, Boz. I'm about to get the dirt on you.

CHAPTER EIGHTEEN
Boz

I excuse myself from the after-dinner drinks for two reasons: One, I am quite thirsty, and being around Stella this evening is proving more difficult than I thought. All throughout dinner, as I pretended to eat a very rare steak—just about the only solid food I can tolerate chewing before discreetly spitting it out—I felt something in my chest. An odd sensation. A tightening or squeezing brought on every time I gazed into Stella's warm brown eyes. Then a loud pulsing sound began, as if I were listening to her heart pumping inside my own chest.

She is my mate? It cannot be. It simply cannot. But what other explanation is there? I have heard many tales of a vampire's heart beating anew when they find their one true love, but since I have never personally witnessed it or known a vampire who experienced the phenomenon, I simply dismissed it as legend or wishful thinking from inexperienced new vampires who are unfamiliar with the process of feeding. There is a moment when the victim's pulse begins to quicken and their blood courses through your veins with a pulsing heat. The sensation can be so engrossing, so utterly hypnotic that one loses themselves in it.

Which results in snack time becoming hide-the-body time. Bad vampire. However, that was not what I experienced tonight.

Christ. I run my hand over the top of my now short hair while walking casually along a narrow street, attempting to deal with reason number two for not joining Stella and Neli for a nightcap: one of those damned vampire hunters followed us here! He must've seen the itinerary in Neli's office back at the castle. Or perhaps he overheard one of our conversations. If the team of mercenaries back home are as good as Neli claims, they are setting up and cleaning house, including Stella's attic, this very evening while the employees are away; however, that does not help us here in France.

Now I will have to deal with two problems: Keeping my hands off Stella, and killing this pesky hunter myself. Unfortunately, I have come to learn that Neli was right to warn me about the technolog-enie, which I now understand is simply a term for a very large system of intrusive electronics. Perhaps calling it a genie makes humans feel more at ease with being spied on by their leaders, because these watchful electronic eyes, called cameras, are every-where—stuck on the sides of buildings, inside those Beemer storage buildings, and even married to those lights that direct traffic. Why do modern humans permit such a lack of privacy? *Makes it very difficult to be a vampire.* The only thing in my favor is that this city has many old neighborhoods, where the streets are dark and the buildings are free of these electronic eyes.

I plan to take a nice long stroll and hopefully lure the vampire hunter. After he is dealt with, I must decide what to do with Stella. I am only one heartbeat away from losing control and making her mine.

Her father would be very cranky with me.

Several hours later, despite circling back toward the hotel multiple times, in hopes the hunter would see me and follow, I abandon the plan and turn my focus on dinner. I cannot deny that the women in this town are very yummy—they drink such good wine—but I am left with a hunger I cannot sate. It is a hunger for a woman I do not wish to harm. I can only hope the warm Bordeaux-infused blood flowing through my veins is enough to keep my other urges in check.

In any case, it is nearly one in the morning now, and Stella should be asleep. She and her family will attend the competition with Neli tomorrow, and I will meet everyone after sunset to congratulate them on their win. I am confident that our entry will be given very high praise. Afterward, I will excuse myself and try once more to find this hunter and turn him into potting soil. *Perhaps, while I slumber, Neli can find out where he is staying.*

I enter the grand lobby of the Argent de Doigt d'Hôtel with its oversized indoor trees, vaulted stained-glass ceilings, and elegant crystal chandeliers. The man behind the counter greets me with a nod. I am almost to the elevator, a very ingenious closet that moves one from floor to floor, when I catch the most exquisite scent of roses. *Stella…she is near.*

I turn my head and spot her through the open doorway just off the lobby, sitting at a table near the bar, one leg crossed over the other in a way that exposes one bare leg from knee to ankle. *Do not go to her, Boz. Do not do it.* I cannot seem to leave. The soft lighting in the wood-paneled space bathes her skin in a radiant glow, and her long dark hair shines as it cascades over the back of her pale pink floral dress. I clench my fists and shut my eyes. If the witch's curse is real, giving in to my desire will result in my destruction. Not to mention, the very real possibility of Stella's. If she is truly my mate, then I will be driven to turn her. And to destroy such a precious creature is not my wish. I know this is what Neli wants. She likely ensured Stella would be here for me to find. I quickly pull out the Summoner and send a note:

Prince Bozhidar: *You and I will have words tomorrow, little matchmaker devil.*

I notice the squiggling dots indicating that she is

responding. I turn and quickly make my way toward the elevator while she likely composes an apologetic reply.

> **Neli:** *Don't look at me, dude. Destiny is all. Can't outrun it.*

> **Prince Bozhidar:** *Don't you dare quote Uhtred. He is a great warrior!*

Uhtred is that fellow we were watching on the tiny portable theater during the *aeroplane* ride here. I rather enjoyed the way he beheaded his enemies in his *Last Kingdom*. It was also nice to escape to the gritty, filthy warmth and simplicity of the medieval era. *Ah, nothing like home.*

> **Neli:** *And you were once a great warlord. So stop being such a wuss, and go claim your woman! She's waiting for you in the hotel bar. Chicken. Bock. Bock. Bock.*

I growl. *I knew it!* Neli is my trusted ally, but like any female, she cannot be discouraged from her goals once she sets her sights on something. It is very annoying.

> **Prince Bozhidar:** *Your fowl words do not sway me. Now, please try to find out where our hunter is staying so that I may address the issue properly tomorrow evening. Good night!*

The elevator chimes, and I am about to step inside when I hear Stella's voice. "Boz! Hey."

I groan, feeling the push and pull. I should go to my room. I should break into the Musée d'Aquitaine to see the Venus of Laussel—a stone carving of an ancient woman scratching herself. I should find a café table in the plaza, sip wine, and compliment the fashionable American tourists passing by and showing off their Must Have Tees. I should do anything but go to her.

"Boz?" she calls out again.

Against my will, I feel a smile curl on my lips, and my body turns. "Stella, you are awake." *What am I doing? Dammit, man. No!*

Stella makes a little wave, and her face lights up with a smile. I am done for.

I stroll over, my resolve melting away like a piece of ice on a hot, sunny sidewalk.

"I think I slept too much on the plane, and now I'm wide awake. Join me?" She glances at the chair directly to her left. The ambiance is dark, cozy, and romantic. A couple sits closely in the corner, whispering very erotic words between them— vampire ears hear all. Three women and a man, wearing formal clothing, sit at the long mahogany bar, sipping a fine red port with notes of caramel and currants. I can smell it from here. But nothing is more delicious than the woman before me. Roses. Purity. *My little virgin…*

I take a seat next to her, and our eyes lock. My heart jars inside my chest. Dear gods. The beating in my chest feels even stronger now. It must be true that a vampire's heart beats anew when they are with their one true love. She is my lobster, to quote my wise friend Phoebe.

But I cannot dine on my lobster.

"So, where did you come in from?" she asks. "I thought you were going to bed early."

"I meant to, yes; however, I could not sleep. Went out for a stroll."

"Oh. Maybe I should have done that. It's just, I'm so nervous about tomorrow. Everything's riding on this competition."

Why must she say the word "riding"? An image of her doing just that hits me like a spike to the brain and lodges there: Her creamy soft skin glowing with the light of a crackling fireplace, her hair wild and loose down her back, her pert young breasts bobbing as her hips rock while she rides my cock and—

I clear my throat, feeling my shaft press uncomfortably against my trousers. "I am confident our wine will do well in the competition."

"You're just saying that to be nice."

"I would not put my eight hundred years of winemaking reputation on the line if I did not feel it was worthy."

Stella tilts her head to one side. "Eight hundred years?"

"I meant my family's reputation. I come from a very long line of Romanian winemakers."

"Oh wow. Is that where your family is originally

from?"

The beating sound in my chest is so loud I can hardly hear her words, and the stiffness in my cock is not helping my listening abilities.

I nod. "Yes. We are from Romania, as is our wine. The vines we grow today are from the same seeds I planted—I mean my great-grandfather-many-times-over planted."

"That's fascinating. And it explains why your wines are so delicious." She reaches out and sets her hand over mine, her lips dancing with a seductive smile. "Just like the winemaker."

A jolt of electricity surges through me, and I jerk my hand away.

The look of shame on her face is instant. "Oh God. I'm so sorry. It's just that Neli said—I just thought that—never mind."

"No. Please do not misunderstand me." I lower my voice so only she can hear. "You are a very beautiful woman. But I am a very complicated man with a very complicated life. I do not wish to embroil you in it."

Stella gazes down at her nearly empty glass of wine. Why she is drinking the house wine, I do not know. "Allow me to get you another glass of wine, and then I shall see you to your—"

"No. I'm good." She smiles, but I see the corners of her lips struggle to remain lifted. She is upset. "I should go."

I catch her wrist as she stands, and the electricity

that was just now buzzing through me gives her a jolt.

Her eyes go wide. "Ohmygod, Boz. What was that?"

My face contorts awkwardly. "Static electricity?"

I think my secret is out. She knows there is magic between us.

CHAPTER NINETEEN
Stella

I stare at the spot on my wrist where Boz is touching me. My entire body hums with an odd current that amplifies right as it passes over my—

Whoa! I pull my wrist away. Did he just reach all the way down to my magic button? There's a lingering tingle between my legs and a delicious ache.

I step back. Was I imagining it? *Must be the jet lag and wine or something because his hand never left my wrist. Magical seduction.* Probably all in my mind, except I definitely felt…*something.*

My mind quickly hops to the conversation I had earlier with Neli. I was looking for dirt and clarification about their romantic status, but what I got was a mile-long list as to why Boz and I would be perfect for each other.

If that's not a green light from Neli, I don't know what is.

She then assured me that Boz's attraction was mutual and that all I had to do was make the first move, because his gentlemanly ways would prevent any action on his part until I make the "deepest desires of my timeless soul and fervently beating heart known to him."

I swear, sometimes when Neli talks, I feel like I'm listening to an old woman from some classic romance novel. The part of our conversation that stuck with me most, however, was when Neli said, and I quote, "His supernatural gifts of seduction will leave you breathless. You will forget all other men until end of days are upon us." What a weird thing to say. And how does she know about his "gifts" if they've never been together? She says it's just what she heard, whispers over the years. Either way, I'm intrigued. And now, my entire body is trembling with need. I can't help wondering if this is what Neli meant. His rep is so well deserved, and I'm dying to experience more.

"Boz," I say in my firmest voice, "I know you're old fashioned about certain things, so what I'm about to say might sound forward, but Neli said I have to make my intentions clear." I lift my chin. "So that's what I'm doing. I have intentions. And they are the sort that take place in private." I swallow hard. "Naked," I add, in case it wasn't clear.

He looks up at me from where he's still seated, stifling a smile, but the hungry look in his dark seductive eyes tells me Neli was right. He *does* want me. But then why the speech about him being complicated and pushing my hand away? And that spark when our hands touched? Phew! I always thought that "the spark" thing was a metaphor, not an *actual* physical reaction. I *have* to follow through.

"Are you truly prepared to be naked in my bed?" he asks, his voice gruff and low, for my ears only. At my sharp intake of breath, he continues, "Perhaps you are not ready for this *experience*." That last word comes out gravelly, seductive and challenging at the same time.

My toes curl, and my nipples tingle into sharp points beneath the thin fabric of my pink floral dress. His words are almost as sexual as the sinful tone of his voice. *Supernatural gifts of seduction? Yes, please. Ruin me for other men.* "I'm ready," I say.

He is about to speak, but something in the window behind me catches his attention. A hard, fiercely bitter gleam in his eyes replaces the carnal hunger I saw just a moment ago. I turn my head and catch a glimpse of a man staring at us. He's in a tan trench coat with a black fedora pulled down low, leaving his face in shadow. Little warm out for a trench coat.

"Wait. Isn't that the guy from the restaurant?" I ask.

"Let me walk you to your room."

Um. That wasn't an answer, and I'm about to say so when Boz stands. He takes my hand and tugs me out of the bar.

I stumble along, catching glimpses of the other patrons immersed in their conversations.

"Boz, what's going on? Who is that guy?"

"He is—he is an old nemesis." Boz punches the

button for the elevator, keeping his eyes focused directly on the door in front of us. For a moment, I think he's avoiding eye contact with me, but then I realize he's looking at the reflection in the shiny stainless steel. He's watching everything behind us. His shoulders are square, his back is rigid, and he looks like he's about to rip off someone's head. A vision of Boz as a warrior flashes through my mind—fierce, strong, victorious.

"Is he from a rival winery?" I whisper, actually finding this whole thing a little exciting. Or maybe it's the weird buzzing sensation flowing from our touching hands, into my body. The space between my thighs begins to heat.

Oh, God. What is that? I squeeze my thighs together, wanting to release the pressure, but it only makes the sensation intensify.

The elevator chimes, and the doors slide open. Boz quickly shuffles me inside and presses the button for the fourth floor. My floor. My body hums in anticipation until he presses the button for the penthouse. His floor.

I deflate at the ego punch, disappointment making my limbs heavy.

I pull my hand away and keep my lips clamped together. I'm confused and hurt, but most of all, I'm angry. It's not nice to play with a woman's heart like that, and I expected more from him.

"I will see you to your room," he says as we step out, "and please stay there until morning. It is not safe to wander about."

I stop and turn to him. "I can see myself to my room. Thanks and good night." I turn and start walking down the hallway. "Gentleman, my ass," I huff under my breath.

"I heard that," he calls out.

Supernatural hearing to go with his supernatural gifts of seduction? Isn't he special? I grind my teeth. Neli was wrong about him, about us. I feel like a fool. *I mean, wow. I really put myself out there with the flirting.* It's something I've never done for anyone. *And won't do again!*

I continue down the hall, silently seething. Just as I turn the corner, Boz is standing there, and I almost crash into him.

"Ah! Where'd you come from?"

He ignores my question and frowns down at me, those dark eyes drilling into my soul. "Do not be upset, my sweet Stella." He raises his hand and cups my cheek. His skin is cool yet makes the spot warm and tingly. "As I said, I am a complicated man, and I truly believe you deserve better—afternoons of sunshine, beautiful babies with rosy cheeks, scuba diving in turquoise water with colorful fish."

Huh? "Scuba diving?"

"Yes. I saw it in a magazine while on the *aeroplane*. It is when you strap a large container of oxygen to your back and—"

"I know what scuba diving is, Boz. I just don't

understand what it has to do with us or this conversation."

A sadness fills his dark eyes. "Because, Stella," he says is a quiet voice, "it is a life I could never give you." He brushes his thumb across my lower lip.

"Why?" I ask breathlessly. He's so close. Need rushes through me.

"My work keeps me very busy," he says brusquely.

Work? This is about work? What an asshole! Stung, I take a step back. He doesn't want to sleep with me because he's a workaholic? It sounds like an excuse.

He stares deeply into my eyes. I can practically feel the despair. I know I'm missing something. He's not being honest with me. I can sense it in my gut.

I go for complete honesty, trying to reach him. "I'm fine without scuba diving, and I don't need all of your time. I just… I think there's something here worth exploring. I'm willing to take a chance." My brows knit. "It's a little early to talk about kids and all that. Can we just take it one step at a time? I'm fantastic at making plans if we get to that point. Most everything in life can be fixed with a good plan."

"My sweet, sweet Stella. If only it were so simple." He takes my hand, places a kiss on top, letting his lips linger, before he rises to his full height. "But I am afraid that as lucky as I would be to have you, a gentleman must always know right from wrong."

He bows. And I don't mean like a little head dip. He literally bends his body in half. It's the move of a courtly gentleman just like Neli said. "Good night, Stella. Sleep well."

He turns and leaves me standing there, my head spinning and my body on fire. I have never wanted a man so badly that it hurt. The worst part is that something in his voice sounded so final. *Was he saying goodbye just now?*

In shock, I turn and go to my room. Once inside, I plop down on my bed and stare at the cream-colored wall. What just happened? In one fell swoop I was carried away in the hottest moment I've ever experienced, only to have it end with a bucket of ice water poured over my head. I know it wasn't one sided. None of this makes sense. What am I missing?

I stand, planting my hands on my hips. We're not done, Boz. I refuse to be shuffled off to my room without an explanation.

CHAPTER TWENTY
Boz

My loins burning with need, I quickly return to my suite on the top floor and begin running the shower. I will have to service myself tonight—something I have not done for, well, I cannot recall. When I have needs, it is never difficult to seduce a woman to my bed. Tonight, however, and possibly for the remainder of my existence, there is only one woman I desire.

Phew. That was close. There was a moment when I did not believe I could walk away from Stella. Her delicious scent lingers in my lungs and calls to me like none other. And when she looked up at me with pain in her eyes, I wanted only to make it disappear.

Damn that Neli. I grab the Summoner and tell her to come to my room immediately. She and I need to get on the same page. I cannot be placed in such tempting situations again. Also, we must devise a plan to take care of the hunter.

I hit send and strip my clothing to prepare for my shower. My cock is so hard, I fear it might never abate. I poke the thing. *Like granite.*

I turn to go into the bathroom and hear a light knock on the door. *Ah, finally.* For once Neli is being the obedient servant. She must know she is in the pigsty. I go to open the door. "Neli, we must talk—"

Stella is standing there, her eyes wide as she takes in my naked form, my cock jutting out like an arrow directed at her.

"I-I just came up to…" Her words fade, and she licks her lips while staring directly at my manhood.

My heart starts to beat once more like a loud drum, demanding action. *Take her. Take her. Take her.*

"Fuck it." I grab her wrist and pull her inside, pressing her firmly to my body.

She says nothing with her mouth, but the desire in her eyes speaks volumes. I bow my head and press my mouth to her soft lips. The need inside me is overwhelming. But it is not for sex. It is for her blood.

No. You cannot do this. You will not be able to stop. But my mind is not in control any longer. It is my thirst, begging for one last taste of her virgin blood before I take her.

Stella

The nerves were racing through me as I made my way to the penthouse suite. I knew I could be facing a harsh rejection, but I deserved to know why. I didn't mistake the desire flowing like an electric current between us, or the pain in his eyes when he turned from me. Whatever the problem is, I want to fix it together.

Then I knocked on his door to find him naked, fully erect. He pulled me inside and pressed his mouth to mine. Now I can't remember what I came here to say, but I know it was important.

I push back and stare up at him. The way he's looking at me takes my breath away. There are no words. There's only primal need. I lift my face to his, my heart hammering against my rib cage. His dark silvery eyes smolder into mine for a crackling moment before he dips his head and presses his mouth to mine again. *Yes, yes, yes.* His hand grips my hair, tugging my head back as he deepens the kiss. I welcome the fiery heat, consumed by it. Desire unfurls within me, and I wrap my arms around his neck, urgently pressing all of my softness against his hard powerful body. I want with an intensity I've never felt before. I roam my hands over his broad back, a needy moan escaping.

He breaks the kiss suddenly, his breath ragged. "Remove your clothes and go lie on the bed."

The note of command in his voice excites something deep inside me. I've never been with a man who wants to take control like that. I comply, making my way to his bedroom. He follows, and when I reach the large bed, I keep my eyes locked on his, wanting his reaction as I unveil what I know he wants. I reach back and unzip my dress before slowly sliding the cap sleeves off my shoulders. The dress falls to my waist, and I shimmy it down over my hips. It pools at my feet. His dark eyes gleam as I step out of it, wearing only black lace panties and a matching bra I wore just for him. I wanted this moment and now I finally have him.

"And the rest. Take it off," he says, barely restrained need in his voice.

My lips curve up, loving the effect I have on him. I unhook my bra, sliding it off and tossing it carelessly to the side. His hot gaze never leaves my breasts, and my nipples form hard points under his attention.

"Everything else," he commands.

My breath quickens in anticipation. I slide off my heels and push my panties down, stepping out of them and letting them dangle from one finger.

His gaze is hooded, taking me in from head to toe. My body heats in response, and I drop the panties, my need spiking.

"Now what?" I ask softly.

"Lie down in the center of the bed."

I pull the covers down and do as he says, letting my legs fall open. He approaches, his gaze eating me up, yet still he holds back. He needs some enticement. I slide my hand between my legs, touching myself. "Is this what you like? You want to see me pleasure myself?" I've never done anything like that before, but something about this man makes me want to step outside my comfort zone. Our connection is intense on every level, and I welcome it.

He doesn't answer, his hungry gaze glued to my fingers. I like him watching more than I thought I would. His massive erection throbs as I continue, my fingers stroking lazily at first. But then his smoldering eyes meet mine, and my fingers move faster, wanting release, wanting him to see how close he's brought me just from a look. That's how powerful this thing is between us.

My head arches back as my climax hits. Suddenly he's on me, his powerful naked body covering mine as his teeth clamp on the cord of my neck. I pant as my pleasure builds again. "What are you doing to me? Oh God, it feels so...sooo...good." I'm dying of pleasure, lost in it.

My hips rock against his hardness, needing more, and then suddenly I'm there, crashing over the edge. "Yess," I hiss, rocking helplessly against him.

A harsh knock sounds at the door. "Boz!" The knocking turns into pounding. "Boz!"

It sounds urgent, but I'm light-headed in the aftermath of the heat of the moment and the most incredible pleasure I've ever experienced in my life. I'm having trouble catching my breath.

Boz releases my neck, lifting his head. "Neli," he says.

I close my eyes, so drained I can't move. *Whoa.*

He holds my jaw. "Are you all right?"

I smile what I'm sure is a goofy smile. "That was amazing. Let's keep going so you can have your pleasure. I'm ready for more."

Neli keeps pounding on the door. "Boz!"

I sit up, wrapping the blanket around myself. "It sounds urgent. I hope everything's okay."

"Her urgent is not my urgent," he says, getting out of bed. "I'll get rid of her."

I follow him, grabbing his pants on the way, and hand them to him with a pointed look. I don't want Neli to see what only I should get to see. I hope this will be an exclusive thing.

He lets out a manly sigh, pulls them on, and stalks to the door.

I stick close by, wrapping the blanket tighter around my shoulders, hoping everything is okay with Neli. Especially because I really want to do that again. Boz's abilities in bed were not exaggerated. And I still ache to feel him inside me. All I got was a love-bite orgasm. *What was that?*

Boz yanks the door open. "Neli, you are disturbing my supreme lovemak—"

Neli's eyes dart to the side. Suddenly a man jumps out with a wooden stake, screaming, "Die, vampire!"

It's that man who keeps following us!

Boz moves with such speed he's a blur. Suddenly the man is flat on his back on the floor. Boz pins him there with one hand and bites his neck. Neli's urgent voice is drowned out by the man screaming.

My hand flies to my throat, shock rendering me immobile.

A moment later, the man goes still and deathly silent.

Boz lifts his head, blood dripping from his mouth. That same mouth that bit my neck. My vision dims at the edges, my heartbeat roaring in my ears. I open my mouth to speak, but nothing comes out.

And then the world goes black.

Boz

"Shit," Neli says, walking into the room and shutting the door behind her. "How are we going to come back from this one?"

Stella is unconscious on the floor, the blanket falling off her. I scoop her up and tuck her into bed. I stare at the bite marks on her neck. I stopped myself. I don't know where I found the control, but I did it. It must be that I could never destroy my true mate. I'm sure that's what she is. Our heartbeats were in perfect rhythm while I drank from her, and when she climaxed, I could swear I felt it too. Her every moan and quake were like my own.

I'm done for. From this day forward, I somehow know my entire world will revolve around her.

I look over at Neli, who's now standing on the

other side of the bed. "You were right. She is my mate."

"No. Really?" Neli rubs the back of her neck. "Well, you know I love to hear I'm right, Boz, but now we have a teensy problem: She just saw you kill a man. That might not be so easy for a modern person to handle. This isn't like back when you ruled eight hundred years ago with unlimited power. Back then you were the boss, and it was accepted that you had the right to punish as you saw fit."

"I never stopped being the boss."

She grimaces. "Okay. Fine. But there are laws against killing. And those laws apply even to you."

"I do not have to obey human laws. I am a vampire."

"I get that, but the laws are a reflection of human values. They are not okay with witnessing people die. It really freaks them out."

We both stare at Stella looking so innocent lying in my bed, her lashes fanning over her pale cheeks.

And then I understand what Neli is trying to say. "She'll think I'm a monster."

"That's what I'm afraid of," Neli says. "But maybe if you explain. Tell her who and what you are; she'll understand the way of it."

She sounds as uncertain as I feel. But what choice do I have? She will walk away if she believes I'm a killer. But vampires have a code. We never kill those who don't deserve it. This vampire hunter deserved to die. He and his cohorts violated Stella's family home, putting her and her family at risk in his zeal to stalk me. I had to rid the earth of him.

Stella stirs with a soft sound. "She's waking," I whisper to Neli, who gestures for me to get in there and try to undo the damage.

I sit on the mattress next to Stella. "Hello, my sweet. Are you all right? Can you hear me?"

"Gah!" Stella scrambles to a sitting position, yanking the covers up to her chin. "Get away from me! What. Are. You?" The terror and confusion in her eyes are palpable.

I will break the news gently. Which part would be less terrifying to her? Is she more afraid of vampires or killers?

"What. Are. You?" she repeats.

"I am Prince Bozhidar Alexandru of Transylvania." I rise and bow.

"I-I thought your first name was Prince. You're an actual prince?" Her gaze darts to Neli for confirmation.

I find it odd that her mind is skipping over more pressing matters, such as, I just killed a man in front of her. She must be in shock.

Neli backs up a step. "I'll leave this conversation to the two of you."

"Don't go," Stella says, fear laced in her voice. I can hear her rapid pulse.

"I'll be back in a few," Neli says, shooting me a

significant look. She will take care of the body. This top floor has my room and Neli's servant quarters next door so she can see to my needs. I'm sure that's where she's taking him.

I hear her grunt and then grumble as she attempts to move him. She's not as strong as I am. Stella's eyes widen at the sounds even she can hear.

"I will be right back, sweet Stella. Everything will be explained."

I use my speed to lift the body swiftly up and out the door. Neli follows me, opening the door to her room for me.

Just as I return to my room, I notice Neli has followed.

"Maybe I should stay in your room while you talk to her, Boz," Neli says. "For moral support. While you wipe her memory. You can explain who you are when you think she's ready."

"I will not resort to trickery. She's my mate, and the sooner she understands what that entails, the sooner she can come to terms with it. Now, go."

"But she's terrified of you."

I clench my jaw. Perhaps for once I should listen to Neli. I have never dealt with a mate before, and I wish for this to go smoothly. "Very well. Stay. She will learn by your calm example. She trusts you."

We return to the bed, but Stella isn't there. She's fully dressed, staring out the window. At least she didn't leave.

"Stella, you might want to take a seat," Neli says.

I watch as my mate moves in a daze and sinks heavily into a nearby chair.

I sit on the bed across from her, but she refuses to meet my eyes. Neli remains standing by my side, showing her loyalty. "Stella."

She slowly lifts her head. "You killed a man."

"Stella, I am very aware of your feelings on the shocking matter we are about to discuss. I merely ask that you keep an open mind and hear me out before jumping to any conclusions."

Stella continues staring, but doesn't argue. Perhaps a good sign.

I clear my throat. "The supernatural world you once spoke of is real. It is not fiction. It is not an invention of wild human imaginations. It is very real, and I am an eight-hundred-year-old vampire, but I only kill those who deserve it. And you, my sweet Stella, are my mate."

Stella's brows shoot up.

"It's true," Neli puts in. "All of the signs are there. The witch's curse was lifted when you returned home. He woke from the five-hundred-year nap he was forced into."

Stella blinks rapidly. "Witches? Vampires? You expect me to believe any of this nonsense? I know what you are, Boz. You're a killer." She narrows her eyes at Neli. "And you're an accomplice."

"I know it's hard to process," Neli says gently. "I

told you he had supernatural powers of seduction. You felt that was true, right?"

Stella strokes her neck where I bit her, her brows furrowed.

"Stella, with time—" I start.

She stands abruptly. "I'd like to leave now."

"Of course you are free to go," I say.

She nods once and walks briskly to the door. I appear at her side in a flash and open it for her. She does a double take at my swift movement. I want her to see my powers in small doses until her mind is ready to accept the full truth.

"I will see you tomorrow at sundown at the competition," I say.

Her mouth opens and then closes before she bolts, her heart hammering loudly enough to make my own chest ache.

"Well," I turn to Neli, "that went better than I imagined."

Neli groans and shakes her head. "I'll go take care of the body."

"Shouldn't you go speak to Stella? Pre-immortal woman to post-immortal woman?" Couldn't hurt for Neli to do a little selling on the perks of being mated to a vampire. For example, the sex is amazing and we have excellent taste in wine—something that could only prove to be advantageous to her family.

"Give her some space to digest; she'll come around." Neli sounds more hopeful now, but the look in Stella's eyes gives me cause to worry.

"But you will talk to her. Yes?" I press. "You will make her understand how important she is and that her feelings for me are real." I know Stella senses our connection. She has to. The question is, will she embrace it, or will her fear of the supernatural destroy a love that I now know has been missing from my life for over eight hundred years?

Neli's green eyes are intense. "Trust me, Boz, there is nothing more important to me than this. I want to be free. And if that means getting her on board, then consider it done."

CHAPTER TWENTY-ONE
Stella

The next day, Friday, I tour the exhibition hall with my parents for the competition that means so much for the future of my family's vineyard, and all I can think about is Boz. He's a killer, yet he claims this fantastical story, trying to convince me I'm his mate. I could never be his mate. *Who even says that? Does he mean wife?* I could never marry a cold-blooded killer.

The judges are making their way through the tables set up for tastings in their three-piece suits and fancy dresses. Our fate lies in their hands. My parents are talking excitedly about some of the tastings they've done at a table set up with last year's winners. The wine is available for sale there. What if that's us next year? How huge would that be to return in triumph and dazzle all the fellow vintners?

And it never would've happened without Boz's help. He went above and beyond taking the time to work on a blend for us using his award-winning wine, arranging for this trip, paying for everything. I can't reconcile the man I thought he was and the man I saw last night. My mind rebels instantly at the idea of him being a vampire, sucking that man dry. That can't be what I saw. He must've broken that man's neck using his powerful jaw. That's the only thing that makes sense. He bit me too, but that was sex play. I'd be dead if he was a bloodsucking vampire, right? *Just like that man.* Chills rush through me, and I cross my arms, rubbing them.

"Stella, are you okay?" Mom asks. "I thought you'd be more excited about today. There's so much we can learn from these other wineries."

"Sorry. Jet lag. I'll get some coffee and be good as new."

My parents give me matching looks of concern. "You just don't sound like yourself," Dad says. "Your voice is monotone."

"There's a lot riding on today. I'm anxious."

My dad rubs his hands together. "Me too, but we can only go up from here. I'm so thankful to Boz and Neli. Have you seen them?"

Boz's voice echoes in my mind: *I'll see you at sunset tomorrow.* Vampires awaken at sunset.

I shake away the bizarre thought. There's a reason I've been terrified of vampires since childhood, and it all comes down to a late-night movie and the poor timing of my cousin scaring me. Everything is perfectly explainable and in the realm of reality. Boz is not a vampire.

"I'll get us both coffee, Stella," Dad says. "You want one, hon?"

My mom shakes her head. "No, thanks. I'm

going to check in on the twins. They wanted to explore the shops. Stella, take notes on the marketing materials over at the winners' table. There might be something useful for us."

"Sure." I wave in farewell as they leave the exhibition hall. I head over to the row of winners' tables.

I taste a few wines, chatting with the representatives, and take some brochures. I need to focus on business, not last night. I'd like to erase last night from my mind completely. I shift to the side, discreetly taking pictures with my phone of some wine labels, and head to the next table, taking a brochure. Wait. I know this medieval castle.

My head jerks up, and I meet Neli's eyes across the table. They won last year, so of course she'd be here representing them.

"Ever wonder why there's a medieval castle sitting in the middle of California wine country?" she asks.

The illogical pieces slide together in my mind as I stare at the picture of the castle on the brochure. This isn't a reproduction. It's the real deal, an eight-hundred-year-old castle belonging to an eight-hundred-year-old man, who used to dress in a top hat and cape. Like in olden times.

Not an eccentric billionaire recluse.

Not a goth musician in hiding.

An eight-hundred-year-old man. There's no question in my mind he's a man. I saw him in his full naked glory. Somehow he found the fountain of youth. That must be it.

I pinch the bridge of my nose as I feel a head-ache forming. Neli's suddenly at my side, signaling for a young woman to take her place at the table. She must've brought an assistant. Of course she couldn't run an award-winning vineyard single-handedly. I focus on this fact instead of the larger one that makes my head hurt. It's just not possible. No human can live that long.

"Let's go someplace quiet for a chat," Neli says, guiding me from the noisy exhibit space. "We'll sit outside. There's a nice bench under a shade tree. How does that sound?"

I follow numbly, grateful for her soothing voice. My nerves have been jangled all day. I barely slept last night, and when I did sleep, I had nightmares of blood everywhere, a man screaming while I watched in frozen horror, knowing I could be next.

A short while later, we're seated on the bench. It's a warm day with a light breeze. The spot is secluded, no one else around. A calm oasis.

"How are you feeling today?" she asks.

"Exhausted, frazzled, stressed out of my mind."

"Competition has that effect on everyone."

I lift my brows, giving her a pointed look.

"Okay, okay, I'm here to talk you through a different kind of reality. Let me start by saying I am *so* sorry about the way you found out. That was a shock to the system, and you didn't deserve that."

"Thank you." *Why am I being polite to a killer's*

accomplice? I should be running straight to the authorities. But something stops me. I want to believe they're the good people I've come to know.

"Let me start at the very beginning…"

I listen as she tells me the most fantastical tale about Prince Bozhidar, how he came to be the form he is now from his humble beginnings, how he took her in when she was a child and treated her well, and how life has been for them in the centuries they've been bonded together.

"No human lives eight hundred years," I say stubbornly. "You're human. Completely normal." There's no way Neli is a vampire. She's a beautiful woman in her twenties. Someone I would consider a friend. "And, to be totally honest, I don't appreciate being lied to like this." Especially because I don't understand why they're doing it.

"I'm not lying, Stella. I'm immortal," she says. "I'm bonded to Boz, and I can only leave him when he releases me."

I snort. This whole thing is an insult to my intelligence. Vampires. Immortality. Bonds. Stupid! "Oh. And I suppose you're hoping I'll step into your place and be bonded to him for the next eight hundred years. And then what? He bonds with someone else and sets me free? That sounds like slavery."

"I am his slave," she says on a sigh.

"What? That monster! You do all this hard work making his vineyard an award winner and he doesn't even pay you? Neli, you can't allow him to treat you like that!" *And why am I even having this conversation?* It's not like I can believe a word she says. She and Boz are liars *and* killers.

"I'm going to explain slowly and carefully. All I ask is that you keep an open mind, okay?"

I nod, but really I'm thinking about how I'm going to keep my family safe from these two psychos who've become entrenched in our lives.

"When my parents gave me to him as a child, he never used me or turned me. He bonded me to him with a blood ritual. Our lives are tied, and now I cannot die unless he kills me. And, Stella, I want to die. I've been around longer than I ever dreamed possible. I want my freedom even if it means through death."

I squeeze her arm. I might not believe in this whole vampire thing, but I believed her just now about wanting death. "Oh, Neli, I don't want you to die. Is there someone I can call? Do you have a therapist?" Maybe she's supposed to be on meds and forgot them back home. That would explain her state of temporary insanity and longing for death.

"I'm not suicidal, Stella. I'm immortal, and death is different when you're immortal. Death is a relief. I have lived in that same damned castle for over five hundred years, doing the same damned thing year after year—take care of vampire, run vampire's business, move vampire's castle, hide vampire and myself from world. I'm tired of working! And, honestly, my only other option is to become a vampire, which would happen if I tried to end my own life or someone else killed me."

"Let me get this straight. You believe your options are to die, become a vampire, or be his slave for eternity?" She needs help.

"I'm actually Boz's majordomo."

"What's that?"

"I run the household," she says proudly. "I'm at the top of the servant hierarchy." At my confused look, she adds, "It's a medieval thing."

"But I never saw other servants."

She huffs. "Can you give me a little dignity here? I prefer having a title to being called slave."

"Oh, of course, sorry." I try not to let my true feelings show through—she's nuts!—and she should be in therapy. As for the fantasies she and Boz share, I think they're engrained in some sort of delusion to justify their psychotic, killer tendencies.

"You still don't believe me, do you?" Neli asks.

I stare blankly. I hate lying. I truly do. But I don't know if she's mentally stable enough to hear the truth.

"Fine. Here." Neli grabs my hand and sandwiches it between hers. The look in her green eyes is suddenly intense, almost hypnotic. In an instant, I feel an energy pulsing through my hand, up my arm, and into my body. My heart starts pounding, and images of Boz flood my mind. Him dressed in a black velvet suit, riding under a moonlit night, slashing his sword at a pack of hissing men with long incisors. "You feel that? That buzzing? That's Boz's blood in my veins. You can feel it because you're his mate. You're destined to be with him."

I jerk my hand away. She said nothing about the vision I just had, but yes, the buzzing was there. And just like that, something clicks in my mind. I know she's telling me the truth. I feel it in my heart, like I feel Boz. It's almost as if he's always been there, but my mind couldn't see it.

"Holy shit," I mutter. "Boz is a vampire." And that means Neli is an immortal human. I swallow hard and mutter, "Majordomo is a very nice title."

"Thank you." She blows out a breath. "So now that you believe me, I'm sure you'll have lots of questions?" Her voice turns cheerful and she starts clapping. "And now you can understand how excited I was to realize you're his mate. All the signs are there! So once you accept your place with him, I'll be free, and you'll have everlasting love and happiness."

"Hold on. You really were serious about dying." I flash a worried look at her. This is all too much to take in, but two things are certain: I haven't accepted my "place" with him—there's a lot to think about, including what that means for my family and for my future. And two, I do not want Neli to die.

She smiles. "Yes. It's a gift for me, not a sadness."

My mind flashes to Boz lifting his head, blood

oozing out of his mouth, the dead man lying on the floor.

"He didn't just kill that man; he ate him," I whisper as it all starts to sink in.

"That man was a vampire hunter and was about to drive a wooden stake through Boz's heart. It was kill or be killed."

There *was* a wooden stake gripped in the man's hand. Neli takes my hand and gives it a squeeze. In that moment I understand the gravity of the situation. She's bonded to a vampire who's claimed me as his mate. And she wants to die.

My breath turns shallow, my vision dimming at the edges.

"You're looking a little pale," she says, guiding my head down. "Head between your knees. Can't have you passing out here."

I stay that way for a few moments until my breathing evens out. I slowly rise and face her, my eyes intent on hers. "Be honest. Are you a vampire?"

She bares her teeth. "No fangs. And I can eat real food. I told you I'm his majordomo." Fancy title for a sad state of affairs.

"Wait. Do vampires eat anything besides…" I can't even say the word. It's disgusting to think of Boz drinking blood.

"They can't ingest human food. Wine is just about the only exception."

Now that she mentions it, I never really saw Boz eat anything, though he did take a bite of steak at dinner last night. Then he spit it out in his napkin. I thought he was diet conscious or didn't like his food. *But not being able to eat? How awful.*

"Sorry, Neli. I like eating. I don't want to be his slave. And, even if I could accept that, what if he bonds with me and then lets me die to bond with another?"

"Excellent question. I'm glad you're thinking this through. The mate is special. You wouldn't be his slave, and it's a forever bond. Boz would never force your hand. He wants you to come to him of your own free will."

My mind drifts to the odd conversation I had with Boz before I went to his room. He wanted me to have sunshine, scuba, and children of my own, something he thought I couldn't have with him. At the time I thought it was an excuse, but under the new circumstances, more and more is making sense to me. "And he can't have children?"

"*You* can't if he turns you."

I gulp. "Into a vampire?"

She hesitates before saying in a rush, "Yes. But the good news is all that everlasting love and happiness! You'd live forever, sealed to each other in an unbreakable bond. It's better than a human marriage, which can be dissolved so easily nowadays."

I take a deep breath, my mind finally calm enough to think this through. "So you're saying I'd become a vampire and live forever with him. What about my family? Can they live forever too?"

"If he turns them, sure."

I look down. My entire family and me, vampires. How would that work? Would we all have to sleep in coffins? Would Eliza and Mabel still want to bake? *Wait. No more eating and enjoying their famous chocolate chip cookies? No. I can't ask them to follow me into the unknown supernatural world.* I'm not even sure I want to be there. "So, reality is, I'd have to watch my family and everyone I know die of old age, while I'm left behind never to have a family of my own. Is that the gist of it?"

"Yes, but—"

I stand. "I've heard enough. I'm sorry, Neli, but I can't take your place. He'll need to find another mate."

I hurry back inside, ignoring her frantic pleas. "Wait! Stella! There is no other mate. It's only you!"

I duck back inside the exhibition hall and then keep going out the door, racing to the ladies' room. I need a moment to pull it together.

I turn the sink on and splash cold water on my face, my charm bracelet jangling with the movement. I stare at it and then frantically undo the clasp and throw it in the garbage. He put some kind of spell over me with this thing, and I refuse to be drawn in anymore.

I'll forget Boz, even if it kills me to lose the only man I've ever had these kinds of feelings for. That is, until I discovered he's a vampire. My stomach churns. This is awful. I thought our connection was straight out of a fairy tale. He was even a prince!

Now I know the horrific truth—he's a prince of the night.

CHAPTER TWENTY-TWO
Boz

"What do you mean 'Stella left'?" I clench my fists, having just woken from a very restless slumber. Things had gone so poorly with Stella last night that I could not stop replaying the entire scene in my mind. One moment, we were in the throes of ecstasy, the likes of which I have never known with any woman, and the next, I was taking a vampire hunter's life. The horror on Stella's face made me see the evil monster I am.

Or was? The truth is, I do not know who I am anymore. *Killing people used to be so much fun.* But now I find myself wanting to enjoy life in other ways. For example, helping Stella's family. Knowing I can bring that kind of joy to Stella's existence has lit a satisfying warmth deep inside me. Is it because she is my mate? Is it because when I am near her, my heart beats anew? I am unsure, but I suddenly have the desire to commit acts of goodness.

I never want Stella to look at me like she did last night. I want to be the sort of bloodthirsty, danger-ous, supremely handsome, well-endowed, and highly intelligent vampire who can make her feel loved. I want her to feel safe.

And now she is gone!

Neli stares down at her heels in her elegant black satin woman-suit. The crowd files past us, dressed to the nines for the cocktail reception and awards ceremony.

Once inside the large open modern space, I notice the floor-to-ceiling windows Neli warned me about are blocked by large black panels. The floor is black, and the lights overhead are dimmed. The result is a comfortable ambiance that reminds me of the last rays of sunset. They've cleared most of the space for the mingling humans, leaving only a few tables to the edges of the room for the judges' panel. The ball tomorrow night will be in another venue, which I am no longer looking forward to. My Stella is gone. I was meant to win her over in a romantic dance while I whispered sweetness in her ear.

"I'm sorry, Boz," Neli says sheepishly, likely noting I am stewing. "I really am. I tried to talk Stella through everything, but she's in shock."

"Sorry? Do you think *sorry* is good enough? You lost my mate," I growl.

Neli's head whips up, her green eyes tearing and shooting poison arrows. "Do you think I wanted that? Do you? I'm the one who'll have to listen to you whine and moan for the next eight hundred years because you decided to kill some idiot vampire hunter right in front of her. But yeah. It's all my fault." She whisks away a stray tear and sighs. "I wanted this more than you did."

I note the pain in Neli's gaze and realize that her disappointment comes from a place of friendship and loyalty. And also deep-seated, codependent, obsessive tendencies. *As is common when one is in the presence of such magnetic masculinity.* I've been reading up. *Psychology Today.* I'm currently on issue No. 2, 1971. Very riveting, this concept of feminism. Do women truly find being in charge satisfying? *Only five hundred and eighty-four more issues to go.*

"I am sorry," I say. "I should not have blamed you. If I had wanted a successful outcome, I should have done it myself instead of leaving it to a simpleton."

Neli takes my hand, opens my fingers and wraps them around her throat with both hands.

"What are you doing?"

"What does it look like?" She squeezes harder, pushing my fingers into her neck. "Trying to free myself."

I jerk my hand away. "Stop it. People are looking, and now is not the time for your odd, twenty-first-century parlor games. I am not down with this...this...Sixty Spades whatever thing I read about in *Cosmo*." I really should fly more often. I learned so much from all the "bingeing" and "chilling," internet surfing, and magazines.

"It's Sixty Shades, Boz. Sixty Shades of Hay. Not spades of hay. Wait. Or is it Socks?

Or…Shades of Gray Socks?" Neli groans and scrubs her face with her hands. "Balls. Who can keep up with humans?"

"Irrelevant. I am the only one you must keep up with. Please try. I know it is difficult."

"Why did I have to go on a rampage in your honor and kill all the witches? I probably could have paid one to free me," she mumbles.

What was that? "You did that for me?" I ask, feeling quite touched.

"Never mind. It's all watery broomsticks under the bridge."

Sometimes, I feel as though Neli is in her own world. "As you wish. So what is the plan? We must have one to win her back."

"How should I know? After my nightmare of an attempt to get her to come around, I figured you could lay on the old Bozzy magic and charm her tonight. And the ball tomorrow night would've sealed the deal with your grace and elegance on the dance floor." My chest puffs with pride until she continues, "But she flat out skipped town. She told her parents she had food poisoning and that you offered to fly her home to recover. Really, she bought her own flight."

This is a disaster. "Her family is broke, and Stella cannot afford such an expense." My mind quickly shuffles to images of Stella having to sell her maidenhead at the local market simply to pay for her passage home. *That was my maidenhead. Mine!*

"Uh-oh. Your right eye is twitching. That's your warlord face. What are you going to do, Boz?"

"After I find out the name of the scoundrel who deflowered my bride next to a pile of gourds and tie his legs in a knot?"

"What the *hell* are you talking about?"

I shake off my anger. "Never mind. I will allow Stella time to digest. Perhaps the distance will make her long for me."

"That's it? That's your grand gesture to win her heart?" Neli's mouth falls open.

Not enough? All right. Thinking… I scratch my scruffy chin. If I cannot win her over directly, then perhaps there is another way to her heart. *I know!* "I will focus my efforts on the very thing that makes her heart happy. The one thing she values most in this world."

Neli's face turns sheet white, a startling contrast to her black dress that makes her look nearly vampirific. "Oh no. Please don't tell me you're going to take her family hostage and force her to marry you."

"No. Although that is a very fine idea. However, I think winning them over is a more prudent plan if I wish to spend eternity with her and not worry about being staked in my coffin each night."

"Agreed. So…?"

"So, you will point out the judges to me."

"Boz. No." Neli groans.

"Yes."

"No. Stella will not be happy if you do what I think you're doing." She shakes a finger at me, and I notice she's painted her fingernails red.

Still can't resist her whoring ways, I see. She is lucky I care for her so much, or I would have her fingernails removed to teach her a lesson.

"Then we will make sure she never finds out," I say. "So cool your jets." Read that helpful phrase in *Men's Magazine.* Right after I laughed hysterically over an article about pills for human men who can't get "stiffies." *Losers. Do they not know they simply have to fill a clay jar with walnuts and leave it on their windowsill under a full moon, as an offering to the God of Erections?* That's what the men of my time used to do, and look at all the people we have now!

Neli makes a little growl, displeased by my plan. "Boz, if you hypnotize the judges to give the award to Stellariva, and it's not actually the best wine, I guarantee she'll know. She's too smart not to figure it out. The wine will be slammed by connoisseurs and wine snobs around the globe. Thousands will wonder how their wines beat out the better wines."

"Wine preference is subjective."

"Said no judge *ever* at this contest."

Grrrr... I loathe when Neli is right—I mean *disagrees* with me. Nevertheless, this is war. War for love. And every vampire knows that one must use every weapon in his or her arsenal to win wars. "Not to worry, Neli, I know what I'm doing."

"Please, Boz. Please reconsider. Stella wouldn't

want our little project to win through cheating. She's a good person, remember?"

That urge to be a stand-up vampire for my mate kicks in, and I feel my heart start to beat like a drum inside my chest. But Stella is nowhere near me.

What does this mean? I do not know, but I feel something shifting deep inside me. "Very well. I will find another way."

She lets out a sigh. "Good. That's good. Because if you're going to break the curse, you're going to have to step up and be the unselfish hero who's learned his lesson about what it means to be a good man. I read it in your character arc."

"Neli, have you been licking toads again? I thought I made it clear that the use of hallucinogens is not permitted by staff. Please cease immediately. Oh, and thank you for reminding me of the curse and my imminent destruction at the hands of the woman I am meant to love for all eternity." *Prince Bozhidar, I curse you to sleep until a woman is born who will teach you humility and kindness, whose beauty is so majestic, it will bring you to your knees. She will break your heart, and you will feel the misery, same as I.*

"Boz, I can't speak for Olga, but I do know one thing: If she'd truly wanted you to suffer, she would have tied you to a stake in the town square, let her evil crows pick you apart piece by piece, then covered your raw flesh in flammable liquid, and used your severed manhood as the torch to light you on fire."

I cringe. "So vivid."

"I know." She smiles with a satisfied glassy look in her eyes. "It's my go-to happy place."

I snarl at Neli.

"Sorry." She clears her throat. "The point is, Boz, I don't think Olga wanted to destroy you. She just wanted to mess with your head and teach you a lesson—she was in love with you but probably knew she could never have you. Witches and vampires can't be mates. And she probably knew her magic couldn't keep you asleep once your mate came onto the scene. Destiny waits for no man. Or wo-man."

Could Neli be right? Could this entire curse business have been a bit of a ruse? Yes, Olga put me to sleep for five centuries, but the rest was just nonsense. My destiny is Stella, and that means I must stop playing games with token gestures to win her heart and acceptance. I must go all in. Hold nothing back.

I look at Neli. "Thank you, Cornelia. You are truly the best major-dorko a vampire could ask for."

She smiles and dips her head. "My pleasure. Just as long as you keep your end of the bargain."

When major-dorkos fly, Neli. "Of course. I would never go back on my word," I lie. I never said I was a completely changed man. I am, after all, still a vampire.

"Good. Let's have some wine," Neli says.

"Yes. Let us." We walk toward one of the tuxedoed waiters. I know what I must do tonight—how I will show Stella I am not a monster and would do anything for her happiness and safe...safe... I glance over at Neli. "You did call the mercenaries to inform them that one of the residents would be coming home early, yes? I wouldn't want Stella to come home and find a stranger in her house. She's had enough excitement already." We took care of the lead hunter last night, but there were still several back home, staking out our castle from Stella's attic. I assume they're all taken care of by now, but those little buggers can be slippery.

I turn my head and Neli is gone. "Neli?"

Where has that girl gone now?

I shrug. I suppose she went to check in with the mercenaries. Yes. That is what she is doing. I can always count on Neli.

Stella

I can't believe how long that trip was. I drop my suitcase in the foyer, go into the living room, and plop down on the plush blue sofa. Home sweet home. Sadie lifts her head and wags her tail, but like the true ball of laziness she is, she goes right back to sleep. *I bet Max overfed you with lots of treats as usual.* He kept her dog bowl full and checked in on the winery while we were away—not that there was much to do. We've hardly had any customers lately, and sadly, things aren't looking like they'll change. France was a bust.

I groan with a headache and press my palms to my eyelids. What should have been a sixteen-hour flight with a layover in New York turned out to be a thirty-hour nightmare.

I seriously can't believe I was detained. It had been the strangest thing too, because the officers had been waiting for me when I disembarked at JFK to go through immigration and customs. Then they put me in a room and made me watch while a dog sniffed his way through my suitcase. But hands down, the worst part was the strip search. I had no clue they even did that kind of stuff.

Ugh…I feel like I just went to prison. Of course, they didn't find anything, so they had to let me go, but I missed my connecting flight. The next available seat wasn't until the following morning. Just my luck. I even had to pay the change-ticket fee! *Jerks!* For the life of me, though, I don't understand why I was picked. *Like someone tipped them off.*

The bittersweet lining out of the entire thing was that when I finally landed in San Francisco and turned my phone back on, I got five messages from Eliza. The messages had somehow been delayed, maybe because of the whole overseas roaming thing? Anyway, our wine got a ribbon, basically a respectable nod, which is great considering it was our first international competition, but we didn't make it to the final round. Castle Sangria's solo entry, however, placed gold again in the full-bodied red category, where all the heavy-hitting merlot and cab blends compete.

I can't imagine the look of disappointment on my parents' faces. I should have been there for my family. I shouldn't have run. But I didn't know what else to do. There was no way I could have sat through another dinner or stood anywhere near Boz during the awards and kept myself together.

Boz is a vampire. Boz is a freaking vampire! Vampires are real! All I can think about is that image of him sucking the life from that guy. On the other hand, I can't stop wanting to be near him. The pull feels like it's coming from a part of me I didn't even know existed. It's needy and hungry. But only for him.

That's why I left. That's why I had to put as much distance as possible between me and Boz. The conflict is tearing me in two.

How can I want someone who utterly terrifies me? I just can't see it working. I can't see our two worlds coming together in a way that could ever make me happy. I love my family. I love sunshine and fresh air. I love coming home to the smell of Eliza and Mabel's latest baking creation or to an enormous puddle of Sadie's drool on the floor and the sound of my parents stealing kisses in the living room when they think we can't hear. My life might not be perfect, but it's warm and filled with light. I'd hoped to add to it one day with children when I found the love of my life.

But Boz? He's…he's…an eight-hundred-year-old vampire! He's the night. He kills people and drinks blood.

My fingers longingly reach for the spot on my neck where his fangs gave me the most incredible orgasm of my life.

Really? Really, Stella? I berate myself. *You're willing to overlook all of the bad stuff just because of an orgasm?*

"I'm hopeless!" I sigh, feeling like my head is about to explode. I need a hot bath, a toothbrush, and a long nap. Tomorrow, my parents should be home. Neli and Boz will likely arrive with them. As soon as I see him, I have to tell him the truth. There is no us. There is no future I can see with a man whose love would require me to become a vampire.

I can't ever see him again.

CHAPTER TWENTY-THREE
Stella

The next morning my family is back. And lucky them, they did it without a strip search. Not that they needed one to feel down. Everyone is putting on a brave face, talking about what a great trip it was, but I can read between the lines. We all know the ribbon isn't enough to save Stellariva. I don't see another way around declaring bankruptcy. My parents will lose everything they've worked so hard for, and it's doubtful anyone would approve loans for the twins to go to culinary school. I've failed them.

My sisters volunteer to go to the grocery store after breakfast, which gives me the chance to talk to my parents alone. They're sitting at the kitchen island, sipping coffee, and talking in hushed tones. I take in my mom's ratty old beige cardigan and my dad's faded chambray shirt—signs of financial distress I should've noticed. They probably haven't bought anything for themselves in years. Everything was for me and my sisters. My throat clogs with emotion.

"Mom, Dad, I'm so—" my voice chokes "—so

sorry. I failed you. I did everything I could think of with marketing and the labels and blends." I wipe tears from my eyes, overwhelmed by the past couple of days. "Everything you worked so hard for…it's just—"

"Stella," Mom says, rushing over to hug me, "none of this is your fault."

My dad peers at me, hovering over Mom's shoulder. "We know you tried your best. We never should've put so much on your shoulders. We're the ones who failed you. This was supposed to be your inheritance."

"No, Dad, you gave me a legacy to be proud of, but now…"

My dad wraps his arms around both of us. "My girls, we'll be okay."

I sniffle as we break apart from our family hug. My dad always says we'll be okay, but I just don't see how.

Mom puts her arm around me, guiding me to one of the island stools. She pours a cup of coffee for me.

I wrap my fingers around the white ceramic mug, comforted by its warmth. "What are we going to do?"

My parents exchange a look, and I tense. They've been keeping secrets from me again. "What? Just tell me."

Dad speaks in a soothing tone. "First, just know that your mom and I love what we've created here.

We've loved raising a family at a vineyard. It's given us so much freedom and the opportunity to be part of your lives. We both got to see you girls growing up. Something we would've missed out on if we had to commute to a job."

Mom nods. "It was a gift to have this family time together, living and working on this beautiful land."

"And now it's over," I say flatly.

Dad sighs. "You girls are grown. The twins only have a year left to graduate, and they're both so independent. Maybe it's time for us to move on."

"Bankruptcy," I say softly.

"Actually," Mom says, "we thought if we sold the house and the land, we could avoid bankruptcy. After we pay off our debt, we may have enough to get the twins to culinary school."

The breath whooshes out of my body. Sell Stellariva? It never occurred to me they'd give up our home. The rolling hills of beautiful California wine country that I thought would be my view for the rest of my life—gone. I swallow hard over the lump of emotions lodged in my throat. This house, this land holds so many memories. I can't imagine never being able to return to it.

"Stella, it's the only option that makes sense from a business standpoint," my dad says. "Surely you see that."

Panic takes hold. "What if you sell it to someone who turns it into a parking lot or a shopping center? Or cookie-cutter suburban homes or a gas station! It could be anything. You don't know what they'd do with it."

Mom holds up a finger. "Or…maybe another young family looking to run a vineyard could buy it." She doesn't sound convincing.

I press my lips together. The land will be bull-dozed. Everything ruined.

Dad squeezes my shoulder. "We'll be okay. You have a degree. Start sending out résumés. I'm sure an employer will snap you up in no time."

"And what will you two do?" I ask.

"We'll downsize for sure," Mom says. "Probably rent an apartment nearby so the twins can stay in the same school district. After they graduate, well, we'll have to move somewhere cheaper."

"I'll start sending out résumés too," Dad says.

I worry my lower lip. My parents are in their fifties now after working more than two decades here. I'm not sure the job market will be that easy for them to get back into.

"We'll survive," Mom says with a note of steel in her voice. "Don't worry about us, okay?"

I nod and sip my coffee, but I know I'll worry. Worse, I can't stand for them to sell this wonderful land and house. It means too much to them, to all of us. There must be something I can do.

"I asked the twins to pick up some flowers to give Neli and Boz as a thank-you for everything," Mom says. "It's just a token, I know, but how can we ever repay all that they did for us?"

My gut does a slow roll. We owe Neli and Boz so much. I know how I could repay them both—agreeing to be his mate, setting Neli free—but I can't. It would mean stepping into a supernatural world that scares me. Yet something pulls at me, a need to talk to Neli. I want to understand their world. I hate feeling so conflicted over Boz.

I stand, taking my coffee with me. "I'll text her to see when's a good time to stop by and bring the flowers myself."

"Don't go yet, Stella," Dad says. "Let's just enjoy this quiet morning together."

My eyes sting with unshed tears over what he's not saying—it's one of our last times together here in this house looking out over our vineyard. I don't think it will take long for a sale. There's new vintners popping up all the time, and this is prime real estate in Napa Valley. Even if it takes months to sell, it'll never be enough time.

I take my seat again. "Of course."

My parents gaze silently out the wide kitchen window to our vineyard. I do too, trying to memorize everything about this moment before we have to say goodbye forever to the land we love.

Neli didn't answer my texts, so later that day I decide to walk over to deliver a nice bouquet of fresh summer flowers. Her phone's probably charging after the long flight. If she's sleeping off jet lag, I'll just leave them at the front door. There's a small card attached that we all signed. I cross the road and make my way up the long front walkway to the castle. I know it's cowardly of me to stop by during the day, when Boz sleeps, but I'm not ready to face him. (I really hope he doesn't sleep in a coffin like in that movie I saw. Creepy.) The truth is, I'm both attracted to and terrified by the man. The *vampire*, not man. I'm still trying to wrap my mind around that and all his lies. So many damned lies! *Oh sure…he works nights because the customers are overseas*, I mock inside my head. I know it's weird to get hung up on that, but he and Neli were so good at lying straight to my face. How will I ever be able to trust either of them?

I'm being silly. I know I am. They can't very well run around introducing themselves as immortals. Still, the entire thing is just…well, it's a lot.

My steps falter as a wave of dizziness comes over me.

I bend at the waist, taking a few deep breaths, waiting for the dizziness to pass. Okay, better now. *Just focus on Neli, your friend, who's completely normal, except for the majordomo immortal thing. At least she doesn't have fangs!*

I straighten, feeling slightly insane at my twisted reasoning, but continue on in my mission to thank her (and, from a distance, Boz). I probably won't be around much after this, anyway, since I'll be on the job hunt. I need to wrap everything up, even though it kills me to even think of leaving the only home I can remember.

I square my shoulders and cross the moat, taking in the castle with new eyes. It's real. A medieval castle from Transylvania. My mind conjures Prince Bozhidar in that long-ago time, ruling over the castle and the people on his land. Powerful, commanding, but also fair. Neli said he took care of her when she was a vulnerable child.

She also said I could never have children if I was his mate. What if he didn't turn me into a vampire? Then could I have children? I could still live in the light and have my family. But wouldn't that make our children half human, half vampire, never fitting into either world? Why am I even thinking about this? I swear I'm going crazy. This is *not* normal. None of this is normal.

I lift the knocker on the ancient wooden door and bang it a few times. No response. I wait a moment, listening for movement, and bang it again. Maybe she's sleeping off jet lag. Though I'm a little surprised. She's so energetic, I thought she'd bounce back from the trip and get right back to work. I pull out my phone. Still no response to my texts. She's usually a quick responder. I hope she's okay.

I leave the flowers by the front door and head home, my limbs heavier with every step.

❧ ❦

Boz

I am back at Castle Sangria, which appears to be vampire-hunter-free now. My sweep of both properties upon my arrival revealed that all is quiet. No sign of the mercenaries, and Stella's attic is spotless save for some old boxes of family photos and broken glass on the wood floor.

Oops. I had a bit of trouble with that sticky window.

Otherwise, Neli has done a great job dealing with the issue. Very good news because I must prepare to make the grandest of gestures to woo my mate. It is all my doing, not Neli's. She left France before I could get her assistance with my gesture, letting me know by text that she was worried about Stella, so she went home ahead of our party to check on her. I appreciate the fact that Neli takes my mate's protection seriously.

Speaking of Neli, where is that girl? She has not been answering the Summoner, and I've checked her rooms and the kitchen. Perhaps this is like the last time she didn't answer my repeated texts. She wants me to have alone time with Stella to accomplish my gesture on my own. I don't need my Neli, I mean, my…servant to speak for me.

I know it is wrong, but I cannot let Neli go. We are family.

But now I must secure my mate before she closes her heart permanently against me. First, as is proper, I must go to her father to ask for her hand in marriage. Then I will go to Stella and seduce...no, I will *express* my love and my sincere desire to share a future as equals as per issue No. 62, 1973, of *Psychology Today*. I am fully prepared to love a modern woman as a modern man (with centuries of experience). Yes, let's not dwell on my age. It is just a number, after all, according to many informative internet articles.

I dress in my white collared shirt—the modern one—that brings a healthy glow to my skin, my favorite black leather pants, and my finest black leather shoes. Just a spritz of fresh pine scent, and I am prepared to take the first step toward my destiny. I refuse to believe Stella will ruin me as the curse says. No one as sweet as my mate could ever do anything but worship and adore me unconditionally for eternity.

It is dark as I approach her family's house. The light is on in Stella's room, so I know she's home. In my eagerness, I speed to the front door and knock three times for luck. Not that I believe in luck. *I* create my destiny.

Her bloodhound raises hell from somewhere inside the house, her old claws scrabbling on the hardwood as she races to the door. I was careful to rinse my mouth with fine wine after my evening snack, but bloodhounds can sniff out blood almost as well as vampires. I should have brought a distracting bone.

The door opens to Stella's mother. "Oh, hello, Boz, so nice to see you. Please, come in."

I step inside, pleased by the reception. "I received your flowers and note. Thank you." The dog growls at me, baring her fangs. I remind myself not to rise to the occasion. My fangs are much scarier.

"So sorry about Sadie," she says, pulling her back by the collar. "I'll just put her in my office. She's extra protective since we got home. I guess she missed us."

Stella's twin sisters wave at me from the living room, where they're watching the TV. "Hi, Boz!" they call in near unison.

"Hello, Mabel and Eliza. Is your father home?" I can't tell the twins apart. Though they dress differently, they still look exactly alike. I will get Neli on that. It's important I know Stella's family members.

"Yeah," one of them says. "Dad!"

Stella's father appears at the top of the stairs and heads down to greet me in the foyer. "I thought I heard you, Boz. Would you like a drink?"

"That sounds good, thank you," I say, following him to the kitchen.

Stella's mother goes out the back door with Sadie.

"What can I get you?" her father asks. "We've got wine, of course, beer, lemonade—"

"Actually, while it's just the two of us, I'd very

much like to talk to you about a serious matter."

He takes a seat on a stool at the kitchen island and gestures for me to take the seat next to him. "Of course. We're so grateful to you and Neli for all you did for us. If there's anything we can do to repay—"

"With your permission, I would like to marry your daughter."

His mouth gapes open.

Has Stella not spoken of me? Of our fated bond? "I mean Stella," I add, in case he's shocked, thinking I want one of his young twin daughters.

"I see," he says. "Sorry, I'm just surprised. I wasn't aware you were seeing each other."

"She is my destiny." I wait for him to understand the way of things. His eyes are wide, staring unblinkingly at me.

"Have you spoken about this with Stella?" he finally asks, blinking again.

"I went to you first, as is proper. Of course, I am prepared to cover her dowry. It is my grand gesture to prove my sincerity. I would like to make an offer to buy your land and combine our vineyards in one large estate. Five million dollars." This is above the market price because I take care of those my mate loves.

At his silence, I continue, hoping he will see the greatness of my plan soon. "My award-winning vines could be planted here as well. If you would be willing to stay on as full partner in the entire operation, your wife and Stella included, I would greatly appreciate it." It is the best way I could think of to preserve the family's pride and dignity while saving what is clearly a failing business.

His mouth opens and closes several times, resembling a fish.

Stella's mother returns. "I'm back. Will Neli be stopping by later?" She takes a seat next to her husband, suddenly seeming to notice the silence between us. I am waiting for an answer. Her husband appears to be in shock.

Is this not how it's done in modern times? I should have read up on marriage proposals for the modern woman. Perhaps you don't ask the father's permission. He seems to be caught on that part, as he hasn't granted it. By all that's unholy, there's only so much time in a night to research modern customs! Where is Neli when I need her most? Sleeping the night away. Again. I can only forgive such laziness for a short time. I've been too lenient with her.

"Are you okay?" her mother asks her father.

"Five million dollars," he mutters. "Marry Stella."

"What?" she asks. "You're not making sense."

"Tell her what you told me," her father says, gesturing to me. He stands and pulls a whiskey bottle out of a cabinet, pouring a generous amount in a glass.

Her mother turns to me. "You want to marry Stella?"

"Very much so."

She beams a bright smile. "Wow. I had no idea you two were serious. I mean, I saw the way she looked at you and vice versa, but…" She looks around. "Where is Stella?"

"I am waiting for her father's permission before asking for her hand," I say.

Her eyes go soft. "That is so nice. What a gentlemanly thing to do. You certainly have my permission."

"Thank you."

We both turn to the man who still hasn't answered the most important question of my eight-hundred-year-old life.

Her father turns wide eyes on me, but he speaks to his wife. "Irene, he wants to buy our vineyard and merge into one larger estate. Five million dollars. And we could still be full partners."

"Oh my gosh!" Her hand flies to her chest. "Now I understand. I was so caught up in the marriage part, I missed that." She leaps from her seat and hugs me and then hugs her husband. She looks at me over his shoulder. "This is wonderful news! Of course we accept your offer!"

I cannot join in their excitement because her father has not granted me permission. I stand and make my case once more. "Mr. Baker, I will take great care with Stella. She will never want for anything. I will do everything in my power to make her happy. Whatever she wants or needs, I vow she will have it."

He pulls away from his wife, walks over to me, and gazes directly into my eyes. He doesn't flinch at the power there, like most mortal men, and I am glad to see he's a man of great strength too. "Boz, you have my permission to propose to Stella. We would be honored to welcome you to the family. And I look forward to our partnership in the future."

Joy fills me so powerfully I have to fight not to levitate. "Thank you, Mr. and Mrs. Baker. Now, if you'll excuse me, I'd like to see Stella."

Before I can go, her mother hugs me again. I pat her back gingerly, unused to affection. She looks up at me, her eyes shining with happiness. "Thank you, Boz. Just thank you."

"You're quite welcome." My heart beats proudly. I am a changed vampire, a better one, all because of my love for Stella.

Her mother releases me, and I make my way swiftly to the stairs. I catch her excited whisper to her husband. "We can send Mabel and Eliza to culinary school," she says.

I smile to myself. Stella's family is pleased with my plan. Now I simply need to inform my mate.

"Stella, my love," I call.

Her bedroom door opens, and she walks to the top of the stairs. "I am *not* your love."

It is a dagger to my heart. My knees actually go weak. I lock them and pull my shoulders back to display my manly form. "Stella, we must talk.

Alone. It is important."

She walks downstairs, her gaze locked on mine. "Anything you have to say to me, you can say in front of my family. They deserve to know the truth."

"I have already—" I turn, shocked to find her sisters hugging me.

"Thank you, Boz!" one of them exclaims.

"Mom just told us! You rock!" the other exclaims.

I pat their heads. "Which one is Mabel? And which one is Eliza?"

They giggle.

"I'm Eliza," the girl with the cupcake T-shirt says. "You can tell because I have a scar right here." She lifts her chin, exposing her delicate neck.

"Eliza! No!" Stella exclaims, putting herself between us.

She believes I am a monster. That I would destroy her sister because she offered me her neck. But I do not dine on children, and that goes double for my mate's siblings.

"What is wrong with you?" Eliza asks Stella. "I was just telling him how to tell us apart."

Her mother appears in the foyer. "What's all this yelling?"

Eliza turns an affronted look on Stella. "Stella's acting all possessive of Boz. I wasn't flirting, I swear! I was just explaining how to tell Mabel and me apart."

"Okay, girls." Her mother gestures them toward her. "Let's give Stella and Boz some privacy. He has something important to ask her." She winks at me.

They leave.

Stella crosses her arms. "Fine. What is it?"

This is not going as I imagined. By this point, Stella was supposed to be gazing at me with total adoration. I remember the importance of the close heart-to-heart talk between partners and gesture for her to sit with me on the stairs.

Once we're settled side by side, my heart beats in rhythm with hers. *My mate, if only I could make her understand my love is sincere.* "Stella, I have offered to buy your family's vineyard and run the combined vineyards as equal partners. Your parents have happily accepted my offer."

Her hand flies to her mouth, her eyes watering.

"It is my sincere grand gesture so that you may know that I take care of those my mate loves."

She drops her hand. "Oh, Boz. I'm over-whelmed by your generosity and so thankful, but…" She swallows audibly. "The mate part. I'm not sure I'm ready for what that entails."

She needs more from me, so I continue from the heart. "I did everything properly and received your parents' approval to ask you to marry me."

She blinks.

I gaze deeply into her eyes. "I love you. I didn't realize it until we met, but you are the one thing I have been missing from my life, the one woman capable of filling the dark void in my chest with sunshine. No one could ever come close to your beauty, your kindness, your pure soul. Only you could have broken the curse." I take her hand and brush my lips across her fingers. "Stella, you are my destiny. I do not expect you to be anything but you. I would only turn you if you chose it, when the time is right. I am immortal. I can wait as long as you need."

She sighs. And when I lower her hand, she leans close, her lips meeting mine. A surge of triumph goes through me at contact. I frame her face with both hands, deepening the kiss, keeping my fangs in check. She needs a slow seduction, my sweet virgin.

When I release her, she's breathing hard, staring at my mouth. "I don't see fangs," she whispers.

"I can control when they emerge. Stella, I would never hurt you. Only bring you pleasure."

She shivers. "This kind of love was never in my plan."

I smile. She's seeing her way to a different kind of love with me—fanged love. "Let me see your planner. I have something to write in it." She is quite fond of her plans.

Her lips twitch, and then she goes upstairs to get it. When she hands it to me, I step away to write my most personal grand gesture for tonight before handing it back to her. She must meet me halfway. I want her willing.

"Now it is up to you, my love." I brush a kiss

over her lips, just enough to tempt her for more. Seduction is my strong suit.

I turn and walk out the door to the sweet sound of her sigh. She will be mine.

CHAPTER TWENTY-FOUR
Stella

Boz is gone in a flash, his movements supernaturally fast. I open my planner and read his note written in elegant script: *Meet me in the ballroom of Castle Sangria. Wear your gown.*

It's so romantic. I missed the ball I'd so been looking forward to at the wine competition because of my total meltdown, and now he's offering to recreate the moment just the two of us. I could love this man. I'm just not sure I can join him in his world. It's so different. And my family—

My family! I hurry to the kitchen.

My parents beam at me. "Did you say yes?" Mom asks.

My sisters rush in. "Oh my God, Boz proposed!" Mabel exclaims. "I love him!" She blushes. "Not like that."

"Congratulations!" Eliza exclaims.

"I didn't say yes," I explain.

Everyone's faces fall.

"He caught me by surprise, okay?" I take them all in, looking so disappointed. "I didn't say no either. I just wasn't expecting this." I am still getting used to the fact that he is a vampire.

Mom walks over and hugs me. "None of us were expecting what would happen when we opened our hearts to someone who seemed so different from us. I'm only sorry we weren't friendlier with our neighbors from the start. We were put off by how eccentric that place was, made assumptions about the people in it, but you were right all along, it was his willingness to follow his own path to happiness that made him the success he is. We all love Boz and, if you love him too, we're happy to welcome him to the family."

My dad nods. "I understand the hungry looks he gave you. He was in love with you. Poor guy had it bad."

Mom laughs and elbows him. "Sounds like someone I used to know."

He kisses her hair. "I was a goner from the start. Thank God she married me."

"What will you do?" Mabel asks.

I hold up my planner. "He invited me to a private ball and says I should wear my gown."

Mom sighs. "Such a romantic. Do you love him?"

I take in the family I love, so happy together, able to keep their beloved home and vineyard, working as equal partners with my love. My heart pounds. *My love.* If I love him, shouldn't I love all of him, even the parts that aren't human? Only one way to find out. I must go to him.

"Excuse me, I have a ball to attend," I say.

I rush from the room to get ready for my handsome prince as their cheers fill the air.

Boz answers the door himself, looking impossibly gorgeous in a black tux. "You look beautiful, Stella."

"Thank you. You look handsome."

He offers his arm and guides me to the ballroom, which is at the far end of a long hallway. I didn't even know he had a ballroom until today. Sconces light the way, lending romantic candlelight. It feels like a dream that I'm wearing a beautiful red gown on the arm of a handsome prince in a castle. This could be my home. I would be a princess.

"What are you thinking of, love?" he asks.

"Silly stuff."

"Please tell me."

"I was feeling like a princess."

"As you should." He smiles at me, love shining in his silvery eyes. I let out a swoony sigh.

Once in the ballroom, he uses his phone to play ballroom dance music, saying, "I have discovered a wonderful way to find all types of appealing music. This is my ballroom playlist. I have learned the most romantic of dances for you, my love—the waltz."

His formal speech appeals to me. I can get used to the courtly manners of an eight-hundred-year-old gentleman who looks like a hot vampire of thirty.

Nerves skitter over my skin. *Vampire.*

He sweeps me into his arms, taking the lead in the dance, his hand on the small of my back. It's wonderful. I get caught up in the music, in his heat, his sexy scent. All of it. I never want it to end. We dance to song after song until the playlist ends.

He executes a formal bow to me. "I very much enjoyed our private ball. I was looking forward to it in France, but this is even better. Just the two of us." His eyes search my expression for a long moment, and then his arms wrap around me, holding me close.

I rest my head on his chest, listening to his heart beating. *Wait, I thought vampires were dead.*

I lift my head. "You have a beating heart."

"It beats for you."

I suck in air, overwhelmed by all I'm feeling. I suddenly realize that this is the love I've dreamed of all my life. This connection of ours, this feeling in my chest that tells me he's my destiny, this…desire that won't ever fade. He's changed me somehow, and he's changed my family's fate too. All for the better. Simply put, parts of me still might feel afraid of this—of the unknown—but a bigger part of me knows I couldn't ever walk away from him. Not now. Not ever. I'm in, sunk, fascinated, and completely smitten by this man, and the fact he's not like me—human—won't change that.

"I love you," I whisper. A realization. The strange part is, I feel like he's been by my side for years, waiting in the shadows, loving me too. It just wasn't our time yet.

Boz's dark eyes glow with his unspoken happiness. He goes down on one knee, takes my hand, and gazes into my eyes. "Stella, will you do me the great honor of becoming my mate for life?"

I drop to my knees in front of him. "I want to say yes, but how can I when I don't know what being your mate means?"

"Oh, Stella." He holds me close. "It means I will be so careful with you. I will love you and care for you for eternity. You need never fear me."

He strokes my cheek. "It means I will love you forever."

"No more lies?" I ask.

"There will never be secrets between us again. Please be my wife, Stella. Let me give you a perfect life so that I may experience everlasting happiness. Because living forever means nothing if my mate isn't by my side."

In that moment I know. His love for me is in his eyes, in his touch, in his voice. It's everything I've always wanted. If I can just take this leap of faith and trust that what he says is true, then there is nothing to fear.

"Then I do. I accept."

He wraps me in his arms, holding me tight. "I am so honored in your trust. I will spend the rest of my days making your every dream come true."

"Oh, Boz." *How could I have ever doubted this*

wonderful man?

He pulls back to look in my eyes. "I know you love to check things off your list. The first step was saying you'll marry me. The others will come in time, only when you're ready."

"To become a vampire?"

"Only if you wish. I am prepared to say goodbye at the end of your natural life if that is what you want. I will mourn you for eternity."

A surge of love fills me, pushing out the last of my fears. "I will think about it. I promise."

He grins and sweeps me off my feet, carrying me out of the room, cradled in his arms. "The next step is a slow seduction to initiate you into the pleasures of the bedroom."

"I love that step!"

He nuzzles into my neck, and I tense. "Stella, I'll only bite you with your permission and only for pleasure."

I let out a shaky breath. He did give me an orgasm that way. It's difficult, knowing how powerful he is, potentially deadly. But I know he loves me, and that makes all the difference. "Okay. And what are the next steps?"

"I will write every one of them in your planner. But first, we must plan our wedding. Right away. I cannot wait long to have you." He sets me on my feet by the front door. "And I want you to know I understand if you had to sell your maidenhead for a plane ticket—"

"What! Boz, I used a credit card."

"Ah. Those are very useful, and I am most pleased to hear your maidenhead is intact."

"But—"

He swoops in, dipping me back over his arm and kissing me. A rush of dizzying lust races through me. He rights me again and gives me a little push toward the door. "All in good time, my love. I will get everything taken care of. Good night to you."

I turn back, hands on my hips. *Seriously? He's turning his new fiancée away from his bed?* I'm still aching for him, but he's already gone with supernatural speed. Maybe one day I'll move like that too. *Super Stella.*

I walk home with a bounce in my step, love in my heart. Boz understands me; he loves my family; he loves me. He's not like I ever dreamed my husband would be. I smile to myself.

He's better.

Boz

I shuffle my beloved Stella from my castle in a hurry. This is not how I planned the evening to go. I wanted to dance with her until the morning light and tell her all the ways she has brought sunshine into my very long, very tedious life. She has filled me with a renewed sense of purpose and brought my humanity back. Well, some of it. I am, after all, still a vampire. A little nibble on her neck might have been a pleasant way to finish off the night.

However, all that must wait. While she and I danced, I caught wind of an intruder. "Come out!" I yell. "I can smell your foul stench, vampire!" Why any of my kind would dare to enter my castle is beyond me. I am ancient, which makes me faster and deadlier than most.

I grab a claymore from the stone wall in the hallway. The decorations in my castle are there for a reason. "I will find you! And I will remove your head!" I sniff my way down the hallway, toward the parlor that connects to the kitchen. The trail grows stronger with each step.

Blood. I smell blood. I stand in my parlor and notice the tiny people in the TV box are still awake. They truly are dedicated to their craft, rehearsing at all hours of the day, whether someone is there or not. "Shhh…" I hold my finger to my mouth. "I would not want you to be harmed. There is an intruder."

They ignore me and continue talking amongst themselves. I press the tiny button and close the curtain for their safety.

Two more steps and I am at the door leading to the kitchen. Someone is in there drinking all my snack blood! There are rules among vampires. One, you never touch another's mate. *And two, you do not eat my snacks!*

I push open the door, ready to strike with my claymore. "Relinquish my treat, you foul—" I freeze with my arm in midair. There is a vampire, caked from head to toe in mud, standing in front of the open refrigerator. Its two green eyes stare unblinkingly. "Neli? What are you doing, girl? Where have you been? And what are you doing with my food?"

Her mouth flaps for a moment, and that is when I notice her fangs.

"Neli, you—you're a vampire?"

CHAPTER TWENTY-FIVE
Boz

"How did this happen?" I ask, standing on the other side of the shower curtain in Neli's bathroom. She has yet to say a word besides "I need more blood." I assured her that the ten bags she took from my snack bin were enough. Cold and tasteless, but enough.

"Neli, I asked you a question, and I expect an answ—"

The curtain flies back, and naked Neli is in full shampoo mode, her hair covered in bubbles. "I am not your servant to command any longer!" She closes the curtain.

"No," I mutter to myself, "I suppose you are not." And then the realization hits me; what will I do without her? A problem to resolve another time, I suppose. At the moment, Neli needs my superior vampire guidance. And, possibly, vengeance. "But you are still family, and I demand to know who harmed you. Who is responsible for killing you?"

The water shuts off. She opens the curtain, and I hand her a towel from the rod on the wall. I have seen Neli's birthday suit many times, and it is of no consequence to me; however, the paleness of her skin is like a dagger to the heart.

She is a vampire. I never wanted this for her. Correction, *she* never wanted this and, therefore, I am saddened by this turn of events.

She wraps the towel around her petite frame and then looks up at me. "I did it. It's my fault."

"How so?" I frown with confusion.

"Before I left France, I knew our mercenaries were still here, trying to catch the last hunter. They said they'd almost cornered him, but he slipped away. Then you and I spoke at the convention center and talked about Stella leaving France early. I rushed outside and immediately tried to call them so they wouldn't be surprised and accidentally hurt her—they weren't expecting any of us home until yesterday. But when I called, no one answered. I worried that something was wrong and caught the first plane here."

"Why didn't you tell me you failed to make contact with the mercenaries? You only said you went to check on Stella in case any hunters were at her home." I let out a groan. I hate that Neli did not trust me with this information, but part of me wonders if it is not my fault. I am not so forgiving when it comes to mistakes.

"What could you have done that I couldn't? Also"—Neli blinks, tears forming in her eyes—"I didn't want to disappoint you. You're always saying how inferior I am, which is a total crock, but I knew you would never let me live this down. I'd be hearing about it for the next three centuries."

She is correct, but that is still no excuse. "Stella could have been harmed. You *were* harmed. And that is more important than pride."

"I know." She sighs remorsefully. "I did manage to call in a favor with Vincente and ensure Stella encountered a few travel delays."

"Vincente is still alive?" He is an old acquaintance from my Transylvania days, and as any vampire knows, there really is no such thing as immortality. Just ask Kylgorii. *Sunshine happens.*

"Yeah. He works for Homeland Security now. The night shift. He's apparently very skilled at sniffing out bombs, and the benefits are really great—medical, dental, 401k."

"So, in other words, he is still batshit crazy." Vampires do not require such "benefits."

"Exactly. Anyway, I got home early in the morning and wasn't sure what to expect, so I snuck in through the secret tunnel in the wine cellar. Someone attacked me from behind, and then I woke up buried in a grave the next night."

"So you do not know who killed you?"

"No. But I'm guessing it was one of our private security guys. They probably realized I wasn't the hunter and tried to cover it up. There's been no sign of them."

"Or perhaps it was the vampire hunter who killed you."

"No. He wouldn't have bothered with burying me. I'd be charcoal dust right now."

I am not so convinced. If they thought she was human, they would not have burned the body.

"Either way, I caught that last hunter. He was my first meal, and I'm afraid I forgot to question him before I dined." Neli turns and heads into her bedroom. I follow. "I just wish I'd been more careful. I knew the mercenary guys were setting traps all over the place."

Our own security did the deed? I will have their heads! "Oh, Neli. I am so very sorry that you will no longer be my major-dorko. I know it must distress you greatly; however, I assure you that you can continue to launder my shirts and run my winery."

"Are you for real, Boz? My life is over! I'm a freakin' vampire! And you're talking about your shirts?"

"And running my winery," I point out.

She huffs and shakes her head of wet red hair. "You just don't get it."

"But I do. I do get it." Issue No. 30, *Psychology Today.* "You are experiencing a great sense of loss. You feel as though your identity has been taken from you. I am merely attempting to provide you with a sense of normalcy while you advance through the stages of grief. Denial, anger, depression, and acceptance." I scratch my scruffy chin. "Or is it depression, then anger? I cannot recall. But the point is, I am here for you. And when you are ready and have completed your grieving, I shall assist you in finding your very own slave. Someone who will watch after you and, more importantly, whom you may insult as much as you like."

Neli looks at me from across her bedroom, a frilly pink affair, and then rushes toward me, delivering a firm hug around my midriff. "Oh, Boz." She sniffles, and I feel a rib crack.

"Ow. Ow." I attempt to unlatch her from my frame, but she is very strong. "Okay," I grunt, "baby vampire. Easy on the prince now. Stella would like to marry me in one piece."

Neli pulls away. "You're getting married?"

I nod with a smile.

"Oh my God. This is wonderful news."

It truly is. I get the girl of my dreams, and I no longer have to continue deceiving Neli about giving her the true death. Also, Neli is now free to explore the world and find her own fanged love when she is ready. It may take a while, though. I heard our old friend Nicephorus, widely known as Mr. Nice, has kidnapped the author team of Pamfiloff and Gilmore, forcing them to write my story faster. The crusty old vampire is a romantic and very eager for my wedding. As am I.

"I'll plan your wedding," she says excitedly. "Give me some time to make it perfect. It will be my wedding gift to you both. How's after harvest?"

"But I am quite horny and need to bed my bride as quickly as possible." Neli understands that I will want to wait until the wedding night to give this honor to Stella. "I cannot afford to wait months for such an event."

"Boz. Please. You only find your mate once in your existence. It has to be done right, in the old tradition."

She looks at me with those green eyes. I can deny nothing to her. Neli is like my little sister. Or distant cousin. Or a coveted pet, perhaps. Either way, she is family. "Very well, but please be sure to hurry."

"Give me a few weeks, and I promise it'll be the most amazing wedding since Prince Pamfilovamim-ivich married Meshica Mermana."

"Oh no. All that gold? I prefer something more in the tradition of the Great Kylgorii Gillmoreanu." His marriage to Errika the Impaler still lives in infamy to this day.

"You got it. One Gillmoreanu wedding for the record books coming right up." Neli smiles up at me, flashing a little baby fang, and my heart warms. I can already feel her soul settling into her new vampire body. I know she will find peace. And she will make a very excellent vampire. She had the best to learn from.

CHAPTER TWENTY-SIX
Stella

I can't believe the torture Boz has put me through over the last three weeks. He insisted we wait for our wedding night to be together. I assured him it was perfectly acceptable in this day and age, but true to his ancient, gentlemanly ways, he politely declined. "A vampire only marries his mate once, and it must be done right."

And then he bit my neck and gave me another one of those mind-blowing orgasms.

Seriously, I can't even imagine how he'll be in bed if just nibbling on my neck brings me to the point of insane ecstasy. I'm pretty sure my head will explode tonight.

It's finally our wedding day. I'm dressed, my makeup is done, and Mom is putting the finishing touches on my hair. Mabel and Eliza have been cooking up a storm for over a week. It was Boz's idea to have them cater "the nuptial feast for the human guests." Neli provided a list of traditional Transylvanian wedding dishes to inspire their creations.

Speaking of Neli, I'm not going to lie, seeing

her transformation has given me a new perspective on becoming a vampire. Someday. Maybe? I know it wasn't what she wanted, and it did break my heart that I was partially to blame (had I just stayed in France, she wouldn't have died), but Neli assured me that she felt surprisingly happy. "I love being able to levitate. It's so much fun!" she'd said.

I then asked her if Boz could bond with me, since she was now free of him. I wondered if that might be a way for me to have my cake and eat it too. I could stay human, walk in the daylight, have children, and eat normal food. I would stop aging and be with Boz forever. It turns out it's a possibility.

The only downside of me accepting the bond is that, at some point, we will have to tell my family the truth. They'll notice that Boz, Neli, and I aren't aging. Whether they accept us or not, I'll still have to face the heartbreak of watching them grow old and die. After giving it a lot of thought, I know my parents would never want to become vampires. They'd see it as unnatural, cheating the cycle of life—something they've always felt passionate about. Watching things grow, serve their purpose and die, like the grapevines, is a sort of natural poetry to them. As for the twins, I don't think they'd want to trade their love of culinary arts for anything, and from what I understand, in speaking to Boz and Neli, vampires think human food smells like a giant outhouse. So, yeah. I think I can safely say that vampire land is out for my family.

Someday, I will have to face the inevitable. But not today. Today, I am marrying the love of my life. A man who has waited over eight hundred years for me.

Dad steps into my room. "Sweetie? Everything okay?"

I beam at him, noting how handsome he looks in his red and black tux. "Yeah. I'm ready."

I stand from the vanity stool and take one last look in the mirror. My makeup is understated and natural looking with the exception of my bright red lipstick, which matches my red lace dress. It's not the white I imagined for my wedding day, but according to some ancient Transylvanian tradition, everything must be red. And poofy.

"The red symbolizes life. Passion. Blood of our ancestors," Neli said, insisting we all had to wear red. The poofy stuff, like my huge dress with a hoop skirt, is just some royalty thing from long ago.

"You look gorgeous, honey." My mom whisks a tear from beneath her eye. "And I'm really warming up to the Romanian theme." She glances down at her red pantsuit. Her dark hair is up in a bun.

"You look fantastic, but…I think you should wear your hair down. It will go better with your outfit."

I understand there are over three hundred vampires attending the ceremony and dinner. No reason to expose tempting necks. On our side of the family, it's only sixty guests—cousins, aunts, friends of the family, and my friends from school and college. Neli assured me the vampires won't dishonor Boz by touching his guests, but better safe than sorry.

Hide that neck. I pull the pin from my mom's hair and straighten out the locks. "There. That looks way better."

She gives me an odd look. "I see your nerves are finally kicking in." She laughs. "Ready?"

"Ready." We follow my dad downstairs.

The twins join us in matching poofy red dresses with black shawls. They do a couple of spins to make the dresses swirl. "Take it for a spin," Eliza says to me.

I do a twirl for them, and they clap. I smile. "You both look beautiful."

"You too," they say in unison.

The moment I step outside and feel the cool night air on my cheeks, my heart starts beating uncontrollably. I'm beyond nervous.

"Wow. Would you look at that," Mom exclaims.

I follow her gaze to the enormous horse-drawn carriage a few yards away. "Wow is right." It's like something out of a dream, straight from some old Victorian movie, made for a princess, complete with candles inside lanterns to light the way. Every inch of the outside of the carriage is covered in red roses like a float in a parade.

"Wait. Are those horses dyed red?" Mom asks.

I look. It's dark outside, but I definitely see red. "Yes. Those are in fact red horses."

"Wow. Neli really left no detail undone."

"Did someone say my name?" Neli appears out of thin air with a camera in hand, causing us to yelp. I might've screamed.

"Neli," I growl under my breath, "how about not scaring the crap out of my family with your superhuman speed?"

"Oops! Sorry. I'm just so excited," she whispers before returning her voice to a normal volume for the benefit of my family. "Wait until you see the banquet hall and ballroom. You're going to love it! Now time for pictures." She makes us pose for what seems like an hour. "Okay. I think a hundred pics of this moment should do it for the wedding album. Don't want to be late."

A hundred photos of just that? How big will this album be?

My dad helps me into the carriage, followed by the rest of my family, and then joins us. Neli closes the door.

"Aren't you coming with us?" I ask her.

"I want to get some photos of you driving away. I'll see you in a minute."

I hope she doesn't beat us there and open the carriage door. My family will definitely get suspicious. Or freak out.

The driver, who's sitting outside at the front of the carriage, starts pulling away. "Neli"—I lean my head out the little window—"I forgot to ask, who is officiating the wedding?"

"An old friend, Nicephorus."

What a strange name. I sit back in the carriage, trying to keep my hoop from smacking my chin and showing off my red silk lingerie to my family. Neli insisted I wear some very skimpy teddy outfit made of lace from Boz's hometown. It's supposed to be good luck.

Good luck. Does such a thing exist for a vampire? Luck? Goodness? "Oh, God. I don't feel so well." *I'm marrying a vampire. I'm marrying a vampire! An unnatural creature of the night.* "I think I'm going to be sick."

"Stella, honey, just breathe," says Mom.

"It's normal to have wedding-day jitters," Dad adds. "And just remember, your mom and I would never allow you to marry some creep. Boz is a good man, and I've seen the way you two look at each other. You're making the right choice—and if I didn't believe that, I wouldn't have sold the winery to him."

"Boz is awesome!" Eliza says.

"Truly," Mabel says.

I suddenly just don't know. It's all happening so fast.

The carriage arrives, and there's a photographer waiting to greet us. "Oh, thank God." I'm not up to explaining Neli's supernatural speed. I've got enough to worry about.

I step out first, followed by my family. According to Neli, it's tradition for both parents to give the bride away to her new "vampire lord." Boz assured me that wording was simply the ancient nomenclature and did not mean he would own me: *"We will be equals in every way, Stella. Except in bed. I will be your slave and dedicate myself to your every whim, your pleasure."* I liked that answer. A lot.

We pass through the open front door, and there is music playing that reminds me of something I heard in a movie once. Flutes and drums. It has a Renaissance vibe. I wonder if jugglers and fire-breathers are waiting in the ballroom. I hate that I had no say in planning this wedding. *I love planning! What was I thinking? This is all wrong!*

I stop. "I can't do this." But just as I speak those words, Neli appears just outside the closed doors of the ballroom. I didn't notice before, but she's wearing a strange-looking red and black milkmaid outfit with a little apron. Her red hair is now braided in two pigtails.

"Let me guess," I snap, "your outfit is tradition." I don't want to say anything to insult her because I know how hard she's worked to put this wedding together, but I can't contain my feelings. "I'm sorry. None of this is how I imagined."

She gives me a smile, one that I know is genuine because it lights up her green eyes. "Stella, that's the point."

"Sorry?"

"The tradition isn't red and black or anyone having to wear a particular outfit. The custom dictates that the colors, the theme, the music, and even the food must all be something unique. It is a symbol of the couple. There has never been a love like yours, because there has never been another Boz and Stella. There never will be. Therefore, your wedding can't look like anyone else's."

Oh my God. That's kind of beautiful.

"Awww…how romantic," Mom says.

"Strange," says my dad. "I was researching Romanian weddings and never read anything about that."

"It's a very, *very* old custom from Boz's ancestral village," Neli chimes in.

Yeah. I bet it's old. "I think it's a wonderful tradition." The nontraditional wedding as a symbol of the couple's one-of-a-kind love. "Why didn't you mention it before?"

"And ruin the surprise?" She shrugs. "That's also part of the fun of a Gillmoreanu wedding. It's a symbol for life. The bride and groom don't know what lies ahead, but whatever happens, they're in it together. I mean, obviously, I couldn't keep all of the details a secret since dresses and suits are involved. But the rest, I assure you, will blow your mind. You like clowns, right?"

Oh God. I hate clowns.

"Just kidding." Neli laughs. "You're going to have the time of your life tonight. I promise. So, are you ready? Because I hear a flute playing the wedding march," she singsongs and opens the door to the ballroom. She gestures for the twins to go in to their seats.

I can see straight down the aisle. At the end, Boz waits in his black tux with a red bowtie. My parents are beside me, and there are hundreds of people in there, most of whom I can't see, but it just doesn't matter. All I see is *him* and those dark, seductive, loving eyes. Everything else fades away—my doubt, my fears, my nervousness. I suddenly hear his heart beating alongside mine. How? I don't know, but I hear it. And I know. He is my fanged love. We are a once-in-an-existence kind of love.

I smile at Neli. "Thank you. It's the most perfect wedding ever." With my parents by my side, I begin my march down the aisle, never wanting to look back.

CHAPTER TWENTY-SEVEN
Boz

"Wow. That was some wedding!" Stella jumps into my arms. Now that we are in the privacy of my bedchamber and the guests have finally left, I am eager to spend what remains of the night with her. I did say I'd be her slave in the bedroom. And Neli made sure to include it in my part of the vows: I pledge to share my life openly, speak the truth, cherish her, and encourage her fulfillment as an individual throughout our lives. Clearly, fulfillment is a sex thing, but first...

I pull away so that I may gaze at my bride. Her rosy cheeks are the epitome of a blushing bride. Her beautiful brown eyes are filled with joy. Her skin carries the sweet aroma of roses and fills the air with it. It pleased me to discover that I had been wrong about her selling her maidenhead for a plane ticket—something I discovered the first night I nibbled on her neck after our return from France. She still tastes amazing. So virginal. I shall miss it, but I will enjoy bedding her more.

"Why aren't you kissing me?" she asks. "We only have forty minutes until sunrise."

"Because when you have lived as long as I, you do not want to rush moments like these. You want to savor them."

"Okay, but…can't you savor me in the bed? For thirty-nine minutes?" She smiles, and I cannot help melting on the inside. I can deny my bride nothing. She will be the most spoiled wife to ever walk the earth.

"I will savor you, worship you, and do anything you wish, my love. I am yours to command."

"Oh. I like that. Then I wish you to remove my dress, throw me on that bed, and make love to me. Hard. Well, not so hard that you break anything, but I've got a lot of frustration built up."

I bow my head and place a lingering kiss on her warm, sweet lips. My heart glows from the inside out, pumping heat through my cold veins and down to my straining manhood.

I break the kiss and take another look at my bride. Tonight marks the beginning of a new life. "I think I should be gentle with you the first time, Stella. I know from extensive research reading *Cosmo* that losing your virginity to such a well-endowed man might cause extreme discomfort."

"Virginity? But, Boz, I'm not—"

"Not ashamed. I know. You are a modern woman who embraces her decisions." I bow my head and kiss her hard, this time with intent. This time unleashing my passion. I pick her up and take her to the bed, where I rip off her hideous red dress.

Neli is a prankster, that one. She knows the proper dress for any vampire bride is black leather. But I will let it slide. After all, I have my mate. I have the sexiest woman on the planet. And tonight, I will make love to her until her head explodes.

Or at least for the next thirty-seven minutes.

Stella

If Boz doesn't want to hear that I'm not a virgin, then okay. I'm way too wrapped up in him and our now naked bodies pressed tightly together on his huge four-poster bed. I know he's wrapped up too, because he didn't even notice the lingerie. He tore it away with the hideous poofy red dress and then removed his tux.

He's warmer than I remember last time, and maybe that's because his heart is beating as fast as mine.

His kiss is hungry, and I run my tongue over his teeth, curious about his fangs. I find a small sharp point, but they must be retracted. I personally can't wait for them to come out and play.

God, I hope he bites my neck when I'm climaxing. I can't imagine how good it will feel.

I run my hands down his smooth, muscular back and cup my hands over his hard ass as he grinds his cock against me. He's big. He's thick. And he's hard. I could definitely see it being a challenge if this were my first time.

I raise my hips, silently urging him to enter me, but he likes to tease me, pressing the head of his erection against my entrance, but pulling back each time I rock forward.

My nipples are hard, my skin is tingling, and the ache inside me is so intense. I've never wanted anyone like I do him. My husband. Boz. I love how that sounds.

He breaks our kiss and runs a strong hand down my breast, over my hip, and slides it beneath my knee. Meanwhile, his mouth finds that spot on my neck he likes.

"Yes. Do it," I pant.

"Patience, Stella. We have some time before sunrise. I must see to your proper fulfillment."

"No. No more patience. You said you would do anything for me." *Basically.*

He bites down, and I feel the climax already starting. Each pull of his mouth sends a spike of pre-orgasmic shockwaves through my entire body.

With my knee still in his grasp, he positions himself against my wet, heated entrance and then begins to slide in. One inch at a time.

I suck in a breath and close my eyes, savoring the sensation of him biting me and working himself in.

I love it. I love the friction of his cock, stretching me, pushing me.

He breaks from my neck and gives the spot a

little lick. "Are you all right."

"Yes. Don't stop. Keep going."

He plants his hands on either side of my head, and I open my legs wider for him, wanting him to go deeper.

He takes the cue and thrusts hard, filling me completely. I am lost in the moment, in the sensations of our bodies joined. The ecstasy is unlike anything I could have imagined, as if I feel everything he feels alongside my own bursts of pleasure.

I want it to last. I want it to never stop. But I feel the build happening and I need it. I need him.

"Bite me," I say. "I'm coming."

He doesn't do it. I don't know why. Instead, he quickens the pace, sliding almost completely out and then pounding his way home again. I cry out in ecstasy with each penetration.

"Why won't you bite my neck?" I ask, my words sounding almost foreign. I never imagined myself begging for something like that.

"I am too afraid I will lose control. You are so delicious. So sexy." His mouth is back on mine. Suddenly, I'm remembering the story Neli told me, of how she and Boz bonded. I break from our kiss again. "If I drink from you, I'll be immortal, right?"

Boz stops moving, and those dark eyes focus intensely on mine. "Is that what you want?"

"For now. Yes. At least until I decide about turning."

"But it cannot be undone. And if you were to

die, you would become like me."

I don't know if it's because I'm in the throes of passion and he's inside me, our two hearts beating as one, or because I'm so in love with him that I can't imagine ever living without him, but I nod anyway. "Yes. I want to do it."

He takes his finger, pushes it against his fang, and then gives it a quick suck. He returns his mouth to my lips and kisses me, his tongue dancing against mine. All I taste are roses. Red roses. Not at all what I expected.

I swallow and continue kissing him, more passionately than ever. He slams his cock into me, moving faster. I can feel he's about to come.

His mouth slides back down to my neck.

"Is it done?" I whisper.

"Yes. You are immortal now."

I expected something different. Like my body to go through some sort of painful werewolf-like transformation or a bolt of lightning to crack through the sky like in the Frankenstein movies. But this was nothing like they show in horror films. My fears were all in my mind, and Boz kept his promise. He said he would never hurt me.

I smile in anticipation. "Then what are you waiting for?"

He bites down, and I gasp with pleasure and explode. An orgasm rips through me, hitting my every nerve, rippling through every inch of my body.

I cry out Boz's name as he releases my neck and groans. It's deep, animalistic, and pure male.

He holds himself inside me for several seconds, and I feel my inner walls tightening around his shaft. Each contraction sends my mind spinning into the atmosphere. And he's right there with me.

After several long moments, my mind drifts back down to my weightless body. Everything in the room looks brighter and clearer, and I feel more alive than ever.

"That was amazing," I pant, with him still inside me.

"Yes. Well, I am a vampire. The strongest, deadliest, most sexy vampire ever to live."

"No. You're my vampire."

He raises his head and gazes into my eyes. "And you are my Stella. Forever."

EPILOGUE
Boz

One year later.

"Happy anniversary, my love." I show up to my bedchamber just after sundown with a dozen red roses in my hand. Stella is already waiting for me, naked on the bed, her warm brown eyes glowing with the deepest happiness she's ever known. I can feel it.

"Hello there, husband of one year." She smiles. "Are you ready to take my virginity again?" She chuckles.

"Very funny." Yes, I did realize she wasn't a virgin on our wedding night, but I didn't care. Not one little bit. The fact that she gave herself to me completely and we bonded was far more important than some maidenhead. Besides, as I read in *Cosmo*, a more experienced woman is better in bed and more willing to try new things. Stella is quite the adventurous lover. Just last night, we made love while riding a horse.

"I still wonder, though, why I taste like roses to you," she asks.

I shrug and begin removing my clothes. "Neli believes it is a mate thing—a way for us to identify one another."

"Guess it doesn't matter. I would love you even if your blood smelled like yucky coppery stuff. Oh. Speaking of Neli, have you heard from her?"

I slide into bed, leaving on my leather pants. I know that Stella enjoys her first fuck of the evening when I have them on. She likes peeling them down and cupping my ass as I ride her. Later, after I've eaten, I enjoy taking her on long walks through the vineyard and making love to her there, surrounded by all the smells of the earth and vines. I am a very romantic man, according to the online Facebook quizzes. I've also learned that if I were a potato, I would be a French fry. Facebook quizzes are so very informative.

"I have not heard from our dear Neli, but I assume she is out exploring all of the facets of her new body and freedom."

Stella sighs as I lay myself next to her. "Do you think she'll ever find someone and be as happy as we are?"

"No. I do not. No one can possibly be as happy as we are, yet I do hope she will be."

"Me too. I hope she finds her mate." Stella pauses. "Because I seriously want to plan her wedding. I'm thinking lime green and a seahorse theme."

I laugh. "Our red wedding was quite the spectacle, and the fireworks, mimes and pickpockets were very original. I cannot claim to have ever been to a wedding like ours." I kiss my wife, feeling her contented heart seep into mine. For now, she has everything she's ever wanted. Her family is happy. The wineries are thriving. Her sisters are on their way to New York and Paris as we speak, to learn the culinary arts. Tomorrow, her parents will go on their first vacation in years—to some resort in the Bahamas, where they do this whole fantasy thing. It was very expensive, but they can afford it now.

I just hope they don't run into any mermen. Yuck.

"I wouldn't change a thing," Stella says. "But payback will be glorious."

"Enough talk about Neli," I say. "Tell me what you desire tonight. A good spanking? A candlelit dinner?"

Stella smiles. "I think…I would like to start a family."

"So soon? We just married. How about we wait a few hundred years?" I want her all to myself.

"Yeah, but I've been giving it a lot of thought. I want to become a vampire. After I have kids, and they're all grown."

I am not one hundred percent certain we can have children. The old legends say we can, but I've yet to see such a child.

I crinkle my nose. "As I mentioned, I am uncertain we can have children."

"Why don't we just try?"

"Are you certain? Wait! Did you say you want to become a vampire?"

Stella nods. "I really want to learn how to levitate. It looks so cool."

"I am unsure if that's a reason."

"Well, I have plenty of time to think it over. And if we can't have kids, well, then, I have you. Maybe my sisters will have kids, and I can spoil the hell out of them."

I love that Stella always finds the good in every situation. "I love you, wife."

"I love you too. Happy anniversary." She leans in to kiss me, but stops. "Oh, and tonight, I want to do the levitation lovemaking."

I knew she'd say that. "Then give me your neck. I will need my energy."

THE END?

(But keep reading for free signed bookmarks, an interview with Kylie and Mimi, and other random stuff!)

AUTHORS' NOTE & FREE SWAG!

Hello to all our Winos, Bats, Vamps, and Girls Next Door!

We really hope you enjoyed *Fanged Love* as much as we did! No joke, we had an insanely good time trying to make each other laugh. Did you like our vampire names? Or how we snuck our husbands into the book? How about the little Librarian's Vampire Assistant Easter eggs?

For those who picked up this story and are unfamiliar with *The Librarian's Vampire Assistant* series, here's a brief little background:

In February 2018, I released Book #1 of my vampire mystery series, *The Librarian's Vampire Assistant*. It's the story of a vampire who must solve a murder! There are lots of fun twists and crazy characters, but no one tops Mr. Nice, a very old, very mean, insane vampire.

Anyway, he becomes obsessed with a vampire romance series. That series is, you guessed it, *Fanged Love*. It was a totally fictitious story I never intended to write.

Fast-forward to last year, 2019. I had just released book #4 of the LVA series, and after so many requests for *Fanged Love*, I decided to give it a go. I asked Kylie if she wanted to join in and help bring her special Kylie sparkly goodness to the story, and she said yes!

We penned the first chapters in October of 2019 and have been plugging away ever since! The holidays, several major operations of family members, graduations, a global pandemic, sending kids off to college, and *FANGED LOVE* finally got done. All the while we were writing our other books!

Fanged Love, I think, was a lot of extra work at a time when we probably needed extra rest, but it brought a much-needed distraction and smiles. We HOPE it does the same for you!

If you loved the story as much as we do, PLEASE leave a review and tell your friends about the book! We'd appreciate the word-of-mouth book love!

In the meantime, if you're looking for a FREE SIGNED BOOKMARK (international OK), you know what to do!

STEP ONE: Email me at Mimi@mimijean.net

STEP TWO: Provide your neat and complete shipping info.

STEP THREE: If you wrote a review for *FANGED LOVE* because you loved it more than leather pants, wine, and fangs, be sure to provide a link or screenshot. I will do my very best to include extra goodies. I always warn readers that I do run out! It's first ask, first get!

STEP FOUR: Give me about 3–4 weeks.

Okay! That's all for now. Be sure to keep on scrolling and check our interview, new releases, and instructions for stalking us!

With FANGED LOVE,

Kylie and Mimi

P.S. Want to hear the music both Kylie and Mimi wrote to? Check out the FREE Fanged Love Playlist on Spotify! (Yes, they require you to have an account, but they have a free subscription option.)

INTERVIEW WITH
KYLIE AND MIMI

What was it like working with your co-author?

Mimi: Kylie's mind is a very dirty place. I kept having to rein her in because she wanted to put nooky in every chapter. Sex, sex, sex! That's all she thinks about. I feel bad for her husband. Does he ever sleep? Also, I wasn't aware that she knew so many words for "penis."

In addition, I will add that she's a very disciplined writer, and I'm more of a spaghetti cook. I throw shit at the wall and see if it sticks. So working with Kylie was a great exercise. She kept me in check and made me think instead of just going with my whims. If it weren't for her, this book would be filled with unicorns and a bunch of otherworldly crap that probably doesn't belong.

Kylie: Writing with Mimi is like ha-ha-ha-AAHHH! She's very funny and then suddenly out of nowhere, BAM. Who knew that would happen? Not me. I got a peek inside her brain, and it is a scary place.

The best part was trying to make her laugh, and then she'd try to make me laugh, and so on, and that is why we wrote the funniest book either of us have ever created *in our lives*.

What did you find most challenging about the co-writing process?

Mimi: That Kylie hardly ever has typos. Her first drafts are all sparkly and clean. My first draft looks like someone took a dirty pile of laundry and dumped it on the page. Also, Kylie has better writer snack food (chocolate). All I have in my office are stale crackers. It's really unfair. Why doesn't she share?

Kylie: Mimi, I'm sorry you live in the scorching hot desert where vampires and chocolate go to die. I did send you lots of virtual chocolate! In all seriousness, the most challenging part was stepping into Mimi's world of sexy, conceited but honorable vampires and learning when to let the fangs emerge as the romance commences. Eep! I still don't know how a vampire got into my steamy romcom!

What was fun and exciting about writing *Fanged Love*?

Kylie: At first, I saw my writing and Mimi's writing jump out as two distinct things, but as we got deeper into the story, things changed. That's where the fun began. Our voices danced together, intertwined, and ultimately merged at the exciting climax. *Wait, what?* That sounded oddly sexual. Come on now, I'm a married woman! Fortunately, all of Mimi's typos reminded me that while we are merged on the page, we are also one-who-can't-help-but-correct-typos and one-who-is-oblivious.

Mimi: After a while, I just started putting really huge typos in the manuscript on purpose. Just to fuck with Kylie. That was fun. The exciting part was when I got new chapters back from her. I was like a kid on Christmas morning and couldn't wait to find out what happened next! Kylie never disappointed. Of course, then I would come up with yet another "brilliant" plot twist and mess all her chapters up. I'm fairly sure she'll be buying a voodoo doll to get back at me!

What is your favorite thing about Stella, the heroine?
Kylie: Stella will do anything to save her family's vineyard, including daring to tangle with the reclusive mystery man across the road. I love her loyalty to family, her strength, and her ability to look a vamp straight in the face, turn, and freak out just like any normal person would. :p

Mimi: I LOVE how Stella is the quintessential girl next door. It's really why I asked Kylie to write this story with me. If you've read any of Kylie's books, you know her heroines are smart and funny, but they have a sort of wholesome good nature, too. Even when they're having steamy sex! If you haven't read any of her books, then what are you waiting for?

What is your favorite thing about Boz, the hero?
Kylie: I adored watching an eight-hundred-year-old vampire try to adapt to the modern world. Talk about a fish out of water! But also his deep sense of honor and respect for Stella shines through.

Mimi: For me, it's Boz's transformation. He starts out as a very unlovable pigheaded male (and it's super funny), but as we get to know him, we see that he has a good heart. He's simply not used to showing it!

What's your favorite line(s) from the book?
Kylie: Here's Boz talking to his familiar, Neli, in his dignified way:

Neli: "Find some salty old crow to mess with if Stella isn't the one."

Boz: "I am not into birds, but I do not judge."

Birds and squirrels are *always* funny. Also, not wearing pants.

Mimi: Hands down, the scene where Box tries Stella's wine. It's so rude! And so Boz...

He sips and spews the wine back in the glass. "Horse piss!"

I gasp.

He shoves the glass away, grimacing. "Horse piss mixed with putrid fish entrails."

What makes Boz and Stella's love unique?

Mimi: I'm a sucker for opposites-attract stories, but that's probably not so unique when it comes to romance tropes. What makes this couple special is that they really have almost nothing in common. Different centuries, values, family situations, economic circumstances, and life goals. For this romance to work, they really have to want to make the other person happy and get outside their comfort zones.

Kylie: Love-bite orgasm. 'Nuf said.

ACKNOWLEDGMENTS

A BIG FANGY THANK-YOU TO…

Our readers for continuing to support all of the wild, dirty stories that come from our heads. We couldn't do the leather-pants tango without you!

To team Kylie-Mimi for helping us make the book come to life and sparkle like a vampire in Forks! LD (thanks for all the support), Su (what a fun cover! Thank you!), Stephanie Elliot (I hope you had fun!), Pauline (oops, so many typos!), and Paul (formatting genius). And a shout-out to Mr. Nice for inspiring us to make this story a reality!

A huge thank-you to our families for always supporting us during the long, looooooong days as we slave away on our computers (or take afternoon naps while you're not looking).

COMING SOON FROM
KYLIE GILMORE

Check out my new steamy romantic comedy series, Unleashed Romance, where dogs are part of the family! Book one is *Fetching*!

Fetching

Wyatt

I'm a self-made billionaire with a soft spot for damsels in distress, so when I move to the quirky lakeside community of Summerdale, I immediately zero in on the woman I most want to...ahem, rescue. Only the stubborn woman refuses to cooperate.

Sydney

When Satan moves to town, aka Wyatt Winters, I do my best to be welcoming as the owner of the historic restaurant and bar that he won't stop showing up at, despite criticizing nearly everything about it. *Deep breath.* I might've lost my cool and made a rude gesture in his direction. And told him off. How was I to know he was considering investing in my place?

Did I mention I'm in debt up to my eyeballs and every bank has turned me down?

Still, there's not a snowball's chance in hell I'd ever work with him. Or admit he fires me up in every way.

And then a snowstorm traps us together and—

I'm melting.

For buy links:
www.kyliegilmore.com/books/unleashed-romance/fetching

NOTE: A portion of *Fetching*'s first month's preorders and sales will go to Pets for Vets, a nonprofit that trains shelter dogs to be therapy companions for military veterans with PTSD.

If you love steamy romantic comedy, be sure to sign up for my newsletter and get a free book! www.kyliegilmore.com/newsletter

COMING SOON FROM MIMI JEAN PAMFILOFF

The wait is almost over! More Librarian's Vampire Assistant!
Book #5 Coming October 2020 (Yes! They are still standalones.)

She's a librarian with a dark secret.
He's the broken, cold-hearted vampire king.
Together, they have to solve one more mystery if they want to survive.

FOR BUY LINKS AND MORE:
www.mimijean.net/lva5

ABOUT MIMI

MIMI JEAN PAMFILOFF is a *New York Times* bestselling author who's sold over one million books around the world. Although she obtained her MBA and worked for more than fifteen years in the corporate world, she believes that it's never too late to come out of the romance closet and follow your dreams.

Mimi lives with her Latin lover hubby, two pirates-in-training (their boys), and their three spunky dragons (really, just very tiny dogs with big attitudes) Snowy, Mini, and Mack, in the vampire-unfriendly state of Arizona.

She hopes to make you laugh when you need it most and continues to pray daily that leather pants will make a big comeback for men.

Sign up for Mimi's mailing list for giveaways and new release news!

STALK MIMI:
www.mimijean.net
twitter.com/MimiJeanRomance
pinterest.com/mimijeanromance
instagram.com/mimijeanpamfiloff
facebook.com/MimiJeanPamfiloff

ABOUT KYLIE

Kylie Gilmore is the *USA Today* bestselling author of the Rourkes series, the Happy Endings Book Club series, the Clover Park series, and the Clover Park STUDS series. She writes humorous romance that makes you laugh, cry, and reach for a cold glass of water.

Kylie lives in New York with her family, two cats, and a nutso dog. When she's not writing, reading hot romance, or dutifully taking notes at writing conferences, you can find her flexing her muscles all the way to the high cabinet for her secret chocolate stash.

Sign up for Kylie's Newsletter and get a FREE book!
kyliegilmore.com/newsletter

For more fun stuff check out Kylie's website
www.kyliegilmore.com

Follow Kylie:

BookBub: bookbub.com/authors/kylie-gilmore

Website: www.kyliegilmore.com

Facebook: facebook.com/KylieGilmoreToo

Instagram: instagram.com/kyliegilmore

www.ingramcontent.com/pod-product-compliance
Lightning Source LLC
Chambersburg PA
CBHW072103020726
47501CB00003B/696